1934   *Ten Lyric Poems*
1935   *12 Ethical Sonnets*
1936   *15 Poems with Time Expressions*
1937   *Homecoming & Departure*
1938   *Childish Jokes: Crying Backstage*
1939   *A Warning at My Leisure*
1941   *Five Young American Poets: Second Series* (with Jeanne McGahey, Clark Mills, David Schubert, and Karl Shapiro)
1941   *Stop-Light: 5 Dance Poems*
1942   *The Grand Piano: or, The Almanac of Alienation*
1942   *Pieces of Three* (with Meyer Liben and Edouard Roditi)
1945   *The Facts of Life*
1946   *Art and Social Nature*
1946   *The State of Nature*
1946   *The Copernican Revolution*
1947   *The Copernican Revolution* (expanded edition)
1947   *Kafka's Prayer*
1947   *Communitas: Means of Livelihood and Ways of Life* (with Percival Goodman)
1949   *The Break-Up of Our Camp and Other Stories*
1950   *The Dead of Spring*
1951   *Gestalt Therapy: Excitement and Growth in the Human Personality* (with Frederick S. Perls and Ralph F. Hefferline)
1951   *Parents' Day*
1954   *Day and Other Poems*
1954   *The Structure of Literature*
1955   *Red Jacket*
1957   *The Well of Bethlehem*
1959   *The Empire City*
1960   *Growing Up Absurd: Problems of Youth in the Organized System*
1960   *Our Visit to Niagara*
1961   *Ten Poems*
1962   *The Lordly Hudson: Collected Poems*
1962   *Drawing the Line*
1962   *The Community of Scholars*
1962   *Utopian Essays and Practical Proposals*
1962   *The Society I Live In Is Mine*
1963   *Making Do*
1964   *Compulsory Mis-education*

PAUL
GOODMAN

A CEREMONIAL

STORIES 1936-1940

VOLUME II
of the
COLLECTED
STORIES
EDITED BY
TAYLOR STOEHR

BLACK SPARROW PRESS - SANTA BARBARA - 1978

LIBRARY OF CONGRESS CATALOGING IN PUBLICATION DATA

Goodman, Paul, 1911-1972.
   A ceremonial, stories, 1936-1940.

   (His The collected stories and sketches of Paul Goodman; v. 2)
   I. Stoehr, Taylor, 1931-   II. Title.
PZ3.G6235Co vol. 2   [PS3513.0527]   813'.5'2s   [813'.5'2]
ISBN 0-87685-354-8 (trade cloth edition)   78-16977
ISBN 0-87685-353-X (paper edition)
ISBN 0-87685-355-6 (deluxe edition)

Contents

Introduction

In March 1936 the twenty-five-year-old Paul Goodman, already the author of fifty or sixty short stories, four or five of which had been published, began a new one, with the unpromising title "Prose Composition." Its subtitle was more descriptive—"sustained—rapid—jokes—slow—forthright—and disturbed"—but scarcely adequate to the revolution it represented in his literary method. During the next four years Goodman wrote another dozen like it, most of them with the same generic title, as in "Prose Composition: The Sea! the Sea!" but some merely called "2 Pastoral Movements" or "Ravel"; and all the rest of his fiction in this period shifted in style and manner more or less drastically, depending on just where in the wake of these "prose compositions" it lay. Even his most realistic stories were affected, though the method was essentially an alternative to realism.

Goodman quickly realized that it was a turning-point for him. Before long he had begun to distinguish sub-genres like the "heroic portrait" and had given his new literary manner a more prepossessing name—cubism. Four years later he was thinking of it as his "cubist period"—though he never quite said it so pompously—and was planning a collection of stories to commemorate it, including a preface in which he provided the following theory of his own practice:

"Now by literary *Cubism* let us here understand not abstraction from subject-matter, but in the presentation of subject-matter an accompanying emphasis and indepen-

7

dent development of the signifying means. And in effect this means, if the work hangs together, that the relations of the characters, thoughts, and acts will seem to be partly advanced by the mere literary handling, apart from their natural or imaginary relations. In a scientific work this is of course a dangerous fallacy, the 'literary fallacy'; but in literary works it gives a literary, formal quality to the subject-matter which is to my taste excellent. The classical ideal is so to merge the subject-matter and the literary means that nothing is obvious but the world presented, but this 'world,' on analysis, proves to have no properties beyond what is useful to organize the literary medium. . . .

"The handling of most of the pieces in this volume leans away from the classical in the cubist direction. Thus the minutely varying repetitions in the last part of 'Ravel' are a cubist expression of that subject-matter, the syllogisms in the 'Composition' are a cubist expression of the particular kind of resolved feeling; the reduction of Saul's chase to algebra is cubist; the nonsense-syllables in 'Orpheus' are cubist; and so forth. For the most part, unlike Miss Stein or E. E. Cummings who analyze especially the elementary parts—words, spelling, punctuation—I rely mainly on the larger means of signifying, the sorites in the 'Composition,' the dialectic in 'The Detective Story,' the eristic in 'Tiberius.' (The 6th and 4th parts of 'Tiberius' are parodies of Bradley.)

"Let me make a few remarks about the chronology of these pieces. The earliest of them is 'Phaëthon' [1933]. This is nothing but a mythological account of coming to know something, the temporal sequence of awareness is equated with the sequence of Phaëthon's ride, and apart from this initial device there is little use made of purely literary means in unifying the whole. By the time I came to write 'The Detective Story' [1934-1935] I was prepared to or-ganize the entire structure by a formal device. The great advance, however, came with the writing of the 'Composi-tion' [1936], for here not only the whole but also the parts underwent cubist analysis, and it was therefore possible to find a beginning, middle, and end not merely in a dialectic of objective ideas, but partly in a progress of literary

8

methods, as from continuous exposition to discrete fragments to jokes to syllogisms. 'Tiberius,' 'Orpheus,' 'Ravel,' and 'Saul' are simply further explorations of what I discovered in the 'Composition.' "

As Goodman makes clear, his "discovery" of literary cubism was several years in the making—the earliest hints are in his *Johnson* stories of 1932-1933. Nonetheless, it is important to know that he began self-consciously reconsidering his approach to fiction at the same time that he was preparing the most dramatic and far-reaching changes in his own way of life. In 1936 he left home for good: out from under the roof of the older sister who had cared for him since boyhood, saying goodbye to the circle of admiring friends who had gathered in his apartment every Saturday night for years, uprooting himself from his beloved Washington Heights, the neighborhood in which he had been born and raised, the landscape of his very dreams. Off he went to the midwest, where he had scarcely an acquaintance, to seek his fortune (starting at $900 a year) as a research assistant in English literature and a graduate student in philosophy at the University of Chicago.

Although the opportunity came unexpectedly, this uprooting of his ties with the past was thoroughly willed, an invitation to upheavals of character as well as prospects. No wonder his fiction also reflected the change. The reverberations continued until 1940, when Goodman returned from what he now called his "exile" in Chicago, never again to leave New York City for more than a few months. As if to seal the epoch, he seems to have decided that the possibilities of literary cubism were exhausted for him, and he immediately entered on new experiments in manner.

Of course he was coming back to a world very different from the one he had left, and was himself a different person: he brought with him a wife and baby, a Ph.D. (not quite in hand), and a new sense of himself as a professional. As he abandoned literary cubism, it was not to return to some earlier manner, but to move on to forms and methods that would build from what he had accomplished in the interim. Even before he got back it had become apparent that he would soon break into print with some of the more prestigious avant-garde publishers; New Directions had accepted "A Ceremonial" and "A Cross-Country Runner at Sixty-Five" for the 1940 *Annual*, while the *Partisan Review* had taken a batch of stories and poems, and was soon running his film criticism regularly. It was not far-fetched to think that he might now publish a book of his stories. This was a time for taking stock.

When the collection of stories failed to materialize, the impulse toward self-assessment was channeled into other works—more prefaces that went unpublished, and two important essays, on "Literary Abstraction and Cubism" and on "Literary Method and Author-Attitude." Goodman's theory of literary method or manner was really a theory of art and alienation. The various manners—realism, naturalism, symbolism, cubism, and so forth—were analyzed according to their formal characteristics, and these in turn were correlated with "author-attitude," the social and psychological interaction of a writer with his world. *Realism* was accepted as a sort of norm of fiction, representing the "harmony between the author's sense of what is meaningful and at least the potentiality of the scene accurately described." There is no alienation here, and whatever "problems" come into focus—for instance, as in Jane Austen—are seen against a background of tolerable institutions and reasonable conventions. *Naturalism* however begins to express "latent alienation by a malicious or indignant selection of the pointless or unsavory, tho usually relieved by youthful compassion." Goodman's own early work fell in this category, the tradition of Dreiser and Ring Lardner. The formula of *Symbolism* goes a step further: "it is intolerable that the scene should be merely what it seems, it must contain also some other meaning." This was what he discovered in his novel of 1935, *The Break-Up of Our Camp*, when he first came to revise it in the early Forties: his uneasiness with the naturalistic presentation led him to explore beneath the surface—not so much to causes as to "contexts of causes," the hidden psychic contents looming larger than mere chains of events or even the motives and dispositions of his characters. Finally, the *Cubism* to which he had arrived in 1936-1940

10

represents a further retreat from conventional subject matter, to "inventive play in the literary medium itself, more or less abstracted from the represented scene. . . . One can easily see genetically how the passage from method to method described above would lead to abstraction, if (a) the art seemed more and more worth the trouble and (b) the scene seemed less and less worth the trouble."

Such theorizing can help a reader understand what Goodman was up to in his "prose compositions," but of course the analysis was very much after-the-fact, and certainly too schematic to do justice to his own case. It would be a mistake, for instance, to think of Goodman as distant, embittered, or out-of-touch during his Chicago years, or of his cubist stories as harping on the usual complaints or slipping into the usual rhetoric of the alienated (that, in fact, is what we have learned to expect from naturalism, not cubism). Indeed, the story from this period that made the biggest stir among critics, "A Ceremonial," was lauded for qualities that were just the opposite. Klaus Mann (the novelist's son no less) singled it out from all the stories in *New Directions 5:* "The tone of this young American voice reminds me, admitting the infinite differences in style and scope, of certain venerable accents long-known and everloved—the accents of Goethe's mellow wisdom and fatherly confidence." Hardly a description of alienation. Was it pure spite when Goodman replied that Mann had missed the point, that imaginary celebrations are "the cruellest form of satire"?

We must take Goodman's word for it, that alienation was what he saw when he confronted the work of his late twenties, but surely Mann was not *that* far off when he heard serenity in Goodman's voice. The objective facts of his life also indicate a happier relation to the world, and every photograph that survives from this period shows an irrepressibly beaming face. Perhaps being alienated *suited* him? It is an important ambiguity in a man who twenty years later suddenly gave up writing fiction in order to devote himself to social criticism, appointing himself society's scourge and healer simultaneously. Was *Growing Up Absurd* the work of an alienated artist?

11

In the first place, we must recognize that Goodman's feeling of alienation, at least in the Thirties, was primarily a negative matter. Although he later specified what he was alienated from—"the political economy, the sexual mores, and the religion of the society"—this identification was entirely post hoc, only in 1942 approaching militant antagonism. Before that, he stood aloof. If he paid a price for his non-conformity, it was not by colliding with society but by missing out, a sense of ostracism, exile. This was especially true during his years at Chicago. The academic climate, for instance, was chillier than the wind blowing off Lake Michigan, and gave occasion for poems such as this:

A University City

To travelers I am not far from home,
but I who rode my bicycle and bent
my wheel back on the neighborhood content
—how did I come so far as I have come?
I used to cultivate the children from
the corner school and read the day's events
chalked on a house. . . .
                    I might as well invent
or use a foreign language for this poem,
made so far from the usual deeds that give
words sense; for who knows how they live
hereabouts? what use the gestures of
desire? what are the rules no one breaks?
Dear God, perhaps there is no careless love
among folks merely *studying* the Greeks!

This poem forced itself upon him only a few weeks after "A Ceremonial." And a few days later he wrote a friend back home, "Friday was Lincoln's birthday: I took a long walk along the lake; till suddenly it struck me that I was doing so because it was a holiday. I who always had holidays. Well, I shall fail to attend most of my classes during the next weeks, lest I form regular habits (which are of course desirable). Yet by God, I have no street life in Chicago—& know only people at school or home."

All this edgy self-consciousness, it should be pointed out, transpired after Goodman had been in Chicago only a semester, before he had made any close friends or met his wife. "A Ceremonial" must be seen in this light; it was written out of longing for—not so much a better world, "after the establishment among us of reasonable institutions," but for—Washington Heights! He was homesick. This same month he wrote his most famous poem, "The Lordly Hudson," addressed to the bus driver who brings him back to Manhattan at the semester break: "be quiet, heart! Home! home!"

So one meaning of alienation was simply exile—from home, family, friends, the scenes and habits of his lifetime. Some of these deprivations were only temporary, for soon he had made new friends, had found a street life, had fallen in love. And then what was lacking? The relative poverty of his youth had long since been embraced as "voluntary poverty," so that could not be counted as loss, though it was certainly a case of being alienated from the popular conception of a proper standard of living. Similarly his sexual predilection for young boys as well as lively young women—and especially his openness about it—kept him out of polite society, and ultimately got him fired. But one could not say that he was therefore unhappy, any more than he was discreet. On the contrary, his economic and sexual life in Chicago was if anything an embarrassment of riches. His $900 a year became $1100, then $1500—affluence for the young man who had never made more than a few dollars reviewing a book—and his love affair with Virginia was celebrated in so many poems and stories, one cannot doubt its satisfactions.

Now we begin to touch the quick of his alienation, for when he came to *confront* his happiness, to write not the imaginary but the real celebration, a strange uneasiness welled up. His first attempt, "Virginia," written in the early days of their romance, ought to have been a simple outburst of joy, yet he was already wondering how long it would last, and asking himself why he was wondering. In "Honey-Moon and Archaic Longings" he found himself unable to write the "Olympian marriage-festivities" he had planned;

13

instead, "I see that I am writing the same unquiet strain as of old!" In "The Minutes Are Flying By Like a Snowstorm" he makes an explicit connection between "having sunk into a habit of joy" and a "rage of aggression against my dear self," the desire to be "brought to a pause . . . in the jaws of death." These cubist stories held their subjects at arm's length, as he later theorized, but not so distant that we cannot make out the deeper sources of alienation that disturbed him. It was not society he shrank from, but his own happiness.

His poems show the same ambivalence. They seem to feed on it. On one occasion he writes,

> I've given up punishing myself
> by lonely walks in the park o' nights,
> looking for love where it can't be found,
> where well I know it can't be found.

One effect of the "habit of joy" he had fallen into was that he stayed home nights; but back in New York for a few weeks' vacation, he found himself once again prowling the streets and the parks:

> After those of lust, the pleasures of the chase,
> and by the time I've caught 'n, lust again!
> making daylight a delightful race
> for a week or two at Christmas. It is then

> I learn the idiom of careless love
> needed in poems, and my private parts
> are touched with memory to make him move
> in the dead of winter till the First of March!

"The idiom of careless love"—that was one side of it. "Looking for love where it can't be found"—that was the other side. Together they were the alienation that kept Goodman's art taut between desire and satisfaction. The deepest uneasiness he felt in the very center of joy, when his happiness seemed most likely to persist. If no other circumstances offered obstacles, the uneasiness itself would

14

have to serve as the counterbalance necessary for his art. And so his honeymoon stories turned out anxious plumbings of the unconscious, archaic longings, uncanny dreams.

Perhaps it is misleading to speak of these matters as "alienation." Goodman does not speak of them at all when he analyzes his cubist manner; the political economy, sexual mores, and spiritual death of society were more than enough to account for it. But it is not to be ignored that he never published any of these stories of his fatal encounter with happiness. Instead he printed the more anonymous treatments of his disaffection. "Tiberius," "Saul," and "Orpheus" all have the same theme—the insupportability of happiness, the impossibility of attaining the heart's desire—but the expression is impersonal, muted, "alienated" if you will. Similarly, among his more realistic stories, "The Mean, the Maximum, and the Minimum" spelled out the same message in terms of political economy and the standard of living, while "A Goat for Azazel" explained how the very attempt to take such ultimate desires seriously would turn all against him—a tabooed hero of the libido. Realist or cubist, these too were analogues of his uneasy dreams of perfect satisfaction, the terrifying Golden Age of infant bliss.

Of course he had suppressed just those stories that no one would have printed anyway; no publisher was likely to touch these literal renderings of forbidden subjects— love-making during menstruation, with newsboys, or collie dogs! Goodman knew well enough that he could not publish such outrages on the proprieties. One is tempted to suppose that he wrote them in part for that very reason, to protect his alienation, just as he cruised the parks partly in order to be alone, and to fuel the imagination with fruitless longing. In an early version of "Literary Method and Author-Attitude" he toyed with, but then also suppressed, this conjecture: that "there might be an original relationship between the later alienation and my becoming an author at all."

Indeed there might. It is most clearly envisioned in his story of the archetypal poet Orpheus, who learns at the end

15

that he cannot both possess his heart's desire *and* make his music. Back from Hades, shaken but also somehow relieved, he retunes his lyre and sings a song of mourning for Eurydice, whose loss is now accepted: "Blessed art thou, angel of death, author of every new song."

T. S.

A CEREMONIAL

VOLUME
2

A Cross-Country Runner
at Sixty-Five

The list for the X-country run was tacked up in front of the Post Office; the small boys crowded round, looking for only one name, and there it was:

No. 6–PERRY WESTOVER

"He's going to run again!"

"Look, is the old man going to run again?"

"Let *me* see."

"They say he has run a thousand times."

They crowded up close to the bulletin board, staring at the one name.

"How could he run a thousand times when the race is only a hundred years old?"

"I saw him run last year and before that. I saw him run twenty times!"

"What! you little liar; you're only eight years old."

"He *used* to run, my mother told me so."

"Why does he run; he's too old to win."

"How do you know he can't win? He takes it easy, he's just kidding around. He could win any time he wants."

"I saw him running once in the woods when nobody was watching, and he went like a streak; you couldn't see him—"

"How did you know it was him?"

"If he once put on the steam! They say he has so many silver cups that the whole cellar is full, and there's no place to put the coal. Isn't that so, Danny?"

19

Danny was the runner's grandson. "My grandpa has lots of cups and medals," he said.

"He must be a hundred years old!"

"My grandpa is sixty-five," said Danny.

The Winchester Borough X-Country was one of the oldest races in the State; it was forty-five years old. Runners from all the neighboring boroughs and even from neighboring counties came to run in the event. Perry Westover, however, had run all forty-five times, ever since the inception of the race; he had not missed one year. In his prime, he had once won three times in a row, and twice besides that. Even now he always came home among the first third, probably because of his experience of the course. Other entrants came back eight or nine times; but this was his forty-sixth! A X-country runner at sixty-five!

Mrs. Perry Westover disapproved of her husband's racing.

"I hear that you have again handed in your entry," she said sharply.

"Yes," answered the old athlete.

"Why do you do it, running with a lot of boys! You act like an old fool. Don't you see that you are an old man?"

"I used to run to win; now I run just for the race."

"Running under the broiling sun—you don't know how it aggravates me or you wouldn't do it, to see you come home worn-out and panting. How long do you think your heart can last? One day they'll bring you home on a stretcher. What a shame it is that *my* husband is the one all the neighbors laugh at!"

"Naturally! living close to us and having known us for so many years, they regard us in every respect in the same class as themselves; so I seem eccentric and even comic," said Perry Westover. "But to people farther off, perhaps, there's nothing ridiculous in my devoting myself to a race, again and again; perhaps it's even admirable."

"Do you suppose I care what people say, Perry?" said the white-haired woman. "I am thinking only of yourself. What a pity it is that a person of your intelligence should waste his life away in preparing to run across the fields. Almost every morning you are out before breakfast. The closet is

A Cross-Country Runner

crammed with discarded hobnailed shoes and dirty running-pants hung up forever. And half a dozen tarnished silver cups. Are those proper relics of a life's work?"

"Do you think you could name me a career that is obviously preferable, that everybody would rather choose?" said Perry excitedly, for it was a point much thought of by him. "Don't you believe it! In the long run, the X-country runner is as wise as the banker or doctor—seeing the countryside in rain and shine. One life is as good as another; mine is no worse. Anyway, haven't we done well enough and brought up three children?"

Perry had evolved this doctrine of the indifference among careers partly by a long reading of the book of Ecclesiastes. He kept this book by him so often that it began to infect his speech, and he sometimes bewildered a person talking to him by saying, suddenly, out of nowhere, like the memory of a dream: "Time and Chance happeneth to them all," or "Ere ever the silver cord is snapped asunder, and the golden bowl is shattered, and the pitcher is broken at the fountain . . ."

The Westovers were well fixed, for the village of Winchester, almost rich; this despite the fact that, all his life, Perry had never chosen a career, unless to be a X-country runner for silver cups be regarded as a career. He was "lucky," always falling into money-making ideas, "hunches," "windfalls." One time he saved the State a quarter of a million dollars by demonstrating that a new bridge ought not to be built where they intended building it, at the road, but farther upstream, since the road would have to be made over anyway within a year or two. For this he was paid $10,000 as a "consultant-engineer." Again, he set up his eldest son in a prosperous hardware business by inventing a patent can-opener, sold by mail-order. The secret, of course, was that he alone was not tied down to anything, but could look about him disinterestedly; in a freely competitive society (such as this rural country used to be in his youth) a person like that could always make money.

"I used to run to win," said Perry; "now I run to see the countryside!"

At this moment, Cummings, the eldest son, entered the

21

house—an alert, well-groomed, rather portly gentleman of forty. Like his mother, he disapproved of Perry's running in the race. So did his brothers, and so, aping their parents, did all the grandchildren excepting little Danny. No one could see any *sense* in it, in being a X-country runner at sixty-five! Perhaps they would have felt less ill at ease if he were guilty of some criminal mania, kleptomania or a lust for little girls; then at least one could condemn him. Now, what could one say to him?

"To see the countryside!" cried Cummings. "If you want to see the countryside, papa, I can drive you high and low in a yellow Stutz, and from here to Denver!"

"One need not go so far; a little territory thoroughly explored is sufficient."

"By God, you've had time enough to do that."

"Listen, Cummings," said Perry Westover, "to know one typical thing, it is necessary to return to it again and again, so that each time you change your mind, you also see the countryside afresh. You would not trust to your childhood reading of a poem, would you? Most often, when asked for a judgment about anything, we have no clear present idea of it, but judge it with the same words we once used, although they have lost their meaning; and this is why we so often contradict ourselves, trying to harmonize past words and present knowledge. But luckily we suffer that vague uneasiness of conscience which tells us (though nobody else knows) when our words are opinion and when they are knowledge. By running across the country again and again, I hope to keep my judgments up to date," said the old man smiling.

"What!" cried Mrs. Westover, "is all this philosophy behind a X-country race? I should never have thought it."

"You intrigue me, papa," said Cummings. "What is there to see in the environs of Winchester? Perhaps I have been missing something all my life!"

"Not very much."

"For instance?"

"There seem to be at least five temporal layers of the countryside. When you first pass by, different patches of land seem to have completely different dates—a spot beside

22

A Cross-Country Runner

Beaver Brook has not changed since the time of the Cayuga Indians, whereas the macadam highway, Route 4W, seems exclusively of 1930. But the more you look at each, the more you see all the others emerging from it."
"What are the five?"
"In tabular form:

"1. The rough brook poppling among the green rocks, and under the high pines roundabout, the quiet carpet of brown needles: this is a hunting ground for the ghosts of Indians (since they believed in ghosts).

"2. A stony field baking in the sun, a few cattle penned in with a wall of stones and a wooden fence; the land cleared but full of stumps, planted with wild grass for grazing and four trees where the cows can lie down.

"3. A cultivated field with tomato vines, a sow lying in the mud nuzzled at by seven sucklings; a barn with a nag, a well with a windlass. (You see how crowded the scene now becomes.) A wire chickenhouse strewn with corn grains, and loud with the four sounds of clucking, cackling, crying, and crowing; and a post-box of the RFD.

"4. Next is the tarred road, the tar spattered on the brittle leaves of the huckleberry bushes, and the reek of gasoline; a road turning and bumpy—the wreck of an old Packard with the door in the back; telegraph poles leaning in different directions; a red gasoline filling-pump (painted over for the third time) outside a hut of corrugated iron. (This Age of Iron is the most crowded of all.) The billboard CASTORIA, 'children cry for it.'

"5. And most recent is the concrete speedway, Route 4W, bright buff broad way across the State, crossing valleys and hills with hardly a rise or fall; the road-signs are made of little mirrors that catch the headlights or the sun and burst into brilliance; the bridges are of gray steel. Lying on the road, like a metal jewel, is a smashed radio-tube, the plate, grid, and filament all entangled."

"Bravo, Perry!" cried Mrs. Westover.

23

A CEREMONIAL

"Look, Cummings," said the old runner, "when you skim by in your yellow motor-car, you see all these in a flickering succession, as in a moving-picture: woodland, steel bridge, farm, woodland, pasture, rapidly coming into being and vanishing. But when I break my way through the woods and emerge suddenly on the concrete speedway, a viaduct arching over my head, I am cast bodily into a different time. That is, I am compelled to look. Indeed, sometimes, at the end of a long, hot run, fagged, a little sunstruck, it seems as hard for me to drag my way from a hunting to a pastoral economy as it was for our famous ancestors; I break forth from the forest like a tired replica of the Race of Man!"

"Is it true, what they say, grandpa," said little Daniel, "that you sometimes run so fast among the trees that a person can't see you?"

"Who said that?"

"Alec van Emden."

"Watch out, Perry!" cried Mrs. Westover, "you are becoming a ghost in your own lifetime, and after death you'll haunt the country like the Legend of Sleepy Hollow!"

"What else do they say, Danny?"

"They say you must be one hundred years old."

"What else?"

"They say that the cellar is so full of silver loving-cups that we have no place to keep the coal."

An automobile drove up to the porch. Cummings looked out the window to see who it was.

"It's Roy Wiener of the *County Recorder*."

The reporter came in without knocking, explaining that he was after an interview with the famous X-country runner.

"Is it true, Mr. Westover, that this is to be your forty-sixth annual race?"

"Just so."

"Do you mind if I take a picture?" he said, setting up his apparatus.

Perry likewise gave him a photograph of himself snapped over forty years before, when he was twenty-two or

24

A Cross-Country Runner

twenty-three. A blond, curly-headed youth stiffly posed, with a serious face, in the manner of that time, and holding up an absurd little silver loving-cup in his right hand. The reporter thanked him profusely; this was of course just what he was after. Little Danny kept looking away, fascinated, from the white-haired old man to the boy in the photo.

"In the course of years, I suppose there have been many changes in the itinerary of the race, isn't that so?" said Wiener. "What was the course of the Winchester X-country forty-five years ago?"

"Substantially what it is now. Then also we started at the Post Office, went as far as Hemans Hill, and came back by way of Gaskell. There has been only one considerable change, and I was the one who suggested it."

"What was that?"

"When the road was built through Chapone, I suggested that we run along the road for a mile or two, rather than go out of the way across the fields. It was a X-country race, I argued, and it would be a strange view of the countryside indeed that failed to take in the roads as well as the fields."

The old man searched in a trunk and brought forth a complete set of charts of the course, dating from before 1890 and indicating all the minor variations. The first drawings were rough, blurred pencil-sketches on brown paper; the later ones increased in elegance even to the point of having the printing in red ink. (It was clear that with the passage of the years, the old man had lost not a whit of his interest in the race, except that now he paid more attention to the formalities and perhaps less to the actual running.) Wiener noted the marginalia: "If a warm day, cross at M; if not, at N." " 'Ware of the bull in this field; sprint to get here in the first half dozen."

"You see, there is a certain science to it," said Perry.

"Tell me, Mr. Westover, are you always consulted by the sponsor when there is to be some change in the course or the regulations?"

"Yes."

The reporter thought that this was a good opportunity to ask his most difficult question.

25

"Do you mind if I ask something a trifle more intimate, Mr. Westover?"

"No no. Go right ahead."

"The readers of the *Recorder* would like to know just what you see in X-country running, just what is its peculiar attraction, that you have devoted so many years to it."

Perry laughed briefly. "What crust!" he thought. "How do you mean?" he said.

"Why, I mean, some men go into a thing for the money in it, others because they want publicity—"

Suddenly, for no cause at all, Perry became cross and excited. What infernal crust, he thought, to ask a man for *reasons* for what he has devoted fifty years to!—as if we lived for some ulterior end outside the act of living.

" 'He that observeth the wind shall not sow!' " he quoted, " 'he that regardeth the clouds shall not reap . . . In the morning, sow thy seed; in the evening, withhold not thy hand—for thou knowest not which shall prosper, this or that—' "

"Where is that from? it sounds like the Bible," said Wiener.

" 'Enjoy life with the wife whom thou lovest all the days of thy vanity . . . *Whatsoever thy hand attaineth to do by thy strength, that do.'* That *do.* That DO!"

"My husband is a little tired; couldn't you come back some other time?" said Mrs. Westover discreetly.

"Oh no, thanks, thanks. Thanks very much, you've been too kind," said Wiener, hastily packing up his camera.

" 'VETERAN ATHLETE QUOTES SCRIPTURES,' " he thought viciously, as he climbed into his roadster.

"Is it really fifty years?" thought Perry anxiously.

Next morning, practicing, he slowly jogged over the entire course, glad of the opportunity to move his limbs; he was very disturbed inwardly, very nervous. (He had lost his temper at Wiener's brass and had not yet recovered his mental balance.) At the same time, the realization that he had become an old man made him very thoughtful. He kept withdrawing from the surrounding countryside to the thoughts and memories inside himself, and then moving

26

A Cross-Country Runner

back to the environment as if awaking, shuttling back and forth until the two regions became inextricably mixed. Running year after year over the same course and carefully noting, as he did, the slow transformation of every part of the countryside during two generations, the houses demolished, built, moved from place to place, again demolished, brick replacing wood—it had still not really occurred to him that he also was being slowly transformed. Now, as by a flash of light, he looked at himself with the eyes of all the children of Winchester; he realized that he was not just a runner, but an old institution, extremely ancient, almost fabulous. Likewise, an old man. "Perhaps after all," he thought, "I ought to be thinking about getting ready to die, rather than running across the country again and again." All these ideas obsessed him successively, and kept recurring in various combinations—as the idea that he was a kind of institution led to the thought of Wiener's brass and this to the thought that it was contemptible for such an old man to run across the country again and again; but again, the idea of Wiener's interview led to the thought that he was a kind of institution, an institution something like a house, more permanent than those that had been moved away, soon to be demolished in turn—so that he soon realized that they were all expressions of one basic idea, and it made no difference which one of them he proposed to his mind, anger at Wiener's brass, or bewilderment at having grown old in a second, or the strange humor of being a ghost while still alive. Thus, without a thought of the road, he ground away mile after mile.

But suddenly, in the heart of Winchester Wood, in a little clearing, he found himself in front of a small house of logs that seemed strangely familiar to him; for instance, he knew, without counting, that it was so many logs high, and, without looking, that the fourth log in the rear was pointed on one end as if cut for a different purpose. Then he realized that he himself had built this cabin: he had sharpened the log to drive it into the ground as one of the corner posts, but had finally decided for a different mode of construction. How many years ago, he had absolutely no recollection. During the past twenty years at least, he had apparently

27

passed the house by without even seeing it, as he ran by
(unless indeed he had now missed the train and was lost in
the wood!), without regarding it even as a milestone to
identify the course. But now when he looked at the cabin,
the memory of all the intervening years vanished away . . .

He pushed open the door—which was provided with new
brass hinges—and he went in. The room was in the best of
repair and very clean. There was an unpainted deal table
with a book and a couple of cans of tomatoes on it. The
fireplace had been several times rebuilt; now it was
cemented and mostly of brick; but the two big conical
stones, almost twin, which he himself had built into the
front, stood there still, after many years, the andirons, war-
dens of the fire. Perry picked up the book from the table,
half-expecting to find it a Bible; but it was a tattered copy of
an old edition of the Boy Scout Handbook, with a boyscout
on the cover in khaki shorts and a flat-brimmed hat, signal-
ling semaphore with a pair of red-and-white flags.

The back wall was thick with carved initials:

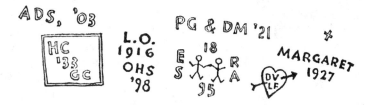

Some were fresh and yellow on the varnished logs, or
stained red, or some were dark, worn, and painted over.
Among these, the 85's and the 92's, Perry looked vainly for
some carving of his own. Quite by accident he lighted on,

A Cross-Country Runner

Cummings, Gerald, Lawrence Westover, his three boys. But there was no P W, no Perry Westover; either he had never thought of carving his own name in the wall, or— what was inconceivable—somebody had scratched out his initials (as the oldest and most worn) to carve over them. To be sure, it was he who had built the wall! . . . To Cummings and Gerald, evidently, this cabin must have seemed part of the immemorial wood; how could it have occurred to them that their own father had built it. P. W. Struxit—Perry Westover built it! For a few moments he became passionately absorbed, fascinated, in the contemplation of each separate carving in the wood—so that he could hardly drag his eyes from one to the next.

On the way to Chapone, he again lost all sense of his surroundings; he clambered over stone fences, his thoughts 240,000 miles away.

"Were Wiener to ask me again," he thought, "I should again quote the passages from Ecclesiastes: *There is a time for every purpose and for every work.*" "But Perry," Mrs. Westover said (he thought), "all the same, perhaps some works are more proper than others." "All are the same! all come to one end!" he cried. He quoted, " 'He hath made everything beautiful in its time; also *He hath set the world in their heart, yet so that man cannot find out the work that God hath done,* from the beginning even to the end.' Even a wise man can't find it out! What does this mean? It means that one thing is as good as another!—

> Strange things I have in head, that will to hand;
> which must be acted ere they may be scanned."

"Is that how you interpret Ecclesiastes?" asked Roy Wiener, arranging his apparatus to take a picture. "The book is a long sermon against idolatry," said Perry; "some men experiment, as it is said, 'how to pamper the flesh with wine'; others make great works, houses, vineyards, gardens, and parks; they gather gold and silver and servants. Others, again, try to become wise. All this is vanity. 'Let me point out,' says the Preacher as I read it, 'that to put your trust in such works is idolatry and vanity. Yet it is proper to

29

turn to something or other,' he goes on to say, 'whatever your strength is capable of, for "to everything there is a season, a time to every purpose under the heaven"—only do not put your trust in *it*.' " "In what shall we put our trust?" asked the reporter. "In God," said Mrs. Westover. "Is this the meaning of the book?" asked Wiener wonderingly. " 'Then,' " quoted Perry, " 'Then I beheld all the work of God, that man cannot find out the work that is done under the sun; though a wise man *labor* to seek it out, yet he shall not find it; though a wise man seek to know it, yet shall he be unable to find it out. Chapter IX. For all this I laid to my heart: that the righteous and the wise and their works are in the hand of God; whether to be love or hatred—man knoweth it not; all is before them. All things come alike to all. . . . *This is an evil that is done under the sun!* " " 'Whether to be love or hatred—man knoweth it not,' " said Mrs. Westover. "Yes, yes," said Wiener approvingly, " 'the race is not to the swift, nor the battle to the strong'—I am a reporter, I have seen it often!—'neither yet bread to the wise, nor yet riches to men of understanding; but time and chance happeneth to them all.' " "Ah," cried Perry, "I see I have convinced you!" "Who would have thought that there was so much philosophy behind being a X-country runner at sixty-five!" said Mrs. Westover.

"On the other hand," said Perry Westover, "although it is certain that one career is as good as another—I mean to say that this can be established by incontrovertible proofs—yet sometimes it is clear to me that the reverse is true. Isn't the Governor superior to his stenographer? If only I, if all of us, had turned to something else—" "*No no!*" cried the Reporter; "Everything seems whole and strong when you look at it from afar; it is only when you take it in your hands that it falls to pieces. It is only when you take it in your hands that it falls to pieces." "Meantime, as you try each thing, you grow older," said Mrs. Westover; "and this goes on from day to day. Perhaps my husband has been right to stick to one thing." "What a snare!" cried the old man, about to burst into tears; "finally you get to be sixty-five years old and ought better to think about dying than about living."

Suddenly, emerging from a copse of birch, he found him-

self at the white fence of the State Road, 4W. A green
roadster, with flashing glassware, shot by at eighty miles.
Perry sat down on the fence for a breather. On the road was
lying a broken spark-plug, the porcelain insulation broken.
There was always some such broken relic on the unending
speedway—just as Perry had previously described the shattered radio-tube on the concrete. He kept staring at this
spark-plug. He knew from experience that by staring long
enough at one spot, and thinking hard, he could revive in
one timeless vision the whole history of the place—the
steam rollers would return and the tar-men light their fires;
the salvos of dynamite levelling the hill; and before that, a
nag dragging a peddler's cart up the grade. He ran on a few
yards, along the road. On the right hand was a battery of
signposts: GASKELL 2½ miles. MIDDLETON 10 miles. MAL-
ORY 15 miles. CICERO 125 miles. From the lowest of these
signs could be seen dangling an old shoe that Perry, having
found it on the road, had hung there, in case the owner ever
drove back that way; but by now it was spoiled by the rain
and shine. The fancy struck Perry that, just as these signs
marked the distances of different towns, it would be a
natural thing, and not useless, to set up signposts of the
passage of time: 5 years ago. 50 years ago. 150,000 years. (As
if abruptly, on a local signpost, there should appear: THE
MOON ↑ 240,000 miles!) . . . At the signpost, the course left
the road, and once again Perry plunged into the wood.

It was the fall of the year, the beginning of October. In the
wood, four urchins, playing hookey from school, had built a
fire among the brightly-colored trees. They were telling
dirty stories and were playing cat's-cradle, passing the in-
tricate cord from one set of fingers to another.

Perry sped out of a scarlet thicket nearby; his white form
appeared and vanished among the tree-trunks.

"Look! there is Perry Westover, practicing for the race!"
cried one of the kids in an awestruck voice.

"Where? where? I don't see him," cried the others; they
were unable to point because of the game of cords between
their hands. "Where is he?"

A CEREMONIAL

Perry kept appearing and vanishing in the wood.
"There he is!"
"There he is!" they cried one after another.

New York City
[January] 1936

Remo

During the days I wrote the argumentative story called "The Boy Scouts of Westhampton," I was in a mood of sobriety, as one who has learned a needed lesson. In this story it was agreed, between the Scoutmaster and the Boy Scouts, between myself and the Boy Scouts, between the reader and myself, that there must be no more deception, no more self-deception, no more lies, no more make-believe. *Why* fool ourselves? I had learned a sad lesson from the summertime with R. and from the springtime with G. and from the last week in February with E. Why fool myself?— even I realized that it was time to return home. The sober truth was that these pretended loves had spread in my soul a zone of death. But now, by a process of reasoning with my pen, I came to set a limit to desire.

I stepped out into the sunlight on the footpad snow, among the brittle icicles and among the rainbows on the trees, on the very day that I released "The Boy Scouts of Westhampton" to the publisher, and the mood of sobriety that had accompanied the composition of this story dissolved into gayety as I moved in the frosty air. I chanced at once upon Remo, the boy who lives in the next house, throwing himself into the silent drifts. This Remo was little more than a child; he was 13 years old; he was at the age of telling lies. Yet on this wintry day as I saw him— seeing him suddenly, as it were—in a snow-caked blue jacket, with a blue cowl concealing his head but not his face, which appeared surprisingly at the border of the cowl, I

33

fell in love with the childish boy; anyway he was tall for his age. No no! I was not fatally struck by such a love, like that writer von Eschenbach who died in Venice of the plague; but his face shone out of the dark cowl in an unusual manner that I could not deny. It was a week of Christmas holidays and we went all day for sleigh-rides with Rippy and Jules.

My Remo lied about everything, to his mother most and next most to me. In school he told lies about the multiplication-table. To win my admiration and especially to make himself seem older in my eyes, he lied to me that he was in the 2nd term of high school. But I was no longer stupid (and why fool myself?) and I learned, by asking the others, that he was in 7A. And in order that he could talk to me about school, and not keep looking daggers at certain remarks of Rippy's, I went to meet him coming out of school.

"Who told you?" he said sullenly.

"Rippy," I said, naming his best friend in order that I could see my boy become angry.

"I'll kill 'im—it's a *lie!*"

"Wouldn't you like me better if you thought I was in high school?" asked Remo.

He told the same lie to other adults, for instance to my friend Mr. Terjesen, the mailman—trying in this way to make people think that my love was more reasonably directed, to a young man in high school! But 13 is the great Age of Lies, when desire is growing more intense, but experience has not yet taught one to be circumspect.

January 29th was Promotion Day at school, and in the afternoon occurred the following amusing episode:

I was standing on the corner with Terjesen, the letter-carrier, who had just finished his round and was leaning against the lamp-post, and I was waiting, of course, for my boy Remo to come by, but was so absorbed in a discussion of mechanics that I had forgotten time and place, when suddenly he appeared and leaned against me. I lightly locked

his head with my right forearm. "Well, were you pro-
moted?" I asked. He said, "Yes," darting at the same time
an apprehensive glance at Mr. Terjesen. "What class are you
now in, in high school?" asked the postman. My boy
pressed closer against me, so as not to have to see me. "In
the third," he muttered darkly to Mr. Terjesen, and breaking loose he moved away, trailing an empty book-strap, for
their text-books had been collected.

But just at this moment, while Terjesen and I were standing by the lamp-post, while Remo was standing with one
foot off the curb, a window opened above us and Rippy
called out from the window on the second floor: "Remo—
what class are you put into?"

"*What?*" cried Remo. "—I can't wait, I have to go to the
store."

I let the postman in on this little comedy, so that he could
better appreciate the attempt made to keep him in the dark.

"I can't hear you!" shouted Remo, trying with these
words to drown out Rippy's voice.

"7B what?"

"Higher! higher!"

"Two for lying," said Rippy.

Perhaps I ought not to have allowed a situation to arise
where my kid felt so disgraced in my eyes (as he thought),
especially since I did not want to correct him. It was in my
power to have forestalled that situation by walking a step in
any direction. But Remo would not find himself in disgrace
with me when I saw him at 4 o'clock and we went on the
pond with skates among a hundred other rainbow sweaters
swaying from side to side; but he would find that I loved
him more. It was, of course, as an effect of loving little
Remo that I complicated the situation by letting Mr. Terjesen in on the comedy and then enjoying it with him—for
the men who love childish boys desire to talk about their
characters and games. But my Remo might have known—
as if he did not know!—that whether he was caught in lies
or was slow in school would not disgrace him in my eyes,
although it might in some people's. What *would* be
disgraceful?—if he no longer looked out from the dark cowl

of his snow-caked blue jacket? No no! we had already advanced beyond that. As the low red sun colored the ice, and as it glinted from the skates of the other skaters far off, little Remo and I skated into Jellico's Creek; and here, all noise and sight suddenly cut off, we were alone.

"All the same," I said to Mr. Terjesen, as we stood beneath the lamp-post, as my sweet lad Remo moved slowly toward his house trailing his bookstrap, as in the window above Rippy disappeared like a portrait vanishing from a frame—"There is sometimes more advantage in seeming to be than in being actually."

"How do you make that out?" asked the letter-carrier.

"Why, when he *is* in the 3rd term of high school—"

"Who is in high school?"

"My boy Remo, of course."

"What! is it *your* son? I didn't know that Mrs. Bairnsfather and you had any son."

"No, he is not."

"I thought it was a kid from nearby, though I have sometimes watched you go bobsledding with him."

"*Have* you?" I said sharply.

"I like to take out a sleigh too, sometimes, and join in with the kids of my boy's age."

"Do you?"

Reaching his house, *my* boy flashed a significant smile in our direction, and disappeared within.

"You ought to teach this boy not to lie," said Mr. Terjesen.

"I am not so sure of that," I said, for I was not in favor of any change in my little liar, any change that might alter our relations, any change in the wintry afternoons. I said: "When he *is* in the 3rd term of high, do you think my Remo will have any more pleasure than he has in 7B-4? No no! that will be his ordinary class, as he has a class now and last term he had a class—"

"Yes, every class is equal, I suppose."

"—Just as you are a letter-carrier, Terjesen, and I the author of 'Here Today, Gone Tomorrow' (do you think I can take pride in that work?—*I* know how it came to be written!); just as Garbo is *used* to posing before the camera, and Honig has *finally* gotten to be the Governor! Am I naming unusual instances?"

"Perhaps not," said the letter-carrier.

"But Lies and Wishful Fancies," I said, "allow us, in other people's eyes or in our own, to skip the intervening stages and to get what we want when we want it!—all those things that will fade into the light of common day as we really approach them little by little."

Somewhat disturbed by my vehemence, by the expressiveness of my badly restrained emotion, by the uncalled-for confession of my easy love, Mr. Terjesen raised his gloved right hand to check me.

I said: "But it is my darling liar, my little Remo, sweet kid, who has taught me again this life of the fancy—with his lies about himself to me, and about me to Rippy and Jules, and to his mother about every one, when I had just invented a long and gloomy argument called 'The Boy Scouts of Westhampton.' "

Out the corner of my eye—as if I had been watching for anything else!—I saw Remo with his poodle-dog Mickey held on a leash reappear from the house.

. . . Alas! it is very true, I thought, that in two years, when he *is* in high school, I shall hardly be able to recognize my Remo; in four years he will be taller than I. Ought I not to act with these facts in view?

Blinking, I dismissed this afterthought to another time.

"Yet you see how it is," said Terjesen kindly, "the boys who lie are always caught in comic situations."

"Do you think any of the others are happier in the long run?" I asked with bravado, for I myself had ceased to think whether they were or were not.

"Happier I won't say, but safer. If he were my boy, I'd surely discourage such reckless habits."

"No no! at present you are talking like the Scoutmaster of the troop at Westhampton, a great proponent of the habit of freedom as he calls it, but no friend of the momentary free act itself."

A CEREMONIAL

At these words Mickey, who had been dashing towards me unleashed (for Remo had let him loose to fetch me), barked, and tore at my trouser-legs.

During these last few moments, while our responding breaths commingled in the frosty air, while I watched Remo approaching from the door of his house, the wintry afternoon passed into a new phase, into an ancient phase that I had come to look forward to during thirty-five days, as a roulette slowing down stops at last: on a lucky number—a phase of pleasure, as at 5 o'clock in the dusk the golden lamps suddenly light. Who was I now, in my ankles and in my heart, in my senses and in my soul? Mickey tore at my ankles, as if to say: "Come away from this dangerous dialogue at the unlit lamp-post where you are thinking too abstractly." My heart was pounding. My sight composed a portrait of Remo loitering at the news-stand, as if spelling out a headline, but he was spying at me through his lowered lashes. My hearing registered these words of Mr. Terjesen's: "Ha! will you advise him to spend all his life *skating* on thin ice?"—and to this my intellect had a ready reply in the form of another question: "And what keen pleasure is there without a risk?"—but my Desire, instead, caught up that idea of Skating from the mailman's metaphor.

Like a face returning to its frame, Rippy reappeared at the window above us on the 2nd floor, and "Remo," he called down, to his friend but to my darling, "are you coming up to play?"

"No no!" said I, "Remo is coming skating at Jellico's Pond."

[New York City]
February 1936

Peter

Walking down Audubon Avenue comes little Peter on the
way to the arithmetic test. He is frightened and has an
uneasy feeling in the stomach because of the test, and his
head is glowing. In his hand he clutches two penny pencils
newly sharpened with long points. Alongside the curb there
is a horse and Peter balances from foot to foot longing to
touch the horse, but afraid; but finally, with a rapid gesture,
he touches him on the shoulder. The animal shies, puts his
foot on the sidewalk. Panicky, Peter steps back and watches
from a safe distance. There is a clock in the store saying a
quarter to ten. With a sinking heart, Peter thinks he is too
late; but it is really only ten of nine, because he mistook the
long hand for the short. In a burst of excitement and relief,
he runs across the street, into the sunlight, unable to
breathe, dangling his books at the end of the strap. With a
last skip, stops running, out of breath, and he walks on and
pulls up his books under his arm. He notices that he has
been running with the pointed pencils in his hand: what if
he fell and dug his eyes out? This thought so numbs him
that he momentarily halts, eyes wide in distraction; but the
sun, shining into his eyes, makes him blink and see everything black, then violet and green. At this he begins to
experiment, staring at the sun with open eyes, then blinded,
shutting them tight and, turning round, slowly walking
backwards watching for the round images of black and
violet, crimson, and yellow-green, to succeed each other in
his teary vision. Preoccupied, eyes shut, walking
backwards—suddenly he steps off the curb and comes

39

down, with a sickening shock and a blinding light, on the back of his head. Immediately he sits up, groggy, his head clearing: he finds himself in the gutter. Puts his hand to the back of his head and finds, with a smart of pain, that there is no blood but a rising lump; his eyes, already teary, begin to be wet. He looks at his hand, but there is no blood on it. A man, bending over, lifts him to his feet; "I'm aw right," mumbles Peter, moving away blindly, trailing his books along the sidewalk. "How much is 15 + 9?" he asks himself in a panic, for the idea has popped into his mind that, perhaps, he has forgotten everything by falling on his head. He sees that one of his pencils has lost its black point and his heart rises into his throat. "15 + 9 is 24, 7 + 9 is 16, 3 + 9 is 12 . . . Those all have 9's . . . 8 x 7 is 56." To make sure he has not forgotten everything, he moves his lips to the song,

> "Oh you nasty man
> takin' your love on the easy plan,
> here an' there an' where you can—"

A ball bounds along the sidewalk, which Peter, dropping everything, corners fumblingly, and with a wild heave sends it to the tall boys up the street. The ball rises, glittering, into the deep blue sky of June. Peter feels as if he has been playing with the big boys. "Is 7 times 8 really 56?" thinks Peter piteously, for now he feels that he has forgotten everything. He tries to add it up—"8, 16, 21, 30—8, 16, 21, 29, 37, 45, 53"—but it never comes out right.

"Tag! you're It!" cries Wally, pounding him between the shoulders. "Aw quit it, I just fell an' hurt myself," says Peter, half-sobbing. "Are y'all ready for th'arithmetic test?" asks Wally. "Wally, how much is 7 times 8?" "7 times 8 is 56," says Wally. "I'll never pass the test," says Peter, " 'cause I fell an' knocked everything out of my head." "You always get a hundred!" says Wally, in jealous anger. "Do you think so?" Peter is proud, uncertain, reassured. "What are you draggin' your books on the ground for, you nut?" asks Wally. "Because it's the end of the term and I wanta use up the covers." At this they turn into the

Peter

school-street, where there are hundreds of scholars running
this way and that. A whistle blows.

[*New York City*]
1936

41

Night

I. Acts of Desire

The hundred thousand incidents of the 5th of June had been ordered to these moments of desire of the night, to these acts of desire, this nocturnal climax of the techniques of seduction. Fantasies so dangerously appearing in the middle of Broadway among the flashing trolley-cars, and painted brighter than the graying sunlight and compelling enough to bring to a pause the animated scene, came to this real reality; and the activities of communicating by telephone and of going from the south part of town to the north, here reached their end. Here was the concentrated daytime, for each episode of the day had boiled over into a vapor of hope and lust, of fantasy, this strengthening daylight, this poison. Loudly rang the bells of the impatient trolley-car, of the Chapel of the Incarnation on 176th Street, and of the insistent telephone in the morning; but from all these the highest overtones were abstracted for these momentary chimes of the intimate night, as dreams are made of memories of childhood and artists succumb to autobiography. A mutual desire charged the hours with impatience, broke off every attempt to organize the electorate, in a brief skirmish and the triumph of impatience.

The night of love is resonant with echoes, but the day before with whispered plans. *Tacet nox:* "the night is still." Early in the morning rang the insistent telephone; and

43

many voices of mid-day—the passage of coal down a chute, the railing of roller skates on the pavement—were urgent whispers, warnings of the passage of time, impatient distractions to organizing the electorate. "Society too is impatient," Arthur told himself crossly; "the issues are very urgent." . . . But at night the street-noise is silent. It is an ancient observation that the stars do not spread rumors of scandal. The unregarded clock-ticks hurry on and on. Only such phrases are heard as "sweet kid" or "little whore" or "give it to me again," amid the acts of desire: these phrases of desire, the concentrated dialect of the activity of daytime. *Tacet nox:* "the night is still." It is resonant with echoes of the activity of the 5th of June, and the seconds of the clock are running, running. They say: "do you like this?" and "kid, make the small sound."

It was not always that the fantasies of mid-day, appearing dangerously in the middle of Broadway, or the impatience of the afternoons led up to the echoing climax of a night of desire. Fancy itself sometimes consumed the fuel of love. At other times occurred the following cycle: Impatience gave way to Longing, as can easily happen; but this, isolated in its purity, apart from the passage from one distraction to another, was soon contemplated with Patience; and Patience passed over into Peace, which is the denial of desire. Thus the cycle ran: from Impatience to Longing, to Patience, to Peace. In this way, often, love turns into art, and we are embarrassed to respond to acts of desire.

Behind the right ear of Joan when her bob was two weeks old, the silky copper-hued hair grew in a whorl, the form of a spiral, of a smooth whirlpool. Here, in this center about to turn, Arthur pressed his lips, protruded his tongue. It is the way of those parts of the body that stand up when erotically excited, her breasts, his sex, to look up like dumb, inquiring animals. The eros of man has no season, it is said (though there is most poetry of springtime, and June is the famous month of weddings); it is also true that there is no region of the human body exempt from desire: for the delicate nerves touch each other off, so that sometimes trivial contacts excite orgasms, which could not happen among animals. The acts of love are literally a fever, or fire: the breathing

44

Night

deeper, the ears ringing, the heart beating stronger, and so forth. The bodies of people are at all times lazy conflagrations, but now—as one flame frees another from the coal or the sticks, in a contagious jail-break—the burning bodies touch each other off. At night, when all the efforts of daytime toward security have retreated to this intimate stronghold, there is a concentrated music. Under the pressure of a usual act, Joan emitted with a hoarse intake of breath a rising note half-way between a sigh and a moan. This sigh was the ultimate signal of the 5th of June, the moan was the audible close of its communications.

No rumor of these climaxes of the night before survived the dawn. *Tacet nox:* the night did not talk; among the innocent whispers of the morning, there were only plans of the day to come. Just so, when the Fall River boat arrives at the dock at 6 AM after its overnight voyage through Long Island Sound, the porters wake the passengers who are surprised to feel the boat not moving, the throbbing ceased, and outside, the morning light and a wagon clattering on the dock; then at once they forget and awake into the world of disembarking and of breakfast at a cafeteria. How completely we forget the feverish night! and the feelings that monopolized attention fade into nothing.

2. Alteration

While the half moon stood on the left of the water-tower, across the Harlem rapidly lengthened the white smoke of a locomotive, slowly expanding. Joan slept. Long, long, from the street rose 2 fading calls of an auto-horn, sounding "Arthur—Arthur—"

"Arthur—Arthur—" these seemed to call (or any other bisyllabic name that was one's own). Hark, this summons! introducing a new variation. Arthur lay with eyes open on the pillow, but with all his attention crowding into his ears, as tho he were a music-critic. The auto-horn sounded again, like the modulating chord that precedes a new variation.

Gently from beneath Joan's shoulders he disengages his right arm. This arm is asleep and has lost the feeling of love.

45

Over the rest of his body he has broken into the sweat of change—yes! just as if he were being summoned to be taken on a long journey. Standing at the window he sees that the white plume of the train, slowly expanding, has lengthened to a mile in the breathless air. Of the 2 lighted yellow squares of windows in the wall across the street, one is blotted out. A black touring-car stands beside the curb with a door swung open.

(Have neither fear nor hope, reader! we shall not climb into that car.)

I am describing the psychology of night-time, the moral meteorology of 1 AM among those animals that make their living by day. The awakening consciousness does not at once enter upon some plan. Those who wake in the dead of night can see somewhat in the dark; their perceptions have peculiar powers.

—Those who wake in the dead of night
   dwell in a different world from ours,
  their eyes can see without the light,
   their perceptions have peculiar powers . . .

A personage came below with a valise, departing on a journey, climbed into that touring-car, and the door slammed shut.

Emerging from the dim-lit lobby, Arthur watched the car retreating down the street, red sparks leaping from the exhaust. But he himself, awakened in the dead of night, yes! having negotiated the journey between day and night, need not travel farther. (It is not my custom as a writer of stories to present more than one movement in each.) The summons of the automobile-horn awakened him to this new life: how much farther could it carry him on wheels?

At this moment the yellow moon passed behind the tower.

Night

3. *Scenes after Henri Rousseau and*
William Wordsworth

When it emerged on the right, the moon was small white and round, like a moon in a jungle painted by that simple heart, Henri Rousseau. Just as among the green fronds in the white moonlight, among the dark lions playing in the shadows, stands a solitary piper with an inscrutable expression on his face: so Arthur stood on the corner of Amsterdam Avenue and 182nd Street where the Boston Post Road,

and the Albany Post Road,

converge.

Conceive this, with the small moon riding high, as the heart of a forest,

       c'était l'heure tranquille où les lions vont boire,

it was the tranquil hour when the lions go to drink. The Knickerbocker Ice Company was a mighty beast dying by the riverside, mortally wounded by the invention of electric refrigeration. The George Washington Bridge was a faithful domestic animal, a servant of the people, that had strayed into these wilds. All thru the night Burns Coal and W. K. Streat blinked at each other with neon eyes, but by day they engaged in a resounding combat for the territory of the Bronx. There were a few of these great interests, such as United States Aluminum or Bell Telephones, that did not fight with any of their own kind, but fed contentedly on many smaller creatures.

"What a piping it would be! what an Orpheus!" thought

47

Arthur, "to hypnotize, to harmonize, all such ravenous monsters. This is not the way to make peace in this forest—do not try it, New Yorkers, but clear the forest by extermination!"

This pleasant machine-age forest, and this megalopolitan fauna for the most part surly. *C'était l'heure tranquille où les lions vont boire.* In a doorway bloomed the flame of a match. On Ogden Avenue rang out a learned argument. And the expanding plume of locomotive-smoke rose, in a milky web, among the stars.

When the white among the stars began to be the light of morning, the atmosphere was that of a sonnet of Wordsworth composed on Westminster Bridge, London, Sept. 3, 1802, and which begins, "Earth has not anything to show more fair—." Returning now from his peregrination about Washington Heights and the Bronx, and pausing midway on any of 3 or 4 bridges, Arthur also might notice how

> the city now doth like a garment wear
> the beauty of the morning; silent, bare,
> ships, towers, domes, theatres, and temples—

a dark-green coal-barge of W. K. Streat in the glittering water and the Golden Dome of Loew's 175th Street Theatre reflecting the sunrise!

Tho bright, it is still night-time. This is why it is possible to unite in one view ships, towers, domes, theatres, and temples. None of these is engaged in its daytime business, and nothing distracts the contemplative eye, the synoptic eye—

> the river glideth at his own sweet will.

Just as the burning, dusty daytime lasts deep into the night (comes to its highest point in the acts of love)—so Night endures long after the sun has risen, especially in cities where there are no crowing cocks; and the hundred thousand street-lamps that glowed all night in rounds and

48

Night

squares burn on into the morning, though decaying. You would not think that the white smoke idly rising and swirling from a thin pipe is about to become a siren—

the river glideth at his own sweet will.

Leaning on the cast-iron parapet of High Bridge, Arthur, who gave up one day to the impatience of love, can overlook the assembled electorate of Washington Heights and the Bronx, asleep: united in a kind of agreement, in the bright sunlight, before the break of day—

Dear God! the very houses seem asleep;
and all that mighty heart is lying still!

Next moment began that busy day, the 6th of June. And no rumor of the night survived this instantaneous transformation—any more than when the Fall River boat has docked, the passengers awakened by a porter remember the nocturnal motion. It was on this day that was founded the famous P.A.W.F., that struck terror into the generals and has kept us out of the war.

[*New York City*]
March 1936

49

Prose Composition
(sustained—rapid—jokes—slow—forthright—and disturbed)

Beginning with some movement drawn-out and more or less beginning over, as walking up a winding road up a fatiguing hill and experiencing at every turning a change of outlook. For it is not interest or variety of scene or of event, reader, that it concerns me to offer now (and perhaps any more); but the movement of unfolding of ordinary occurrences to the tiring soul. And these are more cryptic at every repetition: their fascination and their boredom grow apace—what a strange thing! Meanwhile and meanwhile I am becoming more intimately acquainted with my dear self (if indeed I am), with the cyclical rhythm and with the waning of vigor—and the growth of glory. This progress, slowing down, of perceptions is my literal life, yet I find it difficult to write what will not appear symbolic. At a turning of the road, a familiar scene of the valley is newly disclosed to view, yet I shall omit to describe it, lest these things be interpreted as symbols.

Pausing a moment, to lean against a lamp-post—at this moment I am aware of what I shall call the "factual necessity" of the experience one is having. The hum of this transformer in the lamp-post in the quiet afternoon and the fading memory of my footsteps recently crunching the gravel are together in a unique relation: they *are* together. With a brief click the humming has ceased; and it is clear that this new quiet, in the quiet afternoon, has been prepared by the evolution of the worlds from the beginning of time. The painter Malevich composed a canvas of White on

51

White; we are here describing the event of a new quiet in the quiet of the afternoon.

How should there not be pauses during a tiresome walk uphill? it is to be expected. Driving one's-self, with heavy breathing and troubled pulse—the attention is so centered on these physical difficulties that, at the top, there is no memory of having come up, of having passed by anything whatsoever. Such a void is miraculous, as tho one had fallen asleep on the way up. But where a pause is so spaced—where the weight of the body is so poised—that the attention, animated by the slightly faster breathing, marks out, notes, the aesthetic relationship, the coexistence, of such objects as one's slightly faster breathing, the hum of a lamp-post, and a familiar scene newly disclosed, it is then possible, resuming uphill walking, to keep for a while the sense of the coexisting whole and to regard one's own retarding progress in an æsthetic proportion. This is the growth of glory.

The periodic or cyclical structure of my unfolding apprehension of ordinary occurrences could be expressed mathematically by a trigonometric function.

The progressive fatigue that I am feeling, that brings me nearer and nearer to a pause, could be expressed mathematically by an exponential function.

And oh, as I grow more intimately acquainted with him, I am not without sympathy for my dear soul.

Perceiving ordinary objects (resting on a rail-fence, stepping out of the way of the bicycle accelerating downhill)—they are more fascinating day by day. How frightening the cause is of this fascination of the ordinary! As I grow more tired, my perception is less adequate to cope with what is presented: these facts are withdrawing beyond my reach and control—how cryptic they are becoming! An unknown presentation, a startling occurrence, disturbs the equilibrium of the soul and initiates the quivering of conjecture. These well-known scenes becoming impenetrable to the tiring sight are arousing a state near to terror. And I feel it necessary to run over my oldest studies—of the alphabet and the table of addition—for such things have become most doubtful of all, the child dying before the man, so that

Prose Composition

I am acquainted with the transcendental deduction of the Maxim of Art, but I am not sure how to spell any of the words. A state *near* to terror—for this is not the sacred terror, the *holy* sentiment of uneasiness.

Yet what glory! at the turn of the road, at the disclosure of a familiar scene of the valley, of a moving shadow cast by a cloud, of the skeleton of a half-constructed building abandoned for lack of use! It is *worthwhile* to come to a momentary pause. Out the corner of my eye I spy the retreating back of that accelerating cyclist: this patch of red rapidly withdrawing into itself. At each turning of the road the proportion of extended objects is renewed; the hydrant which once stood on the left of a sumac has swung over to the right. Such a marvellous memory seems about to be recalled as out the corner of my eye I see the red sweater growing smaller downhill.

Again about to begin, and beginning again to move, and on another cycle of perception. For there seems to be one instant when we blink and notice nothing at all—so that our awareness again swells from relatively nothing to a volume of fascination, rapidly fading as the senses tire. The moment of blinking and the moment of pausing and the progressive fatigue of my dear soul constitute this rhythm, constitute this climax. Mathematically representing together the periodic flow and the decreasing vigor of these perceptions, the function is obviously of the sort $y = e^{-cx} \cdot \sin \frac{2\pi x}{p}$,

(which is likewise used to represent the dying away of vibrations under the influence of friction).

I fear that my first stroke of luck may prove fatal!

If *just for a change*, reader, you were *granted* that secret longing, that intimate desire, don't you think the effect of it might prove hilarious? If you were granted at the same time the *two* things you most desire, oh! how would they get on

53

together, those two satisfactions? The lover in the bed and the longed-for husband who walks in with his latch-key returning from Tokyo.

Oh! the oracles in ancient plays that declare "he shall return exalted" and it turns out that he comes back dead on a shield, or that declare "he shall reign until the Earth bleeds at the nose" and it turns out that Gaia, "the Earth," is the secret name of a small girl who falls downstairs chasing a ball.

What a Japanese flower every name turns out to be! There is a variety of tricks and scenes of comedy in confronting whatever exists in the heart with its imitation in the world. My love for Genevieve proved to be a Jack-in-the-Box! Yes, it is not the least surprising thing that I can regard this event so humorously; would I have thought this possible two weeks ago? But not all comic turns are necessarily tragic (unless you think too deeply about them).

The result was not *fatal!*

We have no time to get to know each other. I know that I, at least, never knew my best friend, Frederick—how could I know the secret purpose that was determining what he said and what he did when the public explanation was so obvious? Where did he go when he told us all that he was going home? I am not speaking of anything devious, but of the simple fact that once in the subway one can get off at any station. No one has the time, no one has the understanding to watch over any one but himself. How could we know that that appearance of Dorothy at the party, so neutral to you and me, was to Frederick the highest comedy, the most joyless comedy? Who can tell me why that fellow over there is laughing so bitterly, so heartily?

And it is especially interesting to consider the fruition of two deep desires at once. Don't they interfere with each other? How differently these objects of desire exist in the world from the way they coexist in the heart! O husband returning from Tokyo, O lover half-clad on the bed, shake hands, let me introduce you to each other:

"Ronny, this is my husband Jules. Jules, Mr. Ronny Fairchild."

"What is he doing in the bedroom?"

54

Prose Composition

"Believe it or not," declares the fellow in the joke, "I'm waiting for a street-car."

"What!" cried the irate husband, "I won't let any man say he can get on and off my wife for a nickel!"

. . . (unless you think too deeply about them) was added in parenthesis; no no, I didn't add this parenthesis just to effect an easy pathos—but I was thinking of those thoughts of philosophic men: that these comic turns, tho not necessarily tragic, are still a fatal indication of just how far our freedom extends. We depend a good deal on luck. Who is he? Who? who?—When the wished-for eventuality shocks us by coming to pass, when the oracle is literally fulfilled, when the two objects of our heart's desire unmask themselves, behold each other—there is a comic explosion, *bang! bang!* what has set it off?

What iconography is proper to the Goddess of Fortune, as Justice is blindfold and Love has a bow and dart? Let Fortune have a time-bomb.

Not every turning on the road always presents a familiar scene of ordinary perception. . . .

Alas, I regret having recurred (tho it was not done inadvertently) to the ideas and the movement we began with. For that tired movement puts us in mind—does it not, reader?—of a variety of surprising fruition, a kind of time-bomb, quite different from any of those mentioned above. I mean the desire that is fulfilled, the official recognition that is won, long after we want that kind of thing any more, are too tired for that. (Or on the other hand, the dreaded threat that is finally wreaked and now leaves us unmoved.) We are well acquainted with this stroke of luck, with this not fatal stroke of luck, are we not, reader, you and I? In the shooting off of firecrackers, such a one is called a "sizzler," because of the sound it makes.

Do you want to hear a dirty joke?
—The boy fell in the mud.

Who was that lady I seen you with last night?
—That wasn't no lady, that was my wife.

There were two drunks on a 'bus-top in London and the first said to the second, "It's Wormsley." " 'Tisn't, it's Thursday." "So am I," said the first, "let's get off and have a drink."

Little Audrey was making a cake and the recipe said, "Bake well in oven"; so Little Audrey climbed into the oven and was soon burned to death. But when Little Audrey's mother came home and saw this she nearly died laughing. Why did Little Audrey's mother nearly die laughing?— Because Little Audrey couldn't read.

(These basic jokes are so elegant that they repay study again and again. How melancholy are the basic jokes—you could easily expand each one into a grievous short story. Let the form of one such story be as follows: I tell Frederick a joke and burst out laughing, but he can't see the point. Hereupon I try to explain it, but by the time he gets to see the point and bursts out laughing, I am on the verge of tears as I see deeper into the joke.)

> Hey, you're losing something!
> —What?
> Time.
>
> Hey! hey—where would you be if I hadn't called you?
>
> *Où sont les neiges d'antan?*
> Up-to'n!
>
> Hey, you're losing something!
> —What?
> Time.

When Little Audrey was young, he fell out of a 20th storey window—
Enough.

Prose Composition

*4. A Song of Thanksgiving by one Convalescent—
dedicated to the Memory of Ludwig van Beethoven.*

Enough joyless firecrackers: it is time to make a little effort towards reason. The ones completely surprised are those who lie open to every familiar perception. Those who make a little effort are sure at least of their own efforts.

I was ill, bedridden for more than a fortnight; as I recovered I found out that just keeping my room in order, at home, purified my life. Just making the bed in a tidier manner; just restoring the work-table to right-angles to my typewriter. And every morning, systematically but not by habit, to sweep the dust from the floor, the dust accumulating in the sunlight and settling at night. Do you know where I learned of this sovereign medicine?—in the romance *Leonard and Gertrude* by my teacher Pestalozzi.

I am thankful for such contentment given to me and made by me, given to me to be made by me.

When I had been ill a few days it occurred to me, one morning, how far from health I must have been going about if now, bedridden, I was better off than for many months! In how few nights of sleepless rest enforced (with many thoughts), I succeeded in depreciating the feverish folly of a week ago: the nights of love, the nights of theatres and games! I found that I could hold my hand up to the light and the fingers almost did not tremble. And altho the object of life hardly consists in robust health, in the avoidance of nervous twitchings and trembling; there is contentment in knowing that one's will at least controls the slender fingers. It occurred to me—how soon!—that there had been a time *before* the chequered pattern of seven nights a week in society, each night endlessly engaging some night in the week to come. In less than four days of being ill, I caught a hint of the antique self-possession of my twelfth year! so that I was surprised, opening my eyes, to find my limbs grown so long and my soul so crowded with experience.

When the rays of sunlight slant across the bedroom and are gleaming with filaments of dust—when the May morning is revealed indeed—when I stand, attention caught, in the doorway, for it is there that I often notice changes—

57

when the May morning is indeed revealed—

"Systematically but not by habit," the convalescent makes the bed and arranges the furniture geometrically. Now you might think that such things he ought to do by habit and spare his attention for better problems. That's just it! For him just now there *are* no better problems; what he needs *first* is to learn to do all things in an orderly way.

Peace "given to me *and* made by me": what an exceedingly mysterious formula! You would think, since it is in men's power to bring about, that all men would be at peace. Yet few are at peace. The habit of order *and* the habit of freedom; effort and peace . . .

It is time to make a little effort toward reason. Those who make a little effort—

Those who make a little effort do not lie open to every familiar perception. Those who do not lie open are not completely surprised. Therefore those who make a little effort are not completely surprised. (Barbara.) No one completely surprised is at peace. Those who do not make a little effort are completely surprised. None of them is at peace. (Celarent.) A part of freedom is the effort that we make. Those who are free are at peace. Some of those who are at peace are those who make a little effort. (   ) Those who are free are at peace. No one at peace is completely surprised. No free man is completely surprised. (   )

All we know is orderly. No knowledge is without effort. Some order, at least, is not without effort (for who could deny that something is known?) (   ) There is no order that is not made. What *we* make we make with effort. There is no order that *we* do not make with effort. (Celarent.) What we know we have with effort. No man of knowledge is completely surprised. Some of what we have with effort is a safeguard from complete surprise. (   )

We know the order we have made with a little effort. Some freedom is to be got thru knowledge. Some freedom is to be got thru the order that we have made with a little effort. (Datisi.) One kind of peace is freedom. Some freedom is to be got in the order that we have made with a little effort. Some peace is to be got in the order that we have made with a little effort. (   )

Prose Composition

In how few nights of sleepless rest enforced! In how few nights! In how few nights of sleepless rest enforced, with many thoughts! I succeeded in depreciating the feverish folly of the nights of love, the nights of games; the quiet combustion of seven nights a week in society; the nights of restaurants. The slow consumption of my dear vitality proceeded so far that I took to bed crying Enough! enough! Enough of these joyless firecrackers: it is time to make a little effort towards reason. Those who make a little effort are not completely surprised; they are sure at least of their own efforts. By their own orderly effort they are saved from the surprise that comes over one in restaurants when the bell sounds and he realizes it is his birthday, when the letter falls from his pocket and he realizes he is not at home, when the Western Union boy appears bearing a starred telegram that has priority of delivery because it is a message of death.

When the rays of morning sunlight stand in the chamber orderly arranged, I am thankful for the peace given to me and made by me; given to me to be made by me; given to few; in the power of every one perhaps to make for himself. When I stand in the doorway, attention caught, for it is there that I often notice changes—when the May morning is indeed revealed—

Revealed!

When the May morning is revealed indeed—

Perhaps not all are willing to be thankful. All are thankful who have made a little effort. Not all are willing to make a little effort. (Bocardo.) All who are free are thankful. Not all who are orderly are free. Not all who are orderly are thankful. (Baroco.) But we who are at ease are willing to be thankful. Not all are willing to be thankful. It must be that not all are at ease. (Baroco.)

My good friend Mrs. McDonough, nearing 60, began to complain of neuritis, rheumatism, and all that class of pains. Poor and frail, she had nevertheless brought up 9 children, bearing them from her 18th to her 40th year. (About the husband I could find out nothing.) But now, when the 4th and 5th daughters, who were twins, had grown up and gone into vaudeville, came a certain prosperity for all. Therefore I wondered what pressure kept this old lady always on her feet doing, even when she was most in pain.

"I have not felt rested in 43 years," she used to say.

"Why don't you make her go to bed if she's ill," I said to the oldest daughter.

"She doesn't stay."

"She soon becomes bored with lying in bed."

"Mother is out of practice resting."

"The fact is," I said, "that she has gotten so nervous and on edge in 43 years that it is now an intolerable hardship for her to sit still. All the same, she must cultivate this habit."

I said to the old lady: "Just the way you would take foul medicine, you must now force yourself to be at leisure. After a while you will get the knack of it again and then you'll find that it's a real pleasure. Otherwise, if you don't make this effort, even tho all your children honor you, you may lose the propriety of a peaceful old age."

No no.

With the white on white of this sure peace, made by effort both in private and in public life, with this abstraction of virtue to the perfection of art, I ought perhaps to end the pages that began in fatigue? No no.

Why should I lie? I find it impossible—perhaps each writer finds it impossible—to end, to end on a note that is not the echo of my present soul, of the ever-flowing soul, dynamic harmony, the echo of a changing polytonality; I find it impossible to end; I find it impossible to end on a note.

Confusion and incoherency sometimes creep into my thought after a few moments of reasoning starting from a small problem and leading to "larger issues," as they say; in this situation the resistant mind begins to cloud, apprehension loses the grip for which it is named: and the oldest studies, the multiplication table and the alphabet, are remembered with doubt. Now this is happening to me now. Nonsense-syllables would be the clearest echoes of the polytonal soul: *Skaraw du jaggle*—of the atonal soul: *miniomini kalmus!*

Prose Composition

(Why should I lie about making an effort? about the use of making an effort? I have generally found it easy to make a little effort, yet here am I!)

No no! we have now gone back—how soon!—to before the beginning. You must not expect us, reader, to leave off, to come to a close on any other note than the beginning, beginning over, or *before* the beginning, about to begin. For in each case, *this* is the present harmony of the soul that we honestly echo; and the development of the prose (the evolution of the prose thru pages 1 to n−1), tho it profoundly analyze or ethically transcend, cannot but return to this echo on page n. Cannot but return falling from a height, emerging from a depth, declaring, *"Here am I: I have given myself away!"* Falling like Phaëthon on fire, emerging like Aphrodite wet with love: into the chaos of before the beginning.

Only nonsense-syllables operate in this world, before the formality of beginning. One hears such sounds as *Motokesklio chada,* allo! allo! No no.

One hears such music as an orchestra tuning—premonitory roulade of a flute, approximation of an E-string to its proper tone. It is not really possible to tell from the tuning of instruments what is going to be played, whether they will soon play Vivaldi or Paul Hindemith. No no. Anything is possible before the beginning, at the ending. Nothing is possible at the ending.

The resistant obscurity—the fertile Chaos—Indeed! should not the close of composition perhaps echo this atonal symphony, this tuning-up?

"When the May morning is indeed revealed—" No no.

Like the noises thru the receiver of the telephone when the power is fading: both speakers desperately joggle the hook, crying "Hello! hello!—"

The following conversation then took place:

—"Allo! Allo! fortelor gramellu tid rochar?"

"Deh! deh! miniomini kalmus."

—"Kshatelgo fortelorni gramellu?"

"Stumayvo, atta greerson."

No no.

With the first word (I am speaking of prose composition),

61

everything is determined. Before the first word, anything is possible. (After the ending nothing is possible.) I find it impossible—perhaps each writer finds it impossible—to end, to end on a note that is not the echo of the chaos before the beginning. Beware! Falling from a height are we like Phaëthon on fire, emerging like Aphrodite wet with love: into the chaos of this present moment, declaring: "Here am I: I have given myself away."—Beware, reader! for our honesty is your confusion. Do you know?—sometimes it is only nonsense-syllables that are the echo of the atonal soul, of the polytonal soul before the first word, of the clouding harmony returning to the beginning, of the polytonal soul before the first word.

[*New York City*]
March-April 1936

The Birthday Concert

When I had played the piano part of the Brahms B-flat Sonata—a work tired for us both, but we forced our feelings—I quietly spread my folding chair in the wing and sat down, to hear Herman alone perform Handel's E-minor Partita for violin unaccompanied. Quietly, because I knew what the performance would be; not without a gnawing anxiety at heart, nevertheless, for my friend.

It was again his birthday concert. In the crowd were our many friends, of whom some—I saw Alvin in the front row of the balcony and Husky near Exit 10, staring fixedly, like myself—some had been present at the very first one of these concerts, when Herman was seventeen. He would be thirty. (For it was really the eve of his birthday, the idea being for him to play till nearly midnight, and then all of us would go to a restaurant or roadhouse, to celebrate the incoming day.) Loud applause crowned every number; and the warm atmosphere of the lighted hall was a patchwork of the rhythmic noise of handclapping and the strains of the violin.

The louder the applause the sadder I became. There was no longer a moment of music in the violin, neither tone, rhythm, brilliance nor insight; but only notes, bars, a thin technique and nerves. But on pitch. The applause was in honor of a memory. (As for me! the sadder I became the better I played, but I could not teach this to him.) Now, in the wing, during a moment of silence, while Herman raised his bow—a void moment in which one often sees the unvarnished truth—I realized bitterly that I, the accompanist, could now be considered a better musician than my friend—if it is even right to consider such talents as musical. He was done for, *fichu;* he had, as we say, "shot his bolt."

He started to play, a largo introduction, a quick movement. There was not one moment, I say, when the music was played from within.

I could remember a time when each note fell crowded with the composer's mind, as it had been written down; but now the several tones without meaning slipped into cadences without meaning, and these formed no whole.

"But sometimes when I am alone," Herman insisted to me, "sometimes there is one tone that is truly bowed. Here or there, through no doing of mine, one phrase comes to life and is crowded with the composer's mind. Then we slip back. It is through no doing of mine, one way or the other."

At the concert, I could have wept at the hollow tone and the pitiful brilliance. I saw that there was a difference between *this* bad playing, which was a fall from perfection, and just ordinary playing, which would never mount to perfection. In his great days of fire and form, when he was twenty-six and twenty-seven, Herman had refined from his execution—I remember how he did it, week by week— every last dross of personality, of rhetoric and of technique, so that the natural music glowed with a strong and unwavering light, like a flawless candle. But now, therefore, when the music itself was gone, there was nothing left, nothing material to fall back on. It was all framework, no content, either personal or musical. I was somewhat surprised that any sound came forth at all.

"You see, I have lost my touch." He tried to explain where the bowhand was at fault, and how the fingers of his left hand had for some reason become "too cautious." But the change was not in his hands, but in him; what he needed was not a violin lesson, but a revival of the spirit.

With a cadenza and a flourish, he closed the first movement. There was a volley of handclapping, at which he turned toward me in the wing with a wry smile on his face. Then at once, with his head averted from the audience, as if to conceal tears in his eyes—which were not there, however, so far as I could see—he struck up the largo.

I followed him on a miniature score: it was always the same, a faultless reading and not a note of music. We came to the bottom of the page—I turned.

Then, at the top of the next page, in the midst of a delicate phrase, came one note, a B-flat—

As he had said: "Sometimes there is one note truly bowed. Here or there, through no doing of mine, one tone comes to life and is crowded with the composer's mind—" I knew him well, and as soon as he touched this B-flat dotted quarter note, I looked up from the score.

Herman played this note again and again, a fourth time, a fifth time, a sixth, a seventh.

The music had come to a stop, but was returning, like a nicked phonograph record, on the same groove. An uneasy pause! The audience looked up in astonishment. Those who had been tapping the time on the arms of their chairs, found themselves with finger frozen in the air, for the note was in the middle of a bar; those who had allowed their souls to wander off in an internal revery, suddenly found themselves *fixed*, like a butterfly on a pin, in a picture frame.

A pause! as if nothing could advance this whole situation—my stare, the violinist on the platform, the throng of people in the theatre, the social life of the Americans, the imminence of violence, the configuration of the stars—onto its next movement.

This uneasy peace
could not cease;

we had no power
to break this endless hour by hour;

Plato's thoughts knew no way out
but in the courtyard played about.

Herman, absorbed, out of his mind, played this B-flat dotted quarter note again and again, a tenth time, an eleventh time and a twelfth time. And everywhere about us, in his mind and in mine too, and in the minds of Alvin and Husky out front, under the influence of this one divine note of true music, there revived all the great moments of music that our friend had ever brought us: the Chaconne, the Vivaldi Concerto in A-flat, the Mozart Sonata in E-minor, the "petite phrase," and the cadenza of Beethoven's Concerto—an entire world recovered from one memory, for, as Socrates promises Meno,

> for as all nature is akin, and since the soul has learned all things, nothing prevents one, if he can recollect one single thing, from finding out all the rest—

all the rest! all blooming from this one quarter note and filling the air with a choral sound—all the rest, forever and ever, blooming from this one note, from this crotchet.—

No wonder that our friend, lost to the occasion and to the fact of his birthday, played over and over, a thirteenth time, a fourteenth time, this one note that brought back to him, or rather brought him back to, the realms of music where we had been ceasing to live.

As he played the one tone a fifteenth and a sixteenth time—to him each time it seemed with more power and more glory, but it was already only a monotonous scraping—the audience began to murmur, to laugh; several persons rose.

On the seventeenth repetition the string snapped and Herman fell down in a faint.

They rang down the curtain and there was a scene of confusion backstage, reporters taking notes and a dozen admirers crowding round; Morton-Moses, our manager, wanted to know whether or not to refund the money.

I advised him to. "One note of music, even though repeated 17 times, does not make a concert."

Afterwards, the three of us got Herman outside, into my car. He was pretty much recovered, and we started off up Broadway just as if nothing had happened, for so inertia always takes us a few movements further on. I kept stepping on the gas, and the others sat silent in the rear; but Herman talked in jerky sentences.

The Birthday Concert

"It's all over with me as a fiddler; I'm not sorry.

"How would you like to feel that day by day you're losing power? And after a while you don't even care, for to care about it is part of the power."

"Oh, this is a good motor," I said, by way of a joke. But I knew the feeling nevertheless, going up a dangerous hill.

"No!" he cried, "an electric current! a telephone—" as if the particular machine made any difference. *"Now the connection is cut off*—you act in the distance. Your arms are far off when you play. Can't hear. Can you hear? Can you hear me, Abe?" he shouted. "Hello! Like a telephone that begins to die away—I joggle the receiver, but I don't have the current."

His left hand was shaking—in tremolo.

I stayed on Broadway as it became Route 9, the Albany Post Road, going north through Riverdale and Yonkers; and all through here I was driving too fast.

"No connection between the body and the mind," said Herman; "and that big audience—they're looking. So I remember the old days, and I try hard; can the feelings be forced? They are absent—"

(Who knows? they are already busy *elsewhere*, and it is only later that we shall find out about it!)

"And what if the power is drained from the line by your own doing? I mean if by—excesses—you so coarsen all feelings that they can't give in any longer to the good music. Heh? What is the use of shouting Hello! hello! But anyway this isn't the reason—not *only* this reason—It's *not* for this reason! It's not for *this* reason! It's not *only* for this reason—"

I veered sharply to the right, up a side road. We had reached Harmon, two miles this side of Croton, and it was nearly midnight. We got out at Nikko's, a roadhouse at the end of the turning. The place was moderately filled with a weeknight crowd, about fifteen couples dancing to Cuban music. We sat down at a table to celebrate and we ordered Old Fashioned cocktails.

Herman began to cry and said: "You see, my birthday always comes in a noisy restaurant, or driving over the sleeping countryside in an automobile. Then I sit back, and count out the year, and my friends confound me with congratulations."

At this, a church bell in the town of Harmon rang out midnight.

"Happy birthday, dear friend," I said to Herman, raising my Old Fashioned, and we all drank, including Herman.

Now the liquor seemed to do him good, for at once he said, in a decided tone quite new to him, hard with conclusions and decisions: "The great fact to remember is this: that it is not through our own doing! These inner changes, from childhood to youth, so on and so on—not through any doing of ours! it is something that happens to us! as much given as anything else. So! the magic powers are lost, the dear habits become impossible. Well! there are some who when their bolt is shot—"

I was startled, to hear from his mouth this same expression that I had myself used.

"—there are some who when their bolt is shot, still try, still try, still try, still try—try—" he faltered and we rose. But he *did* not say it again, and he did not fall down in a faint. He said: "Just as if nothing had happened, I mean as if their bolt *hadn't* been shot! But I, friends, shall look around—" he said it suavely and with a smile on his face, suddenly relieving our tension, lightening the atmosphere, just as if he were making an after-dinner speech, "I shall look around at the new set-up, the new situation in which I have been placed, the new chances given to me and not made by me."

He was like a dead man.

New York City
1936

Tiberius

Writing from Capri to the Roman Senate, Tiberius who had usually dissimulated but was now a little older, said: "What to write to you, conscript fathers, or how to write, or what to leave *un*written at this juncture, if I can determine, may the gods and goddesses doom me to destruction worse than is consuming me day by day." (Tacitus, *Ann.* vi, 6). From Capri and from oh! the delicious joys of island solitude, what a sociable picture-postcard to send to the boys back home: "Having a fine time, wish you were here. T."

Hear again what the Emperor of Rome had to say for himself: "What to write? or how? or what *not* to write, at this juncture?—" Do you recognize these symptoms? poet! reader! innocent illiterate who will never read these lines! They are the nervous symptoms of one who has been striving after too much good. Often baffled, not content when not baffled, now he is called on to give an account of his future intentions! then he says, "What?—how?" or he cries, "Where! where shall I put my next step?" And just as a while ago, last year, the year before last, he was hastening in every direction, restlessly pursuing the pleasures of his first to his twenty-first years, the full-grown Tiberius, unwilling to forfeit the oral lusts of infants or to omit any trophy from the conquests of the future—so, the next year, the year after next, baffled as are all, more baffled than is necessary to all, the Emperor of Rome cannot begin to send a picture-postcard, though among the scenic beauties of Capri.

"Dear boys," writes he, "I—" He crosses out this "I" (in dissatisfaction with the thought implied), he crosses out

69

"Dear Boys," and is left with a writing-space at the same time smudged and blank—though the umbrageous leaves aflutter make the small suns flow across the lawn like a ripple of water; and though across the Bay our prince Vesuvius is idly smoking; and the blue tide, ebbing between the islands, tears at the legs of an angler, as rapidly as the drift of time, as rapidly as the drift of time, as strongly as the temptation to descend into vicious practices. In a rainbow the spray is leaping from the rocks, and on this screen is shown in a continuous performance the *Metamorphoses* of Ovid.

At this juncture baffled, when perhaps we have just vomited into the cup of wine (something wrong below!); when we have just received the letter asking: "When do you intend returning home? shall we have the 'phone discontinued? how long can this go on??"; a pressing query: "What do you *intend* in the case of Cotta Messalinus?" At *this* juncture, among so many plans for the attainment of too much good and among so many auxiliary plans for carrying out the plans for the attainment of too much good—what a strange thing to find that nothing is going on! There is an uneasy pause.

Bless you, we are not bored, Tiberius and I, and the reader, and the non-reader! There are more kinds of excitement than extending the bounds of the Roman Empire. There's not much time left over, from all this nothing going on, for a polite reply to correspondents or to play at street-games with the boys of 8 or 10!

Obviously too much is no good. You can have too much of a good thing.

You can't have too much of a good thing.

You can have too much of a good thing. You can't have too much of a good thing. You can have too much of a good thing. You *can't* have too much of a good thing. You *can* have too much of a good thing. (You see how easy it is to come to an uneasy pause!)

That the appetite of man is infinite we hold on the *best* authority. Yet at this juncture baffled, behold Tiberius— when perhaps he has just vomited into the cup of wine (something wrong below!); and is the appetite of this poor

70

soul infinite? of this uneasy soul? the baffled appetite of this uneasy soul?—

"What to write you, conscript fathers, or in what manner to write, or what to leave unwritten at this juncture, if I can determine, may the gods doom me to worse ruin that is consuming me day by day." And this goes on from day to day. Bless you, we aren't bored, Tiberius and I, and the reader, and the non-reader, on the island of Capri!—

And this goes on from day to day on the island of Capri.

What a sociable picture-postcard to send to the boys back home: "Having a fine time, wish you were here."

That the appetite of man is infinite, we hold on the experience of infants. Consider, then, Master Peter Skolides, fat little Greek born on Washington Heights, with gleaming dark eyes, and sucking his thumb. Will he be a fireman? Will he be a virtuoso on ancient instruments? (These are careers that are subject to choice, when there happens to be a choice.) Alas for Peter! it is not likely that he will be *both* a fireman with red suspenders and a divine performer on the viola da gamba. Look, the appetite of this little man is infinite. It knows no bounds. Do you think he will fail to be drawn into little practices of sex? No no, he will fall into the hands of a corrupter. He is corrupted in school by those who mention the species of knowledge, and the restless mind hastens in every direction. Even the writers of the books on Ethics are corrupters, for they draw up a list of human goods, the goods of friendship, the goods of wealth, the goods of good luck, the goods of health and of pleasure, the goods of honor, and the goods of virtue. Do you think he could attain all these goods? The universe is Peter's corrupter: it is aglow with objects of desire.

Yet the next moment, baffled, there is an uneasy pause. We are at a loss to explain what we intend. We start to write a postcard home and write: "Dear boys, I—" Then we cross out this "I" and cross out "Dear boys"—and are left with a writing-space at the same time smudged and blank.

O wondrously gifted family of the Caesars! They say that Julius was able to do 3 things at once, to hear a letter, to dictate one, and to write his History of the Gallic War. Tiberius too had a protean faculty, of striving after too much good, and of achieving the pent-up fury of nothing going on from day to day. For there are more kinds of excitement than extending the bounds of the Roman Empire.

This morning, when I was in the next room, the sonorous strains of a symphony floated in from the phonograph in the parlor; and at once I noticed how the successive notes were drifting into the past and vanishing like foam. At an even rate the mellow calls of horns and the singing strings impartially, the rapid notes and the sustained and the piercing trumpet-cry, slipped into forgetfulness, slipped into memory.

But music has the power of making a pattern in time, therefore in a sense of making time stand still, so that we may have it all at once. But as this thought occurred to me, I noticed that the structure of this symphony as a whole was drifting into the past, breaking up into isolated fragments like a ship going to pieces in the tide, and each fragment vanishing like the bubbles of spray.

How lucky am I! to be in the next room! I thought, so I am not under the immediate spell of these sounds, but can listen to them slipping away, out of attention. But as soon as I thought so, I noticed that the thought I had had was slipping away, out of attention, into memory, displaced by the thought I was now having. The entire structure of thoughts was also vanishing, breaking into fragments, out of attention, into memory. Memory too was part of this dissolving structure.

The words I am writing have slipped away. The somber calls of the horns have drifted out of attention. The words that the reader is reading are slipping away. *Halt, reader! freeze where you are!* This Halt is slipping away. Out of attention, into memory, and memory too is part of this dissolving structure.

I remember my grandmother: when I said I had had no time to do something, she used to say, *"You had all the time there was!"* At that time I used to think that she said this scoldingly, but now I wonder whether she did or not.

Tiberius

A Short Narrative of the Dramatic Death of Tiberius Caesar–After Tacitus, "Annales," VI, 50.

At the first whisper "Tiberius is dead," young Gaius came hurrying ahorseback from Baiae, and assumed the power with loud applause of his cronies continually arriving. There was no pause—though there was an interim of confused murmurs—there was no pause between the whisper and the shout. How should there be a pause? for there had been a grave risk, Tiberius having lingered on till 78, that the youth might never come into the Roman Empire till it was past time for satisfying the elementary lusts of 25. (Beyond a certain point of waiting such desires can never be satisfied, but every satisfaction leaves *"un sentiment d'incomplétude."*)

"Phaëthon!" cried the young women in the court. "Gaius!" cried some. "Phaëthon!" others cried. As in all periods of change, there was necessarily an interim of confused murmurs. And I am here somewhat concerned, as if composing a new college yell to be known as the Creation out of Chaos and to be equal to the Skyrocket or the Locomotive—I am here concerned to exhibit how out of the conflicting noises emerged a determinate Name, with whistling and loud applause.

There were strains of string-music in the court; the calls of hunting horns at the arrivals of new guests; the strains of singing intermitted by shouts. *"Phaëthon!"* cried some. *"Gaius!"* cried others. If any soldier, remembering the old days, cried "Caligula!" he was immediately hushed, for it was felt that this name was disapproved of, though it was hard to be sure of anything during this period of change. The cry was "Phaëthon!" because Tiberius had himself given this name to his grandson, promising that he would yet set the world on fire. (And so he will.) There was no pause between the whisper and the shout, and his cronies were continually arriving. How should there be a pause when it

73

had been almost too late to satisfy with the Roman Empire the elementary lusts of 25?

The body of Tiberius was lying in the next room.

Standing apart, under a portico, were Macro, the new pretorian prefect, and Charicles, an aged physician from Alexandria. They were speaking in low tones of the death of Tiberius. Macro was staring at Gaius.

"It was the heart that gave way," said the physician. "The repeated formula of over-exertion, anxiety, and then shock dragged it down into the abdomen, till it was impossible for it to beat."

"His joy," thought Macro, staring enviously at Gaius, "is now not only complete, but more than enough."

"We all today live under the same strain," said Charicles, "we want too much."

"That's what *you* think!" said Macro, with surprising bitterness for one in the prime of life, and who had just attained a position of great power. "And what of the thought that the past is gone by forever, that the unfinished hopes and the ambitions abased by failure can never be revived? when we become aware that we are growing tired—this is the worst heart-disease!"

"Even yesterday he dissimulated!" said Charicles, with the keenest admiration for his old friend—"prolonging the meal lest any one know that he was about to die. But I felt his pulse and it was slipping away."

"The heart cannot bear any more!" cried Macro—"These shouts—"

"Macro!" said the suspicious Caligula sharply, "do not whisper under the portico.—"

"What luck! what luck!" thought the youth with tears in his eyes, "the time would soon have arrived when all of this would have been indifferent to me, through too much waiting for it to come." But alas for Caligula! the very fact that he could think of it at all proved that for most of these simple joys it was already too late. (But Macro kept looking at him with envious hatred, as if for *him* everything were perfect.)

Now, in a closet, were discovered the various disguises.

With piercing cries of delight the boys and girls seized hold of these—a crown of ivy, hairy legs of a faun, the blue

74

nakedness of a water-nymph—and put them on, no one stopping to wonder whence came this masquerade, it seemed so natural to the occasion. But these were the disguises once employed by Tiberius as properties for libidinous garden-parties. When he felt desire ebbing away, he thought that by painting his face and donning the rough clothes of a young sailor he could again fan into flame the ashes of feeling. Or again, tired of the emperor's couch, he had the idea that he could project himself by costume-parties into a pastoral or even a woodland love. Or again, tired of the very lapse of history and the year A.U.C. 785, when, as the poem says, they had all

> come a long way to the present-day diseases—

Tiberius tried to imagine that his court was the aboriginal haunt of dryads and satyrs, and he himself Faunus,

> *nympharum fugientum amator*

lover of the fleeing nymphs. And indeed there is a kind of desire that is made of memories artificially stimulated, the original sex wholly spent. He longed to extend the bounds of what it is possible to long for; he went beyond what is possible, longing for the lewdness of innocence while he practiced more and more learned gratifications. Kinds of love! As Tacitus points out (*Ann.* vi, 1): "Nor were beauty and grace the only provocatives of his passion, but the modest deportment of some youths, the ancestral images of others. And then, likewise, were first devised the names till then unknown, of *Sellarii* and *Spintriae.* . . ."

Having put on these fantastic clothes, several of the boys and girls momentarily scattered among the sycamore-trees, appearing for an instant in some open space and then eclipsed by shrubbery, to reappear farther on. Except that, for the strangeness of the costumes, it did not seem that they were ever the same individuals, but rather continually renewed creations, flickering in and out of existence.

Observing this, how his friends were continually renewed in new shapes, an idea occurred to young Gaius: the idea of Proteus, of Protean change, of the sea-god who moment by moment could assume a different personality—a rainfall, a herd of cows, or a moss-grown statue standing in the wood. Just as if it were possible to be everything, merely in turn!

The shouts rang out on every side. *"Gaius!" "Phaëthon!"* "Caligula"—"Hush!"

"Obviously *Proteus* is the name!" cried the young heir to the Roman Empire. He saw that there was much more to satisfy than the elementary lusts of 25.

"You would think—" said Macro, on whom this spectacle of the chase among the trees had an indescribably melancholy effect, as though it were the very embodiment of the alternative lives he had lost forever and of the one he had which was rapidly slipping away—"you would think that the word would be not Proteus, but *Halt!* freeze where you are, all of you! . . . *Halt!*" he cried aloud, *"freeze where you are!"*

The name Proteus was at once caught up by those near Gaius, who had heard his exclamation in the clamor.— *"Gaius!" "Phaëthon!"* "Proteus!" *"Gaius!" "Proteus!"* Cries rang out from every throat, so the racket was soon extraordinary, compound of the ululating masqueraders, the noise of the strings, the shouts, and the hunting-horns of guests still arriving.

But amidst it all (as if he alone had heard the outcry of Macro: *Halt! freeze!)* it occurred to Gaius to wonder at Tiberius his grandfather, who up to now had never once occupied his thoughts as a person. What were these costumes? Who had been Tiberius? So in a moment young Proteus passed, but for good, from the masquerading boys and girls among the trees to the soul who had thought it all up.

"Proteus!"—Like a live animal, this name leaped and spread from mouth to mouth. It was just what all had been waiting for: the peremptory word to relieve them from the doubt of the interregnum, when all appellations were shifting in value. What was the new government to be? who knew? . . . Now, with the greatest freedom, all shouted, *"Gaius!" "Proteus!"*

"Phaëthon!" "Proteus!" "Caligula!"

"Caligula!" "Proteus!"

Tiberius

For all now understood the young ruler's chosen name, the avowed policy of the government, so to speak. And so, out the welter of names and noises, pealed, like a sudden clap of thunder, from every throat the name:

PROTEUS!—

At this loud shout, as if summoned by name, the emaciated form of Tiberius, awakened from coma, appeared in the doorway. He leaned against the doorpost and fixed all with one glowing eye. Now indeed, all froze where they were standing, looking over their shoulder, or with an arm half-lifted; so that a most curious optical illusion was to be observed: for at the same time as all froze in their places and no one moved, yet the space about Gaius became suddenly empty, as if the masqueraders had melted into the air. No one was to be seen moving among the trees. But Gaius, young Proteus, without fear stared hungrily at his deathly grandfather, and the tears slowly rolled down his cheeks. And it was poor Gaius, his dear soul, self, that he was grieving for, as do all.

With a soft sound, Tiberius slipped to the floor and lay outstretched.

But Macro speedily walked across the floor, gathered up the paralyzed emperor in his strong arms, and carrying him into the next room strangled him in the bedclothes.

"This one instant too much—this abrupt pause—this extra moment of waiting that I did not count on—" thought Caligula, down whose cheeks the tears were rolling.

"Death! death! how bitter! how bitter!" cried Macro staring wild-eyed at the Proteus he had just stifled.

Standing under the portico, old Charicles watched the youth Gaius with compassion, for he saw that the mental disease was already devouring his brain.

A CEREMONIAL

The Joyous Isle

Those are pearls that were his eyes:
nothing of him that doth fade,
but doth suffer a sea-change
into something rich and strange.
—THE TEMPEST

A perfect island! a dream with a logical plan, a good subject for the scientific but unreal prose. Let us visit the Joyous Isle, creating it, you and I, as we go along.

A rain-shower falls, then bursts of sunlight; there is a rainbow. The air is in continuous animation. Our boat nears the rocks.—

The dainty noise of drop on drop
accumulates to be the oceanic roar;

although we might not hear each tiny collision, the tinkling of the billions of drops becomes the roaring surf.

The incoming billows do not stop
colliding with the ebbing from the shore.
Spray leaps high—

there are steady rainbows built in arcades in the tenuous mist. Indeed, this Joyous Isle is the home of Proteus, of all things changing according to desire!

Round all the island the spray forms a movie-screen on which is shown, in a continuous performance, the *Metamorphoses* of Ovid: the changing of the famous Twins into a starry constellation; Jupiter falling in a shower of gold; a girl changing into a heifer and bounding away; an aged married couple becoming a pair of poplar trees beside a stream; the poor drowned body of Narcissus transformed into a nodding flower. In vivid colors this film is shown continuously from sunrise to sunset, and at special midnight performances when there is a full moon. This Joyous Isle is the haven of Proteus, of all things changing according to desire.

Tiberius

And yet, when once we are inside the bar—we find that the rhythm of the island seems to pause, to move not at all. To the tones that continue sounding, each new tone is added in a continuous chord growing richer, louder, and soon vibrating in the marrow of the bones. Memory is perfect: this is how a musical composition must have sounded to Mozart. Certain patterns of color likewise abide in the air after the colored body is vanished, as the rainbow glows across the unsteady mist, and memory outlives its occasion. And especially on the countenances of the men and women on the island can be seen, across the thoughts now passing over their faces, the expressions of childhood; and in their voices can be heard the ring of childhood.

Why do we construct, you and I, our Joyous Isle according to this pattern? First (a) we found that what constitutes our misery is that each one is limited, by nature, place, age, and occasion: we may envy the satisfaction got by others, by the man of virtue or of art (I refer the reader to the list of those whom *Shakespeare* envies, in Sonnet 29)—but being what each one of us is, we are debarred from those other pleasures. Therefore on the Joyous Isle is each one of us *Proteus;* and he can assume at will, at whimsy (for it is hard to speak of will where there is so little resistance), whatever nature is pleasurable. Places here lose their serial order. Time flows as readily backward as forward. And all things change according to desire.

But (b) in our lives the satisfactions of even our limited natures are, while we enjoy them, in the act of slipping away, and this also constitutes our misery. Therefore on the Joyous Isle every felt quality of pleasure is felt so forever. The memory of the senses is so perfect that there is no difference between memory and presentation. For instance, the ecstatic lust of the suckling infant still persists in every soul. Thus there are these 2 formal principles of existence on our Joyous Isle: our nature here is Protean and our memories are perfect. And we can affirm these of the Joyous Isle because their contradictories are what constitute our misery.

And (c) the substance of experience on the island is gratification, the union of desire and fulfillment (though possi-

79

bly there may be pleasure also apart from desire). Here no lust is thwarted; no hope is unfinished; no expectation falls short. No lust is thwarted. No day-dream fails to pass over into reality. To wish is to have, and every wish is what one would wish to wish. To sum up: *the Protean natures here enjoy in an enduring perception every possible kind of gratification.*

The call of a jay-bird on a birch of the island seems so gay that the heart goes out to it—therefore now we are that bird. We are the father seeing his son single sharply over 3rd base. We are the midnight tom-cat vanishing through the hole in the fence where the tabby has gone before; and we are the tabby waiting with eyes glowing green. We are the embezzler when he has given the detectives the slip, sitting back in a Pullman seat and breathing easy.

We are the hustling fireman with red suspenders; we are the performer on the viola da gamba.

Our immie has struck in the middle of the pot and we cry "Dubs!" *Es muss sein!* we joyfully write into our score, with Beethoven—even when there seemed no reason for joy. We are the Commissioner of Education of an honorable government reviewing a sunlit parade of children in white blouses. *It must be!* we joyfully write into the finale of our score, with Beethoven, even though there seemed no reason for joy.

Tiberius has made a perfect island!

It is the home of Proteus, of all things transforming; island therefore of butterflies; island of desires *breeding,* for the old desires beget new, remembrances of old loves seen on new faces, so that the Family of things desired is always multiplying, as it is said:

"Ἔρως δ'αἐὶ πλέκει μευ
ἐυ καρδίη καλιήν—

Eros is ever weaving in my heart his nest. At best there is one egg of longing sprouting feathers, already half-hatched. Now goes up a continual chirping of gaping chicks: the larger little loves nourish the small, and these straightway are breeding others. What is to be done?

80

Island, almost, of too much good; but how can there be too much of a good thing! Every little feeling is breeding another: what is to be done! The air is in continuous animation. At best there is one egg, at least there is one egg, of Longing sprouting feathers, already half-hatched. Tiberius has made a perfect island. What is to be done!

In a blind alley, street-games of children are going on. And we, we tourists, are drawn by an unknown force to a group near the blank wall. Here, among the grooves of a cast-iron manhole-cover, 3 are playing at immies; and 1, a lad of 8 to 10, quite alone, is bouncing a rubber ball against the ground and the wall of brick, catching it on the rebound, and earnestly counting. He has reached the count of 446; his excitement is mounting as he nears the goal of 500 without a miss! Clearly it is this inward excitement that has drawn us, like a magnet, to this back alley.

This bare-kneed boy has a secret smile.

One of the immie-players circles about and crouches, calling *"Rounds!"* With sharp clicks his glass marble hops about the cast-iron grooves, and has come to rest in the O of P & W IRON INC.

"447," mutters the lad of 8 to 10, expanding into his elastic exercise; what an elastic exercise, of aiming and hurling the bounding ball, the rubber sphere visibly quivering, the wall vibrating a millionth of an inch! till the whole again contracts to its initial poise in the small hands. *"448."*

In the cast-iron O the immie of clear green is shining in the sunlight.

"No backs!" calls one of the players.

"Dubs!" he cries triumphantly, and all rise from crouching.

The vibrating, the sharp clear cry of *"No backs!"* rings out forever in our perfect memory. From down the street, like the swarm of Leonid meteors returning on its orbit, comes a wild and straggling chase, crying *"The White Horse! the White Horse!"* then departs again. How long these cries are ringing out!

"Larry!"

"Next to Larry!"

"449." One is already so used to the 3-fold song of the rubber ball, clicking, booming, and whispering—it is hardly noticed, it occupies the background of attention.

I must not omit the mention of the cloudless sky above the tenements and the rumbling of traffic far off.

The clear green immie has now rolled to rest in a pool near the kerb, where in the yellow water it is shining with a faery translucence. Alongside it now comes an immie of steel—a ball-bearing—glinting in the sunshine. These small boys do not perhaps sufficiently esteem the formal, gemlike hue of the marvelous immies; but we others admire what they overlook, and the good is not lost.

"*Kicks!*" cries an immie player.

"*Kicks! Clearing!*"

"*Dubs! Backs! Everythin's!*" cries the Steelie, crouching.

"*Dubs!*" he cries in joy, for his immie has struck in the middle of the pot, and 2 of the pot go bouncing.

There is a hush . . . "450," says the lad of 8 to 10 with bated breath. Nothing follows. It seems as if this hush, this pause, may be prolonged.

Come, come—what is there to fear? let us not distract our attention any longer from the boy, and from his secret smile. It was this inward excitement that drew us, like a magnet, to the spot. Now we can no longer take our eyes from him! His breath is coming faster and the color is mounting in his face. A mounting joy, what would seem to some an inordinate joy, is flooding the soul. He aims and hurls again—*451!*—and again! Now each note of the 3-fold rhythm—*click* on the pavement, *boom* from the wall, and *ah* in the outstretched hands—has come to occupy the very center of attention. *452!*

Who is he, the lad of 8 to 10? Obviously it is I. How joyous are the recollections of my 8th to 10th years! What a happy sound have they! And how long are those sounds ringing out! Obviously it is I we are grieving for; my precious friend: dear childhood soul, self; joyous friend; enduring soul; dear transient soul, slipping away.

But on this Joyous Isle, our joy is mounting forever—*453!* Aiming and hurling the ball towards the wall, and catching it after the 2nd bounce with outstretched hands. What an elastic exercise expanding! the rubber sphere visibly quivering and the wall vibrating a millionth of an inch. Again! towards—who knows—a world's record, goal of 500!

Fear not, reader, we'll not miss.

"*Clearings!*" announces the green immie formally, and brushes clear a pathway for his shot, clear of dust, of an edge of bottle-glass, a moist cigar-butt. But he shoots and misses.

"*Backs! Dubs! Everythin's!*" cries Steelie. . . .

Drawing nearer and nearer, from up the street, like the swarm of Leonid meteors returning on its orbit, comes back that same wild chase, yelling, "*The White Horse! the White Horse!*" Then departs again.

But meanwhile, with eyes alight and with face calm, and with a secret smile, I am extending into my elastic ritual for the 454th time.

For I, this small boy, it is plain to see, am more mature than I shall be again till I am 70. This consummate child, at the height of his powers, adequate to the cosmos within—before the wilder movements of lust—viewing all with directness and with centrality. How justly the old painters represented children as if they were little men, but more self-possessed than men!—before the rage of exterior and indefinite lust, the division of the soul, and the striving after too much good.

"*White Horse! White Horse! . . .*" come the far-off cries.

"*Clearings,*" announces one of those immie-players formally.

"*455.*"

"*No slips!*"

"*Dubs! backs! everythin's!*" cries Steelie.

"Nix; it's not a free game."

"*456.*"

That's enough counting, we get the idea; it is to count to 500.

The fact about logic in dreams—although surely logic has a legitimate place in dreams—is that if it is pressed far enough, it soon disrupts the dream altogether, shows it up. And we know that this is true of many a waking idea also, which just a little more logic often shows to be mere appearance. Now it might seem an ungrateful exercise that I am starting on, to tear the spiderweb of a dream of a perfect island; but why should I lie?—this analysis, this destructive criticism, is what I most delight in.

Then to be brief: 1. What, precisely, constitutes a Protean nature that could become anything according to desire? To whose desire? to its own? But what is "it," if Protean? Every desire presupposes a fixed, and incomplete, nature that satisfaction will in some aspect complete, as hunger is a lack proper only to a feeding organism; thus, it is only on the basis of a *given limitation* that desire, or fulfillment of desire, is thinkable. But if Proteus is unlimited, what is the basis of the desires of Proteus? But, it will be objected, it is precisely the desire to assume *any* limitation (for the purpose of desire) that is the desire of Proteus. Then what is the basis of *this* desire, of this Protean desire? Is it a limited nature—then where is the advantage of Proteus: he is bound by his own limitation to one kind of desire, and this *ex hypothesi* constitutes his misery. He must then desire to become non-Protean in nature! Thus it seems impossible to be both Protean and to desire. "According to desire," then, must mean according to some one else's desire. To whose? Does *he* enjoy the satisfactions enjoyed by the limited natures which he wills Proteus to assume? clearly not. To what end, then, does he desire Proteus to change his shape? And through what channels, or with what instruments, does he impose his will on Proteus, if Proteus is ever elusive? But in a word, what kind of desire or will "he" might possess is worse than obscure, since we do not know "his" nature, nor even indeed if "he" is.

But similar difficulties arise if we consider the meaning of "a Protean nature that could become anything." Who is it that becomes? If Proteus really has a definite nature beforehand, is this lost in the process of changing? If so, how does *he* become, rather than be destroyed and another nature be created? And if the Protean self is not lost, what relation is it to bear to the new nature? If these bear no relation to each other, but exist (how?) as two selves in one being, in what sense has Proteus changed *into* another? And if they bear some determinate relationship to each other, how can Proteus become *any* other indiscriminately? for it is not possible to be bound by definite relations and yet be unlimited in power to change. And in general: all transformation is based on an abiding nature, and this nature must make a difference both at the beginning and at the end of the process of transformation; but if so, where is Proteus? he cannot be Proteus if he is anybody; yet surely if he is nobody he cannot be Proteus.

2. Then let us go on to inquire about the "perfect memories," about "every felt quality of pleasure felt forever." Each pleasure, it seems, is to endure but not to change; yet other pleasures are to come to join the first. Does the duration of the first go on in a timeless way that excludes succession? If so, how do the others unite themselves with it? Either they are with it from the outset, in which case where is the first particular pleasure? or if they are added on (how?) without entering in any way into the existence of the first, even in thought, then in what sense does *one* soul enjoy these diverse, absolutely isolated feelings? But if the duration of the first pleasure proceeds in time, so as to include the increment of subsequent pleasures in its succession, then inevitably the pleasures are slipping away, out of attention, into memory. No, it is objected, for as the first pleasures slip away, they are immediately renewed, and co-exist with the others, which are thus both later and contemporary. But then again we have the mystery of Proteus, and we must ask: Can the soul which is crowded with the decaying ends of all the pleasures be the same to which these same pleasures are first appearing in their freshness? (what a monotonous round!)—does the state of the perceiver make no difference to the kind of pleasure perceptible? How, in a word, can *Proteus* have a perfect memory?

The same questions may obviously be asked from the point of view of the soul: what is the meaning of the notion "there is no difference between presentation and memory"? Is each pleasure attended to as it is presented? Then it is attended to forever. How then is a subsequent pleasure ever to be attended to, for attention is single, being nothing but the directing of the one mind? This is possible only if the attention is now directed to the co-duration of the two pleasures. But then it is not directed to the pleasures themselves at all, but to some new feeling, compounded of them, and which may or may not be pleasurable in itself (for, as all know, the compounding of some pleasures is pain). If the pleasures are to endure forever, and not lapse to give others a place, it seems that *no* pleasure may be attended to. And if it is out of attention that the pleasure is to exist, then pleasure will be found in its purity only in unconsciousness!

3. But in the last place, are these pure pleasures, enduring pleasures of every kind, what we indeed desire?—these pleasures of *whimsy* (for it is hard to speak of will when there is so little resistance); would they be desired, for instance, in themselves alone, apart from the thought of having them? I think not: for ask yourself, What is really desirable about our Joyous Isle? is it the many pleasures there? then why concentrate them *there?* Or is it not, rather, the idea of the perfection of an island of pleasure, a Sum of pleasures, an ideal, an *answer* to what constitutes our misery—not desirable because misery is absent, but because misery is *solved.* But to desire a *Sum* of pleasures is not to desire pleasure; here, as everywhere, it is Perfection and not pleasure that is truly desired. But Perfection not as such and in the abstract (what would that be?), but *perfecting,* perfecting the world that constitutes our misery, actual world, given to us, and *made* by us! given to us to be made by us, working in the actual world, which is here, insistent, and mine!

Those foreign pleasures!—for in the end nothing is so impersonal as a pure pleasure—are they indeed what we desire, continuous expense of the soul upon so many diverse objects, without even the consciousness that it is *my* soul? But if mine, if for perfection I must realize that the soul is mine, then baffled, as I know; more baffled than is necessary, because of too much thought; poor self struggling, *not* to grow richer, but just to *hold her own* against the ever more pressing questions that I myself keep asking. Yet why should I lie? this destructive criticism, these insistent questions, are in the end what I most delight in.

Tiberius

Is the poor soul really so hateful of Time, time that never fails to make a difference to gratification even when all else, such as prudence or resolution, fails; time that X-rays pleasure—for "Truth is the daughter of Time," as Leonardo used to say. Time asks new questions, time insists, time makes a difference, even when all else fails. Time is the strongest ally of the questioning soul, for it will not let the investigation drop—it cannot be bribed—so that time would seem to be an even dearer force than Conscience. Thanks be to God for time, that delivers us from each pleasure in turn, and never fails.

For is it childhood—to go back again prior to some fatal error—that the soul really desires? If we were asked, could we say that we desire something in our past undone, not to have been completely? But by what nature and by what knowledge do we desire it? is it not on the basis of that very past? must not the satisfaction of *any* desire be a completing of that past? then how are we to desire a part of the very source of our desire, and a part of the very satisfaction of our desire, "not to have been completely!" The fact is that we no longer desire anything in the past to be completely undone. What then! is everything that has taken place completely desirable, since we cannot desire it otherwise? do I hold this? God forbid! but it is our present condition, our unluckily acquired knowledge, our present-day diseases that we have come so long a way to out of the unfortunate past, the necessary past, past that we cannot now desire to have been otherwise, it is the present condition of our hearts that all desire to perfect, not to start again. *(Yet in some sense to start again!)* It is not to return to childhood that all desire. *(Yet in some sense to return to childhood!)* For, what! is the poor self never to become a little wiser? never to learn to ask about herself—and what else is to ask about? never to become just a little wiser?

[*Orson, Pennsylvania?*]
[*Summer 1936?*]

87

A Prayer

Let them beware who challenge to themselves
a strength which they have not, lest they lose
the comfortable support of that weakness
which indeed they have.

—HOOKER

Finally I made up my mind to quit the city and neighborhood where I had spent my childhood and had entered into many people's lives. (It was about time! for I had gotten into criminal complications in the cultivation of my dear childish neighborhood; I had become too expert there, not to do more than those circumstances could warrant. Yet I dislike to think that it was thru fear of the police that I made up my mind to quit the city of New York.) But now, when I had made up my mind and had gone away in intention, cutting short all future plans, nevertheless I was still there in the flesh, for a few days. Here was something most unfortunate. I was no longer responsible. There were no future plans and my duties and social relations now lost all power to restrain me by ostracism or in other ways; and I alone knew that I was going to clear out forever; so that my actions, ill-controlled fellow that I am, now became criminal indeed. I dare not specify further; but I suffered the misfortune—all injustice being a misfortune—of gratification without responsibility, abuse without danger, freedom without terror. Alas! I came thereby to confess to myself, in these outrageous and disrespectful acts, that my dear childhood neighborhood was dead for me, which was something to cry about (as I did not yet).

There was no time left beyond these outrageous acts even to cry, I was so busy in making preparations toward my departure—especially concerned with breaking off relations with the very people whose offspring I was debauching.

89

What difference did it make to say good-bye to them! since there was almost no one, I think, who would have noticed I was no longer there. (Perhaps I have no right to say so for how can I know what role I accidentally played in whose life among my neighbors, just as many of them played roles in my life yet did not know it?) I am sure that it was as an artist that I could not tolerate not finishing each thing off; I am sure that it is because so much has died in my heart unfinished off that I am an artist; I am sure that I am an artist, yet the one thing needful to end off with, I mean to pause awhile and cry a little, I neglected, until now.

Meanwhile some sacred holidays were being celebrated. The obligations of these were certainly far more important for me than whether or not I left home or was making preparations to. These days were sacred also in St. Louis or Chicago. (Yes, it is likely that some responsibilities can nowise be forfeited! yet what these may be is not clear to me; and it *still* seems to me that with a little effort I could quit my desires, or even my native English tongue, just as my town. But what a strange effort to make!) Well, in my extreme business, these sacred holidays were also overlooked. I had no leisure to pause awhile and cry a little. I neglected, as it seems, as well the continuing responsibilities as the forfeited ones (which demanded some mourning). One among those holidays happened to be devoted to just such mourning and reconsideration; there could have been the occasion to do two things at one time—as every action exactly right does everything at stake at once! But I often come around to my duties only a week or two later. I often come around in Chicago to what died in my hands unfinished off; and Memory is strong as presentation!

Yet what glory! at last! in going away, going away! The clicking of the wheels on the rails sounds very joyful and musical during the first few moments. Good-bye, good-bye to Washington Heights! Often I, half-pausing from a street-game or from making a work of art, used to glance covertly toward this rattling, westward-moving train. Well, now I have what I most desired: furiously blushing with glory on this electric hurrying westward. Strange: for it is not often that the actuality (seated at the car-window looking out) comes up to the portent (of covertly glancing away). But I knew myself well when I covertly glanced away from the street-game that I loved, or when I wrote—

> Beginning over! beginning over!
> (Again again again and again.)

What is the occasion, Paul, for recreating in memory strong as presentation, and with hot tears, the childish game that we only apparently loved? Why am I crying on the way to Chicago? No one can deny the glory of the hoarse train-whistle screaming thru the night.—

> Beginning over!

Now has Paul what he most desired! (I hope that it was not thru any fear of the police that I finally made up my mind to quit the neighborhood where I had spent my childhood and entered into many people's lives.)

What a strange effort to make: to be about to quit what I most love—going even as far as the English language. Responsibility is forfeited—so I could disregard grammar and write *Turosh fedalion mi ayvi.* (I dislike to think that it is thru any fear of the police.) It would require immense courage to carry thru this experiment to its logical conclusions. Why am I crying on the way to Chicago?—it is that I often come around to these duties a week or two later, and memory strong as presentation.

Having arrived in Chicago, let me offer a prayer. Prayer, I take it, is nothing else than thinking how and what one is. Obviously prayer is proper to arriving in a new neighborhood. I cannot help, as I think about myself, crying over my imperfect childhood: this emotion is the memory of my unfinished childhood criminal. The unfinished past is a generator of many images. Emotion is bygone desire remembered, that we continue to desire. But art, as is well known, incarnates hopes unfinished and completes each thing. (But oh, we've come a long way to our present-day

91

diseases.) It is desirable carefully and prayerfully to know what one is about and who am I, this artist. I am in Chicago, as if beginning over, and composing what is here in a prayerful—I mean a critical and thoughtful (let us prayerfully make everything accurate and tell the strict truth)—in a prayerful spirit, to the end of making reasonable those nervous street-games over which I have been crying, altho I was only apparently in love, covertly glancing away. In what sense is *this* "beginning over" caught, as it were, with the unfinished past that has died on my hands? I have thus come, a little later, to a sacred holiday of reconsideration, though regrettably not on the same day as the communities of New York or Chicago. Indeed, the first part of my experiment seems at an end. Yet I might, with a little courage, carry thru this experiment to its logical conclusions.—

Wait, wait, my good friends! wait! wait! wait! watch and wait!

This morning, as I was crossing the Midway Plaisance, I was accosted by my old friend Professor H., once my teacher, now my colleague. He was out walking a dog. And now, at this point of mentioning Professor H., I may let my readers in on the delicious fact that in the minds of Prof. H. and, indeed, of many of my dearest friends in New York, my removal from that neighborhood, far from being one step in a desperate experiment (and perhaps due to fear of the police), was really, so they thought, an advantageous opportunity accepted. Instead of a responsibility forfeited, it was, they thought, the entrance upon a mature responsibility. This shows how far the same event can differ in two interpretations; and perhaps—who knows!—in many ways they had the right of it, those others, for I have not always understood myself so well as some of my friends. Yet I think that in this case I understand the uneasy movements of my soul.

"Well, young man," said Professor H. to me, extending his hand in greeting, "I welcome you to our Community of Scholars. Perhaps our life here may at first seem rather quiet to an artist, not so nervous as you are used to. In the end, we have no doubt, those little stories of yours, of which we are so proud, will be even more true to real life for this experience." I murmured an inaudible assurance. "We here take up proper places in the institutions of Society," said he; "I mean to say that each man is part of the Republic. He has his own responsibility and he profits by the responsibility of every other. This is responsibility established." "I am sure it is so," I murmured. "Yes yes! it is quite a change for you; I can well imagine. But having had enough of that other—" ("No no!" I cried out inwardly)—"Having had enough of that other, you are now lucky enough, a little older than some, to step right into this broader way, this Midway, if I may be allowed a bold metaphor! You seem almost to have planned your life." "Yes, I planned it," I lied.

"To the gate of this University!" cried the well-dressed professor in a proud voice.

I gave vent to a bitter laugh. *"Higla maroovio,"* I said, *"ta desh kampulello stumayvis!"*

And so far was I from having had "enough of that other," meantime, that here on this Midway Plaisance and while he was saying so (and I inwardly crying out, "No no!")—I covertly glanced away, down a side street, towards another little Patsy and another Remo, shrilly yodelling. And I am writing what is here, art, not thoughtless of past time, this prayer. The fact is, dear Professor H. and my dearest friends in New York, that if it were responsibility was my good, I should never have quit my childhood neighborhood for this easy life of Universities.

And perhaps I cannot quit my childhood neighborhood (but at least it is something to have a respite from the police!) Dear God, what a strange effort to make!

"Dear Margot," I wrote home to my sister, once I had got more or less settled in Chicago, "Dear Margot: By now we are more or less comfortably fixed and have set up housekeeping in the agreed on arrangement. Esther is hanging the pictures, and I . . . I am afraid there is not much for me in this dull place. I met Professor H. yesterday, walking a dog on the Midway. He is as smart and as ready for all things as ever, a regular Boy Scout, a little older of course; he sends his best, etc. He was *pleased* to see me, as tho I were a work of art; he seems to contemplate me, at the University, at 30, as precisely the right man, in the right place, at the right time. 'A planned life,' he assured me, 'a planned life!' *Well!* you know me, Al, as our poor dear Lardner used to say—so far as I'm concerned you can stick this academic calm and the whole Community of Scholars right up your ass! He assured me that I was taking my place in the Republic!!!! No kidding. Do you know what I answered? *'Higla maroovio,'* I said, *'skara beejung.* BOW WOW!' That was right, wasn't it? . . .

" . . . Margot dear, will you look out the window and see if you see Patsy there, or my lad Remo shrilly yodelling? Tell them—that I am asking for them, and that— (I can hardly express what I want to say)—that sometimes I remember them so strongly that it is as if they were with me in the room. . . .

" . . . What now, what next, Margolio sweetheart? is that what you're asking? is that what you want to know? Oh, nothing—I expect to pause awhile in this dull place, just waiting for something exciting to happen, something unusual, such as I've gotten used to. I feel that even here there are strange beasts, lurking somewhere in this appalling college Gothic."

[*Chicago*]
October 1936

94

Frances

On the death of my aunt Frances, I was not moved. Not much moved although in some ways I suspected that there was a kinship not merely physical between my aunt Frances and me. "Not *merely* physical"—what a thoughtless expression! but I speak in the ordinary manner. Her death was the end of a series of heart-attacks; there were several warnings and her last crises were distributed over more than ten weeks; yet I, busy (as I thought) with my own interesting life (but it was precisely this that I was not busy with), neither visited Frances in the hospital, nor gave a single reasonable thought to her condition, such as: what does this mean to *me*? Yet I too now, in the moments of desire, have felt a warning twinge of the heart.

Indeed, when Frances was dead—"dead at last," so to speak—I was not far from agreeing with those others of my family who said that this was better, not only for herself—a pious kind of solace—but for *us*, whose peace she had always disturbed, and poverty imposed on, especially during her illness. Of course we did not really think so (I hope), for what was our *comfort*, even of many, against her *life*? But all of us at least entertained this thought. (Does it seem to be self-centered to be thus describing not her death but what I felt? Alas! this writing also is about myself.)

I have come more and more easily to see my own life in the lives of my immediate family, in the self-deception of my brother, in mama's unconfident and uneasy smile. (About my sister I dare not talk in a phrase.) I did not think that I was like so many. Delicate emotions and general

95

insights I used to find, perhaps with a certain satisfaction, that I had or had discovered in common with ancient poets or even scientists; but my own *fate,* now that the time has come when I have not so many feelings or ideas, my fate is revealed everywhere at home, or in my memories of domestic episodes of long ago, suddenly fraught with warning. What is strange about it? my ideas, sensibility, even will, belong to me just as to any human being; but this necessity of actuality, fatal coming into existence, pertains to a deadly physical strain. Is not every physical strain deadly, reader? *"Merely* physical"—what an ironical expression for any one to use!

I, like others, had been wont to think of and live my interesting life as only mine, as if no one else had ever known unroll this fate or recognized, like me, how every chance has come in its due place symbolically. But now, what a thing it is, opening my eyes from time to time, and more and more, to see myself, this author, at a loss in mama, or dead in Frances! And there is beauty, I think, to standing under such a family doom—though it be trivial or even sordid; and there is peace in the humility of it, I know.

Last summer at the Vermont camp to which we send our child, it was easy to discern the different family strains, for at such camps there are always groups of three or four brothers, either as campers of 6 or 10 or 14, or as waiters, or as directors of the children's activities. And one day, towards the end of my stay there and when all the brothers were well-known to me, there was a fierce and continuous lightning storm, and the danger that the river would overflow, so that after breakfast every one was kept in the dining hall, where they sang and made speeches. Then it was easy to see, looking from one face to another, how the four brothers Buchanan were constrained all to the same ineffectual excellence in a trivial environment; and how charming Herbert, by far the most lively and athletic of the juniors and the most intelligent, might just as well be his nervous brother Winkie, the waiter (and he will yet be Winkie!) Yet there were other brothers, it was clear when they were seen together, who would all succeed and establish themselves, even though considered individually each

Frances

seemed worthless. Whole families were bound for sexual incontinence or avarice. This was clear as their voices rang out in speech or song, in the noisy dining-hall, amid the thick bursts of lightning, while the swelling river was devouring the bank. I hardly ventured to look at Kenneth.

What a noble and tragic cast each face had, seen in this fatal light, this stormy light! Every family a kind of species, one of the terrible planless experiments of Nature. The fact was that each joyful and intelligent soul, or sombre, or stubborn and ambitious soul, would work out a single physical doom with his undistinguished brethren, though often in a very recondite way. Even if the species *triumphed*, the individual would play a tragic role; but we know for a fact that every physical strain is going to die.

I cannot longer avoid, what the form within me demands, speaking of my aunt Frances. Every day for the week past, reflected not on printed pages or in lamps, where we often see loved objects, but in my own gestures and the ominous fluttering of my heart, I have noticed the presence of my aunt Frances. Dear God, is this what I am? but let me speak no evil of the dead. I thank God who lets me know what I am.

When I was 7 or 8 years old, as I remember well, Frances was divorced from her first husband and married a florist. Now I was horribly ashamed that my aunt had been divorced—I was in this merely vibrating, of course, to the animosity of my mother and uncle—but I was even more horrified that she should marry such a man as this florist, surely for only his body, as the child felt not vaguely but with an oppressive intensity of disgust. O child, are you present with me still (as was Frances today and the day before yesterday), to be stifled with disgust day by day at the dear strange company I keep? *We* are not ashamed, Frances and I, of our lives, given to us and not made by us! But I too am ominously overtaxing my heart, as must be indeed.

If I were to be first stricken tonight—which God forbid, but thanks be to God by whom I know what I am!—I know the peculiar horror that my small boy Kenneth would feel; and it is not likely that he, busy—as he thinks!—with his own interesting life, will come to visit me in the hospital.

Yet consider this fact, Kinny, that while your grand-aunt Frances was dying of the aggravation of contrary desire, I mean desire for pleasure and desire for peace, I, who gave no thought at all to her condition, such as to ask: What does this mean to me?—was similarly committing suicide. Yet there is nothing tragic in dying sordidly—it is not even very sad—except that we see that this is the general fate of Frances, myself, and many relations on my father's side. I know, therefore, that this painful stroke of my poor heart is ominous and tragic.

(Yet I am also suspicious of a man who sees every missed stroke of his heart as ominous and tragic.)

As is a common experience, it is not till just this week, so long after she died, that I am beginning to be haunted by the presence of Frances. And so Marcel, in the novel, did not turn his attention to the death of his grandmother till one morning when he bent over to tie his shoelaces. It has taken me a considerable time, I see, to become so self-conscious as to notice the presence of Frances when I move about. The tears are burning in my eyes for her death and my dying. But a stroke of the heart can soon make any one self-conscious: attention is aroused, inquiry stimulated—head raised, nostrils slightly distended. Who *is* this concrete reminder? what does he mean to *me*? It seems that introductions are in order:

Mr. L., meet your merely physical self (what an ironic expression to use!)

—Why, I am *pleased* to meet you! (Thanks be to God who lets me know what I am!)

This introduction, this thanksgiving, are duly couched in the terms of a prayer—for all prayer is nothing but the thought of what we are. But what a thought it is to suspect, to recognize, that in the opinion of my family, in my own opinion, it might perhaps be better, not only for me, but for the rest of the family whose peace I have always disturbed, whose poverty imposed upon, if I were dead! Hard thought, this most earnest prayer, thought of what I am, of the peculiar perfection of our kind: unusual thanksgiving! "Why, I am *pleased* to meet you"—what an ironic expression! It is not to this hard thought, reader, that you or I could

98

come merely by looking *within* ourselves; for surely there, as the poem says,

Hope fails not, as yet, it seems to me.

Yet many times men are mistaken about themselves when everybody else is not.

For all that, we do not really think so, my family and I; for, What is the *comfort,* even of many, against *my life*? My comfort against my life, as they say: "Your money or your life!" Your comfort or your life! as if contrary life, I mean my double life, could last only on these hard terms. Indeed, I myself wrote, did I not?—"Blessed art Thou, O Lord, who hast taken from me every good thing"—it is put in the mouth of Hagar! I wrote, triumphing over Tiberius, "Thanks be to God for Time that delivers us from each pleasure in turn, and never fails!" Therefore it is *clear* that for me this comfort is not so weighty a matter, not so *very* weighty a matter, at least not the *most* weighty matter; or dear God! perhaps I may in the end not have to choose between my confort and my life, for I do indeed desire too much good, both pleasure and peace—

And Hope fails not, as yet, it seems to me.

"Where there's life there's hope!" Hope fails not, as yet, it seems to me. "Your comfort or your life!" What a hard prayer, for I do indeed desire too much good, both pleasure and peace.

My aunt Frances was of a good height, rather plump and of a pink complexion, and her voice was high and nasal. She wore rimless pince-nez glasses and played the piano. At one time she sold flowers at Healy's Cabaret, and almost my earliest memory (I must have been 4 years old) is of being taken there and of sitting at a table under a pink-shaded lamp while Frances sailed toward us,

Sails trim and tackle flying,

wearing a corsage of tea-roses. When she was stirred, as

often by the resurgence of memory, her complexion became mottled with patches of pallor. One evening she told me of a man, who had married some one else, who had used to call her "Duchess" and "his Queen." She was subject to depressions and emotive transports, which were nothing but the compounding of desire and memory. She lived in a series of pasts. At the same time she was resented, that is to say envied, by her sisters because of sexual excesses which she was, and they were not, allowed. These habits of hers betrayed her into several dishonorable, ill-considered, and unprofitable marriages. And what could be the ending of such a life of excess and sentimentality other than that Frances, ill of heart-disease, discarded by her brutal, lowest husband, came to be a burden on sisters who did not love her in the homes of brothers-in-law who could not afford her? After an increasingly serious attack, she left the house of each sister in turn in an ambulance.

Yet what a difference between the highly evolved living body and soul, originative of movement, receptive of feelings, and the loose, motionless, ignoring aggregate of parts in death. The living animal is breathing, attentive, regulates the actions and passions of its organs, sees, hears, responds, has memory and imagination. As a human being, it can bear with resignation or resist with indignation, make use of conventional symbols, compose formal prose, theorize, be self-conscious, pray. A corpse is worthless by comparison. It is this comparison that we mean by our respect for sacred life—it is given to us and not made by us—and what is the comfort, even of many, against a life however careless?

Chicago
1936

100

Vic McMahon

As our self-contained, soft-lighted bus flew through the gathering darkness, I could not help regarding with admiration the driver, whose name was Vic McMahon. He was the shepherd of the passengers. Confident and easy—our lives were in good hands—the passengers readjusted their seats to the reclining position, prepared for a night of travel. Our lights pierced the darkness; we were borne swiftly onward.

But not too swiftly. When we came to a railroad crossing, Vic McMahon brought us to a dead stop, in accordance with state law, and half-opened the door so he could hear any danger coming. And again we rode on.

Reliable, obedient to the law, the guardian of the passengers bore us onward toward St. Louis at forty-eight miles an hour. And what comfort there was in this steady progress through the starless night! one of the passengers was already asleep. What nervous comfort!

As we rounded a curve, our headlights illumined a great poster depicting a small boy and girl menaced by a motorcar, and with the legend: *"Please! They Cannot Be Replaced."* And this was paid for by the Highway Commission of the Commonwealth of Iowa. Yes! this recognition of danger by the Commonwealth gave us, inside the soft-lighted bus, safe in the hands of careful Vic McMahon, a *thrill* of ease!

Vic was engaged in talk with another driver, named Sheeler, who happened to be a passenger; he spoke over his shoulder, never taking his eyes from the hurrying road; and the conversation was about a new licence required in Wis-

101

consin. Drivers were obliged to go to Madison for a medical examination.

"I had a certificate from a private doctor," said Vic, "but it was no use."

"Stiff exam?" said Ed Sheeler.

"Right down to the bones! Blood test, ears. They hit you on the knee with the little hammer."

"Did you jump?"

We came to a railroad-crossing and Vic brought the bus to a dead stop. Here there was a sign

STOP   LOOK   LISTEN

In obedience also to the last of these, he half-opened the door. Then on we drove again.

"Yes, sure I jumped," said Vic McMahon. "There's a new law so they won't give you a licence now unless you're 5 foot 7 and weigh 160 pounds."

Half a dozen persons in the bus were now sleeping, covered with their overcoats, so steadily and quietly we were flying along at 48 miles. Vic dimmed the inside lights.

Again there loomed that sign of the two children, this time with the legend: *Please! Their Lives Are In Your Hands*—paid for by the Highway Commission of the Commonwealth of Iowa. And this time I could see that the little boy and girl were hand in hand; the boy was about two years older; and they were on their way to school, menaced by a black motorcar.

And almost immediately, at the next bend, as if the roadside were afire among the bushes, flamed a sign consisting of hundreds of tiny mirrors reflecting our headlights, and they spelled out, in dancing glory, the words

TAKE   TIME   TO   BE   SAFE!

But we were safe! borne thru the black night enclosed in our self-contained and dimly-lighted vehicle at forty-eight miles an hour. Poised on faintly joggling seats, more than half a dozen of the passengers were already asleep, covered by overcoats; and the rest of us—all save Vic McMahon—

102

were hovering in that imaginary world between waking and sleep. In the brief space fitfully illumined by our searchlights as we rounded a bend, nothing was revealed but the solicitude of the Commonwealth of Iowa. No thought could escape in any direction the sentiment of cautious comfort.

Vic McMahon, licenced at Madison, more than 160 pounds, and quick to jump when tapped on the knee with a little hammer, our lives are in your hands; *please!* we cannot be replaced. . . .

Half-fallen asleep, I imagined that I was piloting an airplane for the loyalists in the Spanish Civil War, returning to a time of desire; it was the aftermath of a brief battle—the poisonous machine-gun rattle was still echoing in my ears, a faint noise in our bus the occasion of it. But now I couldn't bring the plane down; we hovered in one place, high over the earth; till at last I gave up the effort and was content to remain aloft. Whereat, waking a little, I smiled to feel myself so pleasantly poised on the faintly joggling seat, covered with my overcoat. Yes! both I in the bus and I in the dream were content to be, as Keats was when he read the tale of Chaucer, kept "in so sweet a place"—

> I that do ever feel athirst for glory
> could at this moment be content to lie
> meekly upon the grass, as those whose sobbings
> are heard of none beside the mournful robins.

The fact was—the *fact* was—that this long ride on a bus was my *interval* between an existence, such as it was, in the East, and a new existence, such as it would be, in the West; so that I was *well* disposed, I think, to enjoy by day the quiet variety of traveling through the countryside, and by night the security of the enclosing blackness, half asleep, in the hands of Vic McMahon!

What a rare social peace was there among the passengers of our dimly-lighted bus, self-contained world—every desire arrested. The recognition of danger by the Highway Commission of the Commonwealth of Iowa, confessed in dancing reflectors and in colored posters, gave to us all a thrill of ease.

Wildly swerving, our bus skidded onto the soft shoulder of the road, but with a wrench of the wheel Vic McMahon brought us back onto the concrete highway.

"Oh no, stay a little longer, Ronny!" said the lady from Des Moines, distinctly, out of her dream.

"Steady!" said Ed Sheeler under his breath.

How had it happened? The sudden maneuver of our driver to avoid the lights of a car coming toward us; but one saw clearly, if he happened to be looking, that there was no reason for the maneuver. Yet this little error was the only sign that our Vic McMahon did not have the situation well in hand, not, at least, the *whole* situation.

"Oh no! stay a little longer, Ronny!" Those were the very words spoken by the dreaming woman of Des Moines.

"Victory! victory!" came the words out of our common dream.

Again we were flying thru the night, devouring the hurrying highway at forty-eight miles per hour.

We slowed down for a railroad-crossing and came to a dead stop. The driver half-opened the door to listen. Then on we rode again. . . .

Almost immediately after this we again slowed down and, pulling to the side of the road, came to a dead stop.

Vic McMahon opened the door and got out.

"Now what's the matter?" said a gentleman in back.

"It's where he lives," said Ed Sheeler. Looking out, one could indeed see a house among the trees, with one window lit. "He always stops here to kiss his wife goodnight."

"Very nice; when do we get to St. Louis?"

"Oh for heaven's sake!" I said, annoyed at such selfishness.

"I hope he doesn't take time off for something else!" joked an old bent stick from under his overcoat.

"He has two kids," said Ed Sheeler, "boy an' girl. You'll see. They come out in bathrobes to see him off and then they go to bed. You'll see."

There rose a woman's piercing shriek, followed by a thunderous pistol-shot in the silent night.

"In the name of the Father, of the Son, and of the Holy Ghost—" said Ed Sheeler.

104

Vic McMahon

The wailing of the children now was heard, rising to loud outcries.

The sleepers slept. But we others stared at each other in consternation and climbed out onto the road. At this moment rose the moon, disclosing the landscape.

And now, here was Vic McMahon carrying a white-garbed woman in his arms; her brow was bloody, demolished; his face was pathetically distorted, and he had lost his cap. The wailing children in bathrobes took up their stand on his right.

"She is my wife—" were all the words that Vic McMahon could say.

Another passenger climbed down and took his place amongst us, and so we tended to spread out in three quarters of a circle in front of Vic McMahon.

What a rare social pause there was then, among all. The children stilled their voices. The moon scattered its honest light on all. And I believe that there was no one amongst us (save perhaps the children) who would have wished to end this rest-period forever. It was so still after the nervous joggling of the bus; and all were relieved to be standing on their feet, rather than reclining, so the blood could circulate in its customary way. But besides, there was in the proportioning of these circumstances a loosening of the soul, so flowed the tears. All were relaxed of flying thru the darkness at forty-eight miles an hour, brought instead to a formal way of standing, so the tears flowed easily down the cheeks of Vic McMahon and others. Dear God! as easily as tears flowed down his cheeks, may the words of my mouth and the meditations of my heart be acceptable.

Chicago
January 1937

105

A Ceremonial

Oui, le culte promis à des Cérémonials, songez
quel il peut être!
—MALLARMÉ

1. *Viola and the Alderman*

A breezy May morning (not long after the establishment among us of reasonable institutions), a section of decrepit billboards along the highway was called to the attention of Alderman Manly Morison. He was out walking in the breeze when he came on a small black girl, Viola, letting fly with a rock at the sheet-metal billboard: *Bang!* After this percussion she kept time with her forefinger: "1-1-1,2,3-1-1-1,2,3"; then she screeched at the top of her voice: "*Eeeeee! Iiiii!*" and then again let fly with a rock: *Bang!* while antique flakes of paste and paper showered to the ground.

"*Bang!*" said Alderman Morison.

"Oh," cried Viola, surprised out of music, awakened out of music, "you spoilt the rhythm." She was about to burst into tears, so rudely awakened out of music and dancing; but curiosity prevailed and she asked, "Hey, what all wuh them tin fences for?"

"Those?" Now suddenly it came to the Alderman's memory that they had been billboards for advertising, to make profits by persuading people to buy certain products. As he thought of the advertisements, those curious works of painting and poetry, and of the institution, the Alderman turned pale and lifted his hand to his brow in dizziness, at the ancient madness. The fact was that he could not think of those times without becoming confused. "Oh those," he faltered, "were just used for pasting up paintings and things."

"Paintings!" said Viola contemptuously, thinking of louder and more wonderful noises than the *Sacre du Printemps.*

—One of the billboards had shown a huge sexy pirate naked to the waist carrying off a smirking girl in a gossamer nightgown. Above, in italic type, was the legend: *Nature in the Raw is Seldom Mild.* Below: Lucky Strikes (a brand of cigarettes)— *"It's Toasted!"*

Another billboard had displayed a farmer leaning on a rake with glasses on the tip of his nose and symmetrical patches on his overalls, reading to his pink-cheeked white-haired wife holding in her hands an apple-pie, a letter from their son: " . . . *Am doing swell! just bought a Ford V-8.*" And below: "Consult Your Local Ford Dealer."

The third billboard at Christmas season had borne the poster of a mother in a mauve dress with newly marcelled blond hair and just the faintest suggestion of a halo (perhaps only a highlight), gingerly holding a darling baby with face taken from a contemporary infant cinema-star, Baby Kelly. Against the deep rose background shone two golden candles. Underneath in tasteful Gothic letters was the legend: "Sheffield Farms (milk products) wishes you a Merry Xmas and a Happy New Year."

The fourth billboard merely said peremptorily: Buy Rem (a kind of cough syrup).

"What are yuh *cryin'* about?" cried Viola, astonished to see tears rolling down the Alderman's cheeks.

"Look here, black girl," said Manly, "suppose a huge sign there said 'Chew Juicy Fruit!' what would you do?"

? ? ? ? ?

"I mean, supposing the sign jumped up and down and did acrobatic exercises—" cried Manly, and he broke into a peal of laughter.

"What are yuh *laughin'* about?" said Viola. But she was not unwilling to join in, first uncertainly, then with a high clear peal of laughter. She let fly another rock: *Bang!*

"It's all right, kid," said Manly, "we'll have the fence knocked down this afternoon; it blocks the view along the road."

"Yes, it does," said Viola judiciously.

108

A Ceremonial

"We'll have to get together some kind of program," said the Alderman.

"*Program!* Just to knock down the tin fence—"

These historic sentences, which I have imitated somewhat crudely, I fear, were first spoken on the morning of May 9, 19—.

Manly Morison and Viola clambered through the hedge to see what was behind the billboard. From tatters of paper hanging from the metal Manly could see that one of the advertisements had been the following, founded on an evil sentiment of fear:

A young girl is shown in tears, because no boy could call her, because she had not rented a telephone from the Bell Telephone Corporation.

What should there be in the field behind the antique billboard but the meadowflowers?

—the white-eyelashed daisies and gold buttercups
and devil's-paintbrushes in fire dipt.

There was a linden sapling we must refer to again below. The wind had swept away the last wisps of cloud, and the sky was what one might call a *breathing* blue. So blue, day of lovely glory. The grass and weeds, so early in the year, were almost knee deep. With an exclamation of delight, Viola picked up an antique milk-bottle, full of soil.

"What do you want with that, girl?"

"It has a *squeak* note," said the girl, making it tinkle.

"Don't you have any regular instruments to play, girl?" asked the Alderman.

"Oh yes, I play the viola," said Viola.

2. Address by Meyer Leibow

The afternoon's program began about 4:30. Almost a hundred chairs were set up in front of the billboards on the now little-used highway. The children, for the most part, were playing a ball game in the field a few hundred meters

109

off, but they silently returned whenever anything was of interest.

Three of the billboards were to be pushed down; the fourth, on the right, was to be preserved and it was draped with a yellow curtain.

Our good friend Meyer Leibow made an address somewhat as follows:

"Spinoza said there's no use upbraiding the past. Yet I'd like to point out just how insulting these old signboards were; and I guess I'll have to induce, therefore, that some of us were very undignified to take so many insults without being offended. Finally, perhaps I'll make just a remark about the color yellow.

"All of these advertising signs operated on an hypothesis of how we'd react. Namely, the advertisers believed that if they merely brought a certain name to our attention, we'd pay out money for something. Quite apart from any reasonable persuasion, mind you, but just: Stimulus! Response! Can you imagine such a belief? It was, of course, an *insult*.

"Furthermore, some of the signs used to scream *Buy! Buy!* Yet how many of us ever stopped to say: 'I beg your pardon, are you addressing me? Would it not be more polite to say "If you please—" or wait till you are asked, or even, perhaps, to wait till we are introduced?' But a citizen would walk along the street and jump out of his skin when something shrieked at him, 'Hey you! Do! Don't! Give! Buy! Use! Hurry!'

"Other signs became even more insulting by adopting a familiar attitude: 'Listen, Buddy, let me give you a tip—' or 'Say, don't miss it on your life!' or 'Ain't got time for loose talk, folks, but they got taste and plenty to spare!' The theory here was that if we'd develop a chummy attitude to Campbell's soup, we just couldn't help pay out money.

"But this brings me to what to my temper was always the most irritating insult of all. The idea being to make people well-disposed, the advertisers had a theory as to what would make people feel well-disposed. For instance, one thing that could not fail was to show a picture of a blonde little girl or an apple-cheeked boy with torn pants. As Delmore Schwartz once remarked, whenever a baby appears on a movie-screen everybody says '*Ah!*' (something like the end of the skyrocket cheer the young men do). Therefore folks would pay out money. Another sure way to attract attentive observation, so the fateful name of Hennafoam Shampoo could sink into the soul, was to display some secondary sexual activity, such as the exchange of ardent looks. Therefore folks would pay out money. It was the belief of advertisers that the mind worked in this simple way.

"It was essential in putting the buyer in the right frame of mind to suggest to him the right social status, namely just one grade above (as they used to say) what he could ever attain. The theory was that a person would feel that if he bought such and such an article he as good as belonged to the next economic class. Therefore he would pay out money. This was a sad insult.

"Besides this, there were catchy rimes, such as:

Cooties love
  bewhiskered places,
but Cuties love
  the smoothest faces—
USE BURMA SHAVE!

And there were many deep-thought mottoes and slogans, such as: 'Not a Cough in a Carload' or 'Next to myself I like B.V.D.'s best' or 'Eventually—Why not Now?' It was likewise considered good by these theorists of our common human nature to use elegant diction, such as 'Always Luckies Please.' And to give credit where credit is due, it was they who invented a remarkable usage of grammar, the comparative absolute, as to say: 'I *prefer* Tasty Bread,' or 'Kraft Cheese is *Superior.*'

"Aware that we were rational as well as passionate, they made philosophy, too, the handmaiden of commerce. 'Nature in the Raw is Seldom Mild,' posited one product that had a patent process. 'Nature's Best after All!' countered its rival, displaying the effigy of a miss in riding togs (as they used to wear) feeding sugar to a thorobred horse. Therefore people would pay out money.

"Science and common-sense were not exempt. It was

believed that by sufficient repetition, assertions in the teeth of the most ordinary experience would come to be credited. That is, it was a cardinal principle of the advertisers that they could instil in people a habit of lies. Habit of lies— habit of publicity—This, I take it, was a great insult."

As Meyer declared that this or that theory of the advertisers was an insult to our common nature, some of the older men and women shifted in their seats and their eyes flooded with tears; for sometimes they had not been proof against these very advertisements. They therefore listened with the greater attention to the simple speech.

"What a sad case!" exclaimed Meyer, "that science, ordinary sentiment, painting, our dear English tongue—should all have been made to serve so ruthlessly. Everything, to be sure, must be made to serve—I mean to serve life as a whole and our freedom—but not so ruthlessly.

"We often find, I think, that things serve best by being enjoyed in themselves.

"What a nervous time it was when every perception along the road was designed to influence some far-off behavior! I am surprised that there were not more automobile accidents. But we most often have peace, I think, in enjoying each thing in itself."

He turned to the draped billboard. "This color—this color yellow—this yellow—" he said, turning to regard the yellow curtain with attentive sensation. "No, do not consider it too attentively—it is not important enough.

"But before I begin to wonder," said Meyer, "I'd better bring my remarks to a close. When I'm sitting down I can let my mind roam as much as I please; there is no problem of communication then! Then to conclude: I have of course touched only a single aspect of this ancient evil of advertising. For instance I have not spoken of unproductive effort and the expense of the creative soul; I have not touched on the creation of immoderate desires, the fixing of the habit of publicity, and so on. Yet even with so much alone as I have mentioned, how is it that these advertisements, so insulting, so nervous, were able to survive? The answer, my beloved comrades, is that they *did not!*

"Therefore today we are demolishing these boards."

112

A Ceremonial

Hereat Meyer again took his seat in the audience.

There was, of course, no applause for these remarks, since what was there to rejoice in in such remarks?

3.

The next number on the program was the purpose of it all, and the boys came drifting in from the field. It being nearly five, tea and cakes were passed around.

"Will the gentlemen carpenters please come forward and take charge, and explain the proceedings," said Alderman Morison.

Three fellows rose, rolling up their sleeves, and came forward. Two at once disappeared behind the billboards. Their spokesman, a short stout type, wrapped his cigar in a piece of paper and put it in his breast-pocket. He said: "Well, we first sawed through the supports in the back, leaving a few props. Then we cut through these posts here in front, down on the bottom here." He indicated where wedges had been cut from the posts, just as lumberjacks do with great pine-trees. "Now then, when I push in front, at the same time they'll pull away the props in back with cords—and down she'll go! all except that end one that's being kept." He indicated the one on the right, draped with the lemon-yellow curtain.

When he finished this explanation, the people broke into a volley of applause—until the two in the back reappeared at the edge, grinning.

"O.K., boys—" said Tony Bridges, the spokesman. All the children had gone around the back to watch. *"Ready!"* cried Tony.

"Ready!" cried they.

"Here *goes!* One—two—and *three!"* and with a great shove he gave his weight to the billboard.

With a crack, that made the audience jump, it went down, sounding a dull *bunnnnng!* as it landed, amid a cloud of dust, disclosing the grassy field and the meadowflowers.

But there in the field, center of all eyes, the two young carpenters standing on ladders were holding stretched a maroon curtain. What was behind it? This was the question every one asked himself. (It was of course the linden sapling.) Some observed with pleasure the maroon curtain and the lemon-yellow curtain.

"Our friend—Gregory Dido—" announced Manly Morison, his voice broken with emotion.

And in fact, when this great artist and poet and statesman, this philosopher, came to the front, all stood up for a moment, in token of respect.

"I just thought," said the aged man in his beautiful easy tone, "that when something appears from behind a curtain, or when there is a frame round it, we consider it more easily, peacefully, more in itself, as my friend Meyer was just saying. All right, lads, drop the curtain," he said to the lads on the ladders.

They disclosed the quiet tree with its heart-shaped leaves and a few cream-colored blossoms in the sunlight.

This tree, at first, excited only wonder, almost disappointment; until it became apparent, just by looking at it, that the utmost tiny leaves and petals were expressive, were organs, of the invisible roots. Such as it was, this tree in seclusion had come to its present being, behind a fence. Here it was, this linden tree, when the maroon curtain dropped.

Loudly enthusiastic, the plaudits broke forth. "Bravo! bravo!" cried some. There was thunderous hand-clapping. Even Dido and Meyer Leibow, who had spent a long time considering the tree in the morning, were deeply moved anew. The children, in the field, did not fully understand the occasion for it, but they added their cheers and joyous clapping. This continued for three or four minutes, during which time the linden-tree stood appreciative.

"I see," cried Gregory Dido, "that we'll have to incorporate this as a new act in the theatres: I mean displaying a tree alone in the middle of the stage."

"Perhaps the tree wouldn't be so handsome," said Meyer, "taken away from its natural meadow."

"I am not so sure of that!" exclaimed Gregory.

Many of the audience leaned forward expectantly, hoping

to hear a further exchange of ideas and arguments between these two.

But no! The next number on the program was not a dialectical skirmish, but more fittingly a little poem of gratification composed that day by Harry Walker, 14. Dark-haired Harry, dangling a fielder's glove from his wrist, unfolded a soiled sheet of paper which he took from his hip-pocket; and although the other boys made a few sotto voce remarks, he read in a firm and manly voice, as follows:

> Today in center field although
>   I shouted to the others playing ball,
>   there was not any sound at all.
> The meadowflowers softly grow
>
> in the knee-deep grass; the meadowflowers
>   grow softly in the knee-deep grass;
>   I do not know how many hours pass;
> I do not know how many hours
>
> the meadowflowers grow softly in
>   the knee-deep grass; there is not any
>   sound at all; I do not know how many
> hours pass; there is a present din
>
> of baseball; is no sound at all;
>   I do not know how many hours pass
>   the meadowflowers in the knee-deep grass
> grow softly without any sound at all.

There was no applause for this effort, except from the children, for it was not considered convenient to applaud young boys (all were without the habit of publicity). Having used up his courage, Harry awkwardly stuffed the paper in his pocket; but as he was going away, Dido drew him near and said in a low voice, "It is true, it is true!—the meadowflowers grow softly in the knee-deep grass"; so that the boy blushed deep red, and when the others wanted to know what Dido had said, he wouldn't tell.

"All the same, it's a sad way to play ball!" said Meyer to Gregory Dido; "he probably can't field."

115

"No no, otherwise he'd be put in right-field, not center-field."

"Hm. Tell me, Joey," Meyer asked one of the kids, "what position does Harry Walker play on his ball-team?"

"He? He holds down the hot-corner for the Bears!" said Joey.

Dido roared.

"Little liar!" said Mike.

And now the members of the famous string-quartet, who had traveled over a hundred miles to come to this ceremonial, were already setting up their music-stands.

For it was a principle (one of those established by this very Gregory Dido) generally followed throughout the land, that there was never a public gathering without excellent music of some kind.

But since the music was this afternoon of so serious a kind—namely one of the later works of Beethoven—the children and several of the adults went to occupy themselves elsewhere for half an hour. Tony Bridges took his cigar from his pocket and lit it, hoping to enjoy the music and his cigar both.

The quartet tuned their instruments, dropping the plucked notes and the premonitory strains into the deepening silence.

They played several deep, slow chords—major and minor triads—until the spirit of simple harmony spread among the listeners in the late afternoon: for what advantage is it to surprise with complicated music the unprepared soul? (This also was an idea of Gregory Dido's.)

4. *Cavatina*

The four began now to play the long quartet of Beethoven, opus 130, in B-flat major. And while they are playing let us withdraw from representing their real activity (for there is no describing these tones in words); but just represent the performers, and a few of the auditors, and the power of music.

The second violinist, Dickie M'Nall, was a youth in the

116

period of form and fire. That is, after endless study, taking his work to bed and for long walks with himself, and expounding it in discussions, he would arrive at a formal analysis of the whole; and now, in executing his part, he attacked this form, outline and details, with the utmost passion and precision. Self-centered, centering on this imagined ideal, he sat as if alone, constructing carefully the edifice of the second-violin.

The violist, Maritimus, was a profound intelligence; it was he who was the synoptic soul of this famous quartet, who, in a sense, played the four instruments. Indeed, there was nothing like the experience of seeing Maritimus look up, with a profound glance of dark eyes, at M'Nall or Mrs. Troy—and moderate. It was he who gave the broad lines of what M'Nall studied. (Between the youth and Maritimus subsisted a difficult sexual friendship.)

Mrs. Troy, the 'cellist, was a heroine of the civil war, the mother of two grown daughters and a small son, a strong and simple musician. I do not mention these other characteristics at random, for she held her instrument between her knees and bowed it in a firm and matronly way, as part of life, playing music as if it were drawing breath, and sometimes joking with Maritimus (whom she had first met when he was a sailor!) About such a person as this, one can *say* very little.

The first violinist was Herman Schneider. About such playing, in which there is no distinction between the playing of the sounds and the preconceived form, one can never say enough; for it is like anything in nature growing, as a tree. A strange illusion grew from this playing, namely that after a piece was over and the other sounds faded, the line of the first violin seemed to persist in the air, almost visible, like a kind of ghost. There is a legend that once the other three broke off in the middle, to hear Herman Schneider alone.

So these were the four who were playing: Herman Schneider, 1st violin, Dickie M'Nall, 2nd violin, Charles Maritimus, viola, and Martha Aaron Troy, 'cellist.

Dido, with head bent haggardly on his chest, was hardly listening. He was thinking altogether, with horror and

117

fatigue, of his blighted life. And, I fear to say it, when the quartet came to be the smiling, morosely repetitive Dance, *alla Tedesca*, tears began to stream down his lined cheeks. But the next part, *Cavatina*, would free and relax—and make this poor soul's breath more formal with the song.

At the Dance, *alla Tedesca*, small black Viola, who had been painfully following the score in a book, now laughed and hummed so loudly that Mrs. Troy smiled to her with a queenly air.

I, too, was there, this author; but I have never been less attentive than on that day to my master Beethoven. For besides my task of remarking so many details both inner and outer, I was perplexed by a problem of art: for it sounded to me, although I *knew* that I was in error, that the other players were more musical than Herman Schneider. "So to an incompletely formed taste, the good always seems more powerful than the perfect," I thought. But if I had listened only and not thought at all, I might not have erred; and so it came about when they began the *Cavatina*.

Tony Bridges, with moving finger, intently hearing, was a true critic, his attention *crowding* into his ears.

After the fourth movement there was a pause, a half minute of unusual attentiveness. The glance of Maritimus held us all. (I think now that it was a *kind* glance, one with the feeling of our kind.) When he lowered his eyes, they played the deathless *Cavatina*.

Then any one might, if he came by, have observed the power of music. For the people were as if asleep or dead—relaxed—some with open sightless eyes, as if they had been slain with great violence and suddenness. An arm in an awkward position; no grace left to these mere bodies. Indeed, a passerby would have been amazed if he were unacquainted with such causes (I am describing what is not rare, but may be observed at many concerts). And even I was able to hear the deathless *Cavatina* without evaluation. The power of the impassible musicians was not resented—what a strange thing! for we all had the habit of freedom. (How am I to continue, reader, now the narrative has come to this pause of what may not be described?) A very small child came from the field and started with fright, seeing all asleep or dead. At the turn of the melody,

118

2nd Viol.

some of the dead shed tears, in respect for Ludwig Beethoven brought in his fifty-second year to such a turn of the melody. Music looses the soul so flow the tears; soon the breath is formal with the song. Thanks to these tears, to the turn of the melody, it is possible again to describe the scene. We are often, in touching on what is not proper to words, faced with a grave problem of style, namely: how to begin again; unless by luck what is not proper to words, as the music, freely returns, as in these tears, to words.

5.

The last number on the program comprised the re-dedication of the billboard left standing, in some remarks by Gregory Dido. By this time it was late in the afternoon, the ovoid sun almost dropped behind the hill, tinging all linen. Gregory said: "Why we at all make a point of saving and transforming a portion of this old relic—acceptance of the past! triumph over the past!—is a philosophic question; maybe one of the boys can write an article about it." (Laughter.)

"You do it, Gregory Dido!" cried Mrs. Troy.

"You would not think," I thought, "that this cheerful man, whose entire vocation seems to be these neighborhood ceremonials, is the poet of *Desire and Terror*, who questions every one without exception." But I was wrong, for it was *only* this cheerful man, whose entire vocation was neighborhood ceremonials, could have been that poet.

"Our friend Councillor Morison asked me to decorate the board," said Dido. "I've done so in the simplest way I could. Certainly another could do better, but it doesn't much matter for this country billboard. But in any case, as a more general principle, I should like to suggest the following:

"In the public vehicles we might post an occasional poem, a mathematical theorem, or an account of the reasoning behind a beautiful physical experiment. Anything, I mean to say, embodying a single worthwhile act of thought.

"I am not sure how far this principle can be extended, to billboards and so forth, for we can make too great an effort—who can deny it?—to occupy our souls, to *pre*occupy our souls . . ."

I, and the others, leaned forward to give our best attention to a lengthy exposition. But at this moment the sun set and Gregory, whose habit was never to lose sense of the simple and important rhythms, remarked: "You see, my dear friends, the day has ended again."

But having said so, he could not bring himself to break the silence of the pure daylight of the beginning of evening; so he merely made a gesture and a couple of lads climbed up and loosed the yellow curtain overhanging the board. There was disclosed a sentence elegantly printed and a large circle, as follows:

WHEN A LINE MOVES
WITH ONE END
FIXED THE POSI-
TIONS OF THE
OTHER END DE-
SCRIBE A FORM
INTERESTING TO SEE

This was all that was hidden behind the lemon-yellow curtain, just as behind the maroon was nothing but a linden-tree.

"The word 'describe' is not well enough chosen," thought Miss Campbell, teacher of English.

A Ceremonial

6

High over the hill gleamed the star Venus ("afterthought of the Sun"). The meeting broke up.

I have failed, I fear, to catch the spirit of this first May 9th celebration, which began on that day so casually, and has since become the prototype of every communal "May Ninth." Such was the origin of the maroon and lemon, of the linden-tree, of the customary reading of the poems of Gregory Dido and Harry Walker, and of so many other traditions. But I have failed especially, I know, to imitate the social peace and easy subtility of the day; perhaps what I have described seems even pedantic!

What is the spirit of May Ninth? Different thinkers emphasize different aspects: Some the radical turning away from the centrifugal culture of pre-revolutionary days; others again emphasize precisely the transforming of that culture. Some call May Ninth the "holiday of the Arts." Others, more philosophically, declare it is "dedicated to each thing enjoyed in itself alone."

But to my mind, no explanation is adequate that does not *begin* from the sense of social peace that existed first at that time among such critical and exact minds (even profound and sad minds) as Gregory Dido, Meyer Leibow, Martha Aaron Troy, and Charles Maritimus. Just what is new in May Ninth (it is as old as music and science!) is the unique coupling of fastidiousness and love. And yes! to my mind—as evening fell on the first May Ninth, and the planet Hesperus was in the sky, there was most of love.

Chicago
January 1937

Orpheus in the Underworld

Beloved Eurydice dead lived in the past.

Here stood Orpheus, speechless musician, at her grave. Accustomed to express nothing but this love, he burst into tears with no form. Hereat, standing speechless musician weeping, he composed a work of art on the theme: Eurydice is in the past forever, slowly and suddenly dying, for everything is always dying, then dead. He sang:

> So slowly dead and now forever,
> Eurydice! Eurydice!—

Yes, his song is intermitted with calls of her name. *Eurydice!* (Do not grow tired of it, but feel kindly to Orpheus and me.) And the lions are still—one last time, the clock-ticks still, though the time is running rapidly. Orpheus himself is soon breathing to the music, and his tears are dry. . . . The wild beasts are its metaphors, the lapse of time is a metrical form, and breath and tears a plot. (Nevertheless feel kindly to Orpheus and me.) *Eurydice! Eurydice!* is intermitted in the song, perhaps not enough a metaphor. (Feel kindly, reader, to Orpheus and me!) All are still; how loud he cries *Eurydice!* Many would not call this monotony music. (Reader, please to feel kindly to Orpheus and me.)—

With a jerk Orpheus tore out the strings of his instrument and stood crying for poor Orpheus.

Now rose on every hand the immoderate outcries of the beasts! the lions in the deeps and the monkeys on high clamoring in no common scale. The hero's teeth were chattering with fear. But still worse was his anxiety for the lapse of time wildly flying (as it seemed) because there were no measured movements. In the screeching overhead and the ragged tumbling of the falls, all time seemed to be being devoured in one gulph, so that Orpheus imagined that he was suddenly white-haired and tottering, all his time gone by. He no longer breathed and softly wept, but gasped and sobbed like the child with night terrors. An abominable roar of a pack of lions shook the twilight, and in this one roar it seemed as though his whole time of life were elapsing—but in fact the physical rhythms of his body were suffering no such confusion but were measuring out the seconds almost as steadily as ever. He was in the act of losing to the past his beautiful youth, springtime of desire; he was in the state of perceiving it gone. State of grief, prelude to anxiety and mourning. Anxiety of the lapse of time and scalding tears of anguish for the loss of his beautiful springtime of desire. Almost! almost among these unmusical terrors he regarded this irreplaceable past as though it were a good in itself. What could he do but weep bitterly, thinking so? overwhelmed by such a sad contradiction. Spent by such unusual fear and exhausted by such a sad contradiction—the roaring began to fade from Orpheus's hearing and he sank to the ground and fell into a slumber, the irregularities of his breathing evening slowly out.

When he awoke from this trance he had made up his mind as follows: "If my beloved Eurydice dead lives in the past, I have no recourse but to descend into that underworld and bring her back as she was into my beautiful youth from day to day.

"Which way is it to the mouth of this hell?"–

Orpheus in the Underworld

When silent Orpheus pursued his descending way into that underworld—where Mercury,

124

Orpheus in the Underworld

leader of the docile dead,

has taken all aside—everything he came on had at first one aspect, then suddenly another as he looked back. For at first he recognized everything with difficulty, but then it became clear and dear: the one-time objects of Orpheus's best attention.

These, in the first regions of descent, were the past we plumb with easy exploration, I mean through souvenirs, household ware, photographs, and diplomas; such things as verbal theories, prize poems, and the contortions one went to to impress a patron. Coveted starvation salaries (as they now seem); honors that, as we now think, made the recipient out to be a fool; and triumphant refutations of facts.

Look at these when on the way down and they are hardly recognizable as existent things; but in the underworld they are breathing and struggling. They are the first strange flora and fauna of the new-found land: those creatures which on one side look like rocks or at most stone images but on the other are living souls.

(But Orpheus flew by, for he knew that he would not find Eurydice in those regions.)

—So a man is seated conversing with his friends, but let a certain thought appear to him and he suddenly seems to be drugged and dragged to dream. Unless he struggles to dismiss the idea (and why should he?), his eyes close. (Preserve, Lord, his unguarded body then.) Meantime the others in the room regard him curiously.—

Such ideas as might recur to one, as the pressure of a hand or a certain whispered term.

What act profound!—so that the friends of the man are startled as they watch him—what act profound in his dream leads him to raise his right forearm to shield his eyes from a blow of light?

In the profounder forest which Orpheus was now more slowly traversing stood a kind of stonelike birds with harps for wings.* Tears streamed down his cheeks because the air

*I am thinking of the stone *Vowels* of the sculptor Lipchitz.

125

was aquiver with whispered excerpts of songs, muffled shouts, as "Hurrah for the boys of eight or ten!"

Indeed, in this region it seemed to be continually raining, so blinded with tears was the hero Orpheus. But the golden birds irradiated a halo of light and a rainbow: pink, gray, cream, and Prussian blue. Strange mute birds! vivifying with their calls—

(Do not analyze too closely these fauna of impossible desire or they turn into contradictory sentences.)

What a power, what weakness, there is in sentences unfinished, half-heard whispers! There is a game in which each one inarticulately whispers to the neighbor on his right what he imagines he has heard whispered to him by his neighbor on the left: the message is curiously refracted through so many minds. (Reader, tshl d' furo ns pits? Pass it on—)

Into contradictory sentences, such as: None of the birds is singing and some of them are singing in muffled voices. The cause of the apparent rain is his tears, and when he dries his tears it is still raining.

Orpheus, weep unrestrainedly but go on; we shall come to the Elysian Fields by and by—there would not be so much passion except in drawing near what has been lost. But now everywhere about are these stonelike birds whispering sentences of the worst dismay, such as: "The confidence of failure spurs me on to error and dishonor every day," or "Blessed are trumpets and all other things that herald a change!" And if you turn from these, the others are saying: "I fear that my first stroke of Luck may prove fatal."

They say: "The Spring! here is the Spring upon us, the ash-blond son of Death and Memory!" and "Each new beginning has a longer past to drag" and "The obvious despair of yearning for disaster day by day—" and "And this goes on from day to day."

Who before ever beheld stone birds with tears streaming out of their eyes?

Emboldened by this sight, Orpheus asked in a loud voice, "Have you seen my Eurydice?"

Yes, just because there is such passion we shall come to

126

the Elysian Fields by and by; we shall not remain in this lapse of time, but very soon arrive before the beginning of any loss—if only we are able to proceed, beset on every side by contradictions.

Some of the gray trees in this wood bore fruit colored grul and black, and their roots trembled in the fluid of underground Lethe. And if you ate of the fruit, shp kir on dz dzz! The stony birds glowed in the brightening wood. And through here came Orpheus intrepid now dry-eyed, charmer of all things that move by nature, composer of many songs. Lordly leader of choruses and inventor of the tetrachord, he gently first appeared, like the gray sun, among the brightening foliage, meandering into contradiction. This musician was like a gruesome murderer, for often when he played you could see the inhabitants of Cos stretched as if lifeless. What a thing it is to be able to finish an English sentence, with a subject and a predicate and expressing a complete thought!

—"What did you say?" I asked the girl on my left. She repeated. Whispering, "Dss oni dz shp furo wings, etc." "Oh that's it!" I cried: " *'Those stony birds with harps for wings have no extensive flight, I think—' "*

O Orpheus, weep unrestrainedly but go on; we'll come to the Elysian Fields by and by; but now everywhere about are these stonelike birds whispering. It seems that we are lost in this drizzle, blinded by hot tears destructive of art, and almost unable to proceed, beset on every side by contradictions.

The Elysian Fields

Now this author cannot resist coming again and again, cannot resist coming, to this delightful description of the Elysian Fields! Only last summer I composed The Joyous Isle; and all these places have similar moral geography the climate of Pleasure and Permanence. Here subsist all gratifications before the beginning of any loss: when the things we love are taken away, they descend unto these Elysian Fields, and when I think of them I seem to be drugged and dragged to dream. So here comes the hero Orpheus in search of lost Eurydice.

ORPHEUS: "Where else except in the perpetual springtime of this part of hell is my Eurydice to be found? Here subsist all gratifications before the beginning of any loss. And even many *forgotten* objects of desire are here, for whose loss I will at some later time come to grieve, be anxious, and mourn. I met my mother. She was seated under a tree, with one breast uncovered and moist and on her lips playing a certain smile. But besides this, there yawned, not far beyond, a desirable dark cave to enter—"

MOTHER OF ORPHEUS: "Child, do not desire this death, and again my pain—"

ORPHEUS: "No no! for it is only Eurydice I now desire. It is not until next year that I'll come to long for the dreamless joy before I was born."

PLUTO: "Everyone is here overwhelmed with unexpected gratification. Do you want to hear of the most remarkable example of unlooked-for pleasure?"

ORPHEUS: "Yes, if I may likewise possess Eurydice."

PLUTO: "There was a man who had suffered the loss of a libidinous object which was indispensable to him, and therefore he was obliged to repress the desire he felt. This repression resulted in the formation of symptoms, namely certain compulsive acts; and these soon comprised a complicated ritual with many fetishes. Now it chanced that one of these fetishes turned out to be just the original libidinous object itself, and in handling this—what a recognition there was! what a glow of rosy pleasure unlooked-for!"

PERSEPHONE: "For God's sake, let us often tell over such stories of unusual good fortune to cheer each other up. But now here is Orpheus—"

ORPHEUS: "O Queen of Flowers and Death! Queen of Art—"

PERSEPHONE: "—is it not time to restore his girl to him, for I cannot bear to see him deprived and perhaps about to begin to cry."

PLUTO: "Hero, would you want to stay with us in these Elysian Fields?"

Orpheus in the Underworld

MOTHER OF ORPHEUS: "Child, do not—"

PLUTO (bitterly): "Be still, Madam! your influence of his first to fifth year is enough to determine him and you need not speak now."

ORPHEUS: "No no! not stay, although it's pleasant here by definition. But far off, in the periphery of my dreaming mind, I hear the roaring of beasts and the rushing flow of time; I must explore in that direction and bring back the Eurydicean peace."

PLUTO: "Alas for Orpheus! he wants to possess the dead not in the Elysian Fields. But everything in the world, including his body and soul, has gone on to another cycle, and his desire is as anachronistic as the girl. (The fact is that it is contradictory to *wish* for anything that the same soul has once recognized as past; it is contradictory to want something not to have happened! These contradictions are the customary products of error and desire.) Orpheus, take thou Eurydice and return to life; but it cannot be done! I impose this one condition: *Do not look back, or she is dead.*"

Hereupon Eurydice appeared; and if only I could make this narrative move slower and slower. Orpheus turned toward her and all the others vanished in consideration for them. Refound Eurydice was smiling in gratification, but Orpheus said: "I love you whom I love with tears in my eyes, be therefore kind. If you kiss me my tears will flow redoubled, for only so my satisfaction is—my present trying to drown away the past. Believe it, beloved, I am standing behind a shiny wall of tears and cannot see you for a while." There was a pause while she kissed away these tears. Let me not interrupt this pause, but in every way extend it. To some it might seem impossible, and against art, to imitate in the flow of words such a pause; but in every way we need only sufficiently avoid referring to the love of Orpheus and Eurydice and hereby we bring our narrative to rest. So again and again the narrative of this poet has come to this perfectly uneasy pause, and he cannot resist describing the Elysian Fields! Here subsist all gratifications before the beginning of any loss. When the things we love are taken away they descend unto these Elysian Fields, and when I

129

think of it I seem to be drugged and dragged to dream. (Preserve, Lord, my unguarded body then.)

Eurydice covered her face with her hands, then, smiling, revealed it again to his joy, doing it more than once, playing a familiar game, in order that Orpheus could learn to experience longing without the accompaniment of despair.

The abominable savage roars and screeching remembered, and the rush of time, made Orpheus turn away his face slightly.—

Oh no! stay a little longer, poet. (Reader, be indulgent to Orpheus and me.) What I most delight in in these desultory paragraphs is that I have nothing to say. What is relevant to say if we look away, modestly, from the loves of Orpheus and Eurydice? But if we looked to them and wrote, they'd soon come to an end. To delay! To delay! it is so delightful in the acts of love to delay! I think I shall not fall into contradiction asserting nothing. (Is it so?)

"Eurydice," whispered Orpheus, "let us soon be gratified and begin to return."

—To delay! to delay! It is not absolutely necessary that we press on to the fourth part. Even Beethoven in his last works, it seems, could not come to the end of the movement marked *adagio cantabile.* Could not bear to come to the end. Could not bear to come. Could not bear to come to the end of gratification. It is so delightful to delay in this uneasy pause. Here subsist all things before the beginning of any loss.

Refound Eurydice was now softly smiling in gratification, and Orpheus's eyes were sealed.

But Orpheus dragged himself from the brink of sleep. "Beloved," he said, opening his eyes heavy with sleep, "isn't it time to start out, as we arranged to start out early?" Thus many, who have closed their eyes for one instant, mistake the circumstances and imagine a long time has passed.

It was impossible in principle for Eurydice to return to Orpheus's world. His world, with its weird noises, was now *founded on the death of Eurydice.* She, like all delights which are gone forever, dwelt now in the Elysian Fields among the oral pleasures of childhood and the dark gratification of the womb. In such a mode she now existed, for nothing exists simply, in isolation, but only in some great system; so that if Orpheus desired now to look at Eurydice, he had to re-enter Hell.

So they came to a dark cavern near the surface of the Earth, and Orpheus, holding up his lantern, turned and said: "Either I do not turn, or she is dead. This was the condition. But unless I turn I do not see her. Therefore when I see her, she is dead—this is why I turn, in order that I may see her dead. Why, thou art dead, Eurydice: I knew this before!" She turned into a piece of statuary near the exit upon the Earth's surface, no longer animated by the living desires unfinished that animate dreams. "Thanks be to the Angels of Death and Life," said Orpheus piously, "who assign to different worlds the objects of desire."

So, what is hard to say, even a loving father does not desire, after a short time, his small child to come to life again. It is out of the question, for his world—with its idle hour—is now *founded* on the death of the child. And I have come to *found* my life on the death of my love for L. so many years ago. And we do *not* desire—(do we not! it seems to me almost a lie as I write it)—lovely youth, springtime of desire.

Now rose—as that famous hero daring, as do all, not to remain in Hell, emerged into daylight—now rose on every side the immoderate outcries of the lions in the deeps and the monkeys on high shouting in no common scale. "Yes—yes—" he breathed with immense satisfaction, "just as I thought even in my dream: it would be possible by a tremolo C# on the trumpet to restore harmony among those noises. Who knows, in the end I might even have to introduce enharmonic intervals. O you untaught beasts, crying together in consecutive fifths! *and why not in consecutive fifths?*" exclaimed the patron lord of counterpoint and harmony. "This is strange music. I am afraid that it expresses only too well the movements of my soul."

He restrung his lyre, lending an ear to the beastly noises, beating heart, the flow of time.

"I do not intend, nevertheless," he said, "to compose anything else just now but a mourning song for Eurydice. It is not often that the thoughts and new harmony blend in my soul so well."

Hereupon, standing but not weeping, he created the song:

"Persephone, O Queen of Flowers and Death, O Queen of Art! and you, Angel of Death, author of every new song! When he saw she was dead on earth, whom he used to love, Orpheus descended into the springtime of longing, and found her there among the dead, as he knew before. Not she, but the pleasure-stained company of the Elysian Fields; and not dead but forever quick in my soul.

"Oh, where shall I dwell now if not among the violent beasts that have no common scale! but my lord Apollo teaches us a new song. If this were not the most frightful morning of my dear life I should not be so amazed to find it musical. Strange music uncertain—I cannot rely on my heart for the meter, for from time to time it misses a beat.

"Eurydice! Eurydice! Eurydice! undesignating sound, for the convention is violated that assigned a thing to this name. I thought that I had had all the three moments of sorrow: I mean the grief of loss, and the anxiety of impossible desire, and mourning as one by one I laid aside dear habits. Why am I still anxious?

"Weeping unrestrainedly: by and by I shall come to the Elysian Fields, where I am living her death and she has died for me my life (as do all). When certain thoughts appear before me I seem to be drugged—dragged—and in those springlike fields cry out: Persephone! O Queen of Flowers and Death, Queen of Art—

"Blessed art thou, angel of death, author of every new song.

"Orpheus, let us not draw out the time with feelings, but allow less than half an hour to mourning, without repetitions. *Eurydice!* oh, undesignating sound, for the convention is violated that assigned a thing to this name."

Chicago
1937

132

2 Pastoral Movements

I.

The Indian path progressing now thru bushes, blackberry thorns and honeysuckle, emerges suddenly round a corner: and the cliff seems cleft and yawning at one's feet, a rocky funnel roaring. Footing is uncertain; stones hop and jump down the gap; the balance is tempted, as by a desire to *fill* this vacuum. Vast and dangerous: the idea of an abyss, with no underfooting, arouses awe: terror and pleasure. (So Faith, according to my brother Barth, is a vacuum.)

But the path at once turns aside into the airy wood where the musical ash-trees stand on both sides and heavy rocks lie on the ground. Here space itself is not absolute, but is characterized by the calls of birds; and walking thru is to cross solids of shadow and sunlight. There is 3-dimensional support. Yet the heart, touched by fear and desire, is still fluttering; when a branch loudly cracks, it is set to pounding and misses a beat. At every window of the body the tiny perceptions are crowding, the soul turns to each one after it has struck. Blood rushes from face and hands; the afrighted person freezes fast, like those beetles that form a tight ball.

Nevertheless, nevertheless the relaxing summertime moist and lukewarm, tepid as satisfied desire but unwilted, looses. It looses and energizes and there is no cause, in the easy adaptation of the weather and the body's heat, but that the organism and its environment should open to each

133

other. In the hot day, every way, in the play of sensations, there is evidence of intrinsic design. Such design, presented as the beauty of colors or proportion of tones and calls, or the choreography of the clouds and grasses, is homoeopathic: the apprehensive heart is relaxed and, as is well observed, "soon the breath is formal with the song"—

—between successive breaths wind-music,
between successive footsteps dancing.

The deep-drawn breath is one time released by the towhee's bell which next time sounds in mid-breath: for towhee and the breathing man have differing organic rhythms, but the clarity and evidence of the difference is itself an evidence of design. The lifted hand flickers in the flowing suns filtered thru the moving apertures of leaves: a cloud slowly moves east and engulfs all in a drifting shadow. *Tow-hee,* calls that bird. The insect-noise is continuous except for an expectant pause. *Tow-hee! tow-hee!* fills the pause.

(So in the sea of conversation among many friends in a small room, the strong tide does not abate, the energizing soul is not set down, even tho one person may pause to catch the rest of a sentence about a certain person.)

The odor of the glen is fresh, cool, not strong. The path is continually descending, broken by difficult let-downs from rock to rock. Rapid progress: noisy unnoticed breathing. (One is now at the phase of physical movement, not unlike the stones that hopped and jumped, but by more organic stages.) The dihedral of the glen is so obvious that there must be a brook at the angle. When the slate cracks underfoot, the outward body slides five yards, but the heart affirmed by evidence of design does not pound; but it is necessary to grasp an oak-branch with the right hand, and have feet on two levels: an elastic system, for the branch is about to spring and the body to relax. Here the air is cool and almost dank, and the trees have large girth. The space is crowded in which, nevertheless, so much moving is going on. The brook is flowing under the porous ground. There is no sound. A serpent is sliding out of the wet moss. The footing is here too soft and wet, so it is preferable to return a little up-slope among the rocks.

The full heat and brightness of the midsummer day settles down: at the River's edge, the immense plain of water glistening. (For when I say "River"—boastful New Yorker!—it's the Hudson I'm thinking of.) In this great heat—immense plain glistening—Limbs fatigued, heart affirmed, senses detaching.

Green water lapping. Seated on heated sand. Willow boughs. Odor of fishes. Fatigue relieved. So bright the billion-glittering plain! Haze of clouds over Yonkers. Seagull sinking (just as black spots slowly move across the eyesight). The ferry boat *Henry L. Joyce* ablaze in midstream.

So Sleep in a room ablaze with conversation overcomes the soul, by detaching sensations in a fatigued body where the heart is affirmed. Sleep is this detaching of the exterior sensations: neither water lapping nor call of birds is turned to by the soul. But what a vast and formless realm is there of the tiny perceptions from within, these now becoming expressive—but it is difficult to translate their judgments into waking-language.

The action of a sleeping person is startling—his sudden cry or gesture. ("Sudden," as it of course only seems.) The idea of such impulsive acts erupting rouses awe: terror and pleasure. They arouse awe when presented, to a man's friends in the room; but the sleeping man himself is not startled by his cry, which fits indeed into the design of his most intimate perceptions. But he is startled if, crying aloud or gesturing, he chances to awake—and hears the echo, or notices his lifted hand.

2.

Sparkling swiftly over the clear sand and smooth stones flows the brook. Only a few bubbles are formed on the gurgling surface and the pebbles at the bottom are rounded and polished. Sometimes there is a ledge and leap, with sparkling drops and bubbles borne on their way exploding into the smooth swift surface flowing on and on. The transparent current has no soul; this is why perhaps so many poets wondering have asked: "Whence? whither?" as the brook sparkles onward over the gold-pointed sand. Only a few bubbles are formed on the gurgling surface. But there is a ledge of rocks, not without a rainbow and a hiss of bubbles swiftly collapsing as they are borne onward in the colorless and sparkling current smoothly flowing gurgling rapidly softly.

—Pastoral Muse! it is because the flow of the brook is like the flow of prose that we are called on for this imitation, we like many famous men of letters fascinated by brooks, writing "On and on" or "Whence? whither?"

Broadening and slowing down a little, the brook is now the medium of vegetable life. Among the hairy green rocks the cool liquid is everywhere slightly held back. Persistent bubbles are borne 4 or 5 yards on their way before they break. All in one direction, downstream, the weeds are pulled and trembling in the foam. Here is a brief stretch of only clear sand, white pebbles, and rapid water golden-shining: it is because the stream is no longer so iced cold that it supports the life. On one side, warded by two mossy stones, is a little bay of water almost still; into and out of this the brook merely *leaks* and the water's luke-warm here. But outside the gates, foaming and tugging at the weeds, trembling moss, with noises of suction (if you bring close your ear), flows the brook. The liquid is cool and persistent bubbles float onward 4 or 5 yards before they collapse. Here among the hairy rocks is a hole with no visible bottom and over which the black water smoothly swells. Warm or icy to touch, this well where the dusty sun hardly penetrates? Seems to be a silvery gleam down there! a fish? The black water smoothly swells—foaming among the hairy green rocks with noises of suction, tugging at the trembling weeds, everywhere held back, cool and dusty-sunny.

—Spirit of animal life! secret principle of locomotion, sensation, and the feeling of desire, which we distinguish as *almost good in itself,* for we call a dead body worthless,

which can no longer move or feel, and we are sorry to see it:
Soul, be present here.

Off the rather sluggish stream has collected a motionless
puddle. Ought we to pause here and not hurry on to the
lordly River? the liquid of the puddle so thick and lifeless.
But look close, and the pond is teeming with animal
movement! Light insects are sliding on the tension of the
surface and slugs are screwing upward into the dusty sunlight and withdrawing. If the spot were magnified, rotifers
and infusoria would grow into vision: so much movement
going on in the motionless water! Part of the brook has
come to this pause, ateem with animal life. Suspended in
their jelly, eggs of frogs hang warming in the region of dusty
sunlight mud-green. Light insects are darting about the
surface; a yellow flower on a stalk sticks up above it. Nothing is borne lightly onward sparkling by this stagnant
liquid generative.

A frog jumps from the puddle out upon the bank, as if a
memento of the primordial vertebrate ever to quit the water.

If we scholars were not now bogged, no longer hurrying
into new studies, there would not be continually generated
amongst us the live and sensible souls, anxious and new-
born souls, crying and seeing. Impure and stationary, breeding illicit desires, this pause in our dear souls' flow from day
to day has let somewhat, I think, jump forth: an animate
frog, not in every way ugly.

In a circumscribed medium not expanding, it is not un-
reasonable if unusable energy stagnating should produce
what is startling: crimes or miracles. At first one might
suppose that no further adventure was forthcoming to
putrefying water trapped off the main course—till out
jumps a live frog, a startling new generation out of the
motionless; inexplicable only to those who judge on a first
view, yet arousing awe: terror and pleasure.

The thick and *breathing* water, lukewarm—not unlike a
man asleep, whose voiceless breath rises regularly from
him. The unusable energies of sensation and desire are
circumscribed in the vegetable cycle of breath, nourishment, and circulation. These energies putrefy into the

boundless realm of interior perceptions, now becoming expressive, but impossible to describe in waking-language. It is not unaccountable if out of this corporal heat emerges a sudden outcry: *"The game's up, Davie, it's no use stalling!"* unfurls some elaborate gesture: eyes opening, forearm raised to shield them from a blow.

Chicago
May 1937

Prose Composition: Virginia (prologue, interlude, episode, interlude, exodus)

In any institution, a style of prose, a love affair, there are these historical periods, the primitive, the classic, the baroque, the decadence. And it is famous that it is only at the end, toward the end, are written the self-conscious histories; who has not heard of the owl Minerva taking wing at dusk? This is the kind of thoughts I have about myself and 'Ginny: and look, I am already writing down this love in my self-conscious prose that has no rhythm. (But why am I so bent on bringing all to a close! Perhaps our love wouldn't die tomorrow if I didn't kill it. Yet I can no longer resist writing. If 'Ginny would 'phone, perhaps I shouldn't write.) The primitive times were those when I didn't remember her name from that ancient, that prior to archaic, introduction of last winter; they were when I almost did not arrive at the appointment we made because I suspected that she would not, she wouldn't even remember it, I thought, wouldn't come, wouldn't phone. . . . The classic times were those nights every one of which seemed different, as if the acts of lust could night by night create a new atmosphere, new rhythms and vocabulary. Black night, comic night, chaste night, the tragic night when I was prevented by hysteric failure; but it is not possible to enumerate the varieties. And that night, solvent of all and different from all—the mature classic. (And does my perverted taste truly prefer to that night these tired and morose ones—just because they are *last*? These tired and self-conscious nights are so dear.) Baroque was a curious night that we saw a bad play in which our intimate speech came back at us caricatured from the stage, so that we could not look at each other, or speak to each other even in bed; but then wild lust, sadistic and masochistic, somewhat sub-human, seized hold of us.

And now we're at this ending: diffidence, insecurity, moroseness, apologetic *pro amore nostro*; and a critical history of the changes of lust. This is the old age of the pleasure had by 'Ginny and me, *anno domini* 1937. (But oh! perhaps this is the old age of only the Prologue! because often when an institution seems to have run its course—grown old and sickened and is about to die—we see that it is at the end of only the first stage—not even Primitive Times; and the nature of the Institution was not what we thought. Why am I so anxious? Where is she? Why don't I hear some word from her? I don't think I should be so impassioned of this diffident atmosphere, find it so dear—yes, so impassioned even of the self-conscious rhythm of this lost lust— if it were really the ending.)

I must think why I am thinking and writing these thoughts.

This is the feeding of my soul, on thoughts, memories and hope, after my body has been so well fed. The remembering and still desirous body's the ground of many imaginations—*pâture de l'âme*, pasturage of the soul. I remember the subjects of cartoons that we invented: *He* (fucking her): "Do you really love me, honey?" Or again: *She* (being fucked): "Do you really love me, honey?"

When 'Ginny was having a period, I wrote a poem as follows:

"Dear periodic Virginia,
let's 'fuck' in quotation marks—
playfully rub bellies
while the moon's overflowing red!"

—"Dear childish Paul,

Prose Composition: Virginia

you are so red and heavy and hot;
lie on me darling,
and pull the cover overhead."

"It is the secret night
when stars watch the furtive loves of men,
the Moon's rising free and white—
O 'Ginny, let me shove it in."

—"Fuck me, fuck me, sweetheart.
Darling. Darling. Darling. Darling.
O Paul—please—no!
darling. Ah."

When 'Ginny and I had the same idea, I wrote a poem as
follows:

We correlate
we fit into each other, kid
I didn't think you'd think what I did
and oh, we implicate.

In the country of Virginia
clement climate of Vaginia
(we fit into each other, kid)
I am a new geographer

but I know all the caves,
the natural wonders of Virginia
and where to spend the night
(and oh! we implicate).

You know what I imply, darling,
because we correlate:
let's fit into each other, kid,
and spend the night.

But hope—memory giving way to longing—is destroying
the calm feeding, calm digestion, of my heart on these
pleasurable thoughts.
    Anxiety! Anxiety has exposed me to terrible surprises.

If I were, even if I were, writing a critical history of the changes of lust: why? Perhaps it is for this reason: I cannot bear not to put her name and such thoughts down on paper in her absence. It is a way of denying her absence. Think of me, Virginia! please to be thinking of me. Because in the end it is this I long for, more than kisses, that some one should be having me in mind—whose thoughts watch over me even if I'm not thinking at all. So that I could prefer absence to presence, even, except that presence is sure. (Why do I lie?) I am not quietly pasturing the soul; I am feeding a ravenous desire. I cannot moderate anxiety by any means. Virginia, please to be thinking of me! because this thought will perhaps bring you to me. And I almost prefer to kisses the thought that some one is thinking of me even when I am asleep; except, how could I be sure? Lord! creator of the heavens and earth (Thou art thinking of me!)—when Thou gavest me first the unlooked-for easy pleasure, I was not dismayed, for I was so habituated to disaster (why do I lie? I never, at that time, lost anything I really wanted, because I never had it!), I was so habituated to disaster that I knew there was no danger I might forget Thee in lust. But now I have such easy joy, and 'Ginny has so often come to me (and 'phoned, in proof she's thinking of me), and scattered notes for me with my name and saying "Do you remember" this or that—I have such easy joy, perhaps I am in critical danger: Lord, perhaps Thou hast given me respite enough. If 'Ginny hadn't come so often, I shouldn't be so anxious now. If I'd never been habituated to disaster, I shouldn't so desire some one to be thinking of me; for offhand, what difference does it make? I know, I know well (if I do, indeed), that I can't refrain from writing about Vaginia and the acts of lust just because I am for the moment deprived. It seems I can't do without for more than 2 days! There has been more than enough easy joy—if the thought of what I am about, which is prayer, is to flicker on a little, and I am not to sink in gentile pleasure.

Alas! there is no danger! My Lord, whose thoughts search me out, has found me in this lust. The terrible enlighten-

ment, amid the noise of bad memories of old, discloses His
Angel, the winged Eros, archer, with bow shot. And there I
lie, victim of pleasures, tangler of arguments, erroneous
historian; and here I stand apart, true seer, poet, and lover,
in the glory of death. By necessity.

Str.   Lord, thanks thanks thanks for peaceable lust
        unbridled and for no unrest
           which Thou, for I was fit to die,
           providently gavest me.

        And Lord, when I in pleasure most
        am feeding, I taste Thy sacred taste
           on her teats and in her ears
           as I have tasted other years.

Ant.   The Angel Eros armed with might
        and Lord Thy Name, how soon has smote
           to the heart of easy pleasure: I
           shall not resist Necessity

        nor fail to thank (for I am hurt
        and reverent) my watchful Lord
           who hath remembered me, to probe
           my entrails with delightful love.

Epode   Glorious and holy God, lo grief
        has gripped me, yet am I safe
           of void of Thee or joy: what new
           dost Thou desire Paul to know?

        What new now necessary, oh!
        if Thou hast guessed (if it be true)
           how unaccustomed easy al-
           ready is the usual.

        Nothing hath yet befallen Paul
        undesigned for the soul:
           brothers, it isn't unafraid
           I utter such a boast of pride.

A CEREMONIAL

Creator of the world and I
do not beguile mutually,
   and I expect with hope and tears
   fulfilling deadliest of fears.

Now by necessity here am I in the horror of love. What an ending, and what a beginning! It is the ending of easy joy. I know well why I am anxious, and my attention crowding into my ears, but not to hear music. I have laid myself open to terrible surprises. I'll turn to each one after it has struck. Already I'm about to cry. You see that 'Ginny has not come. And what else was I to expect except this rage, out of so many joyous easy episodes of lust; for by use we come to know at last? To know! it is famous a man cannot eagerly fuck without igniting soon, body and soul. Lord have mercy, for I see amid the flames Thy demon Archer hilarious.

I shouldn't write if I were not in love. (This is famous.) How interesting it is to write some new thing! one can never predict the new effect of style. A new song. An unexpected movement of life has been allotted to me by necessity and by the Lord; therefore I'll raise a new song.

It's likely that soon Virginia will be here. Oh, how joyous and how lucky is the coming of lovers face to face! My anxiety has been only anxiety. Virginia would never have come to me so very often if she didn't love me. Oh, how joyous and how lucky is the coming of lovers face to face.

[*Chicago*]
November 1937

144

Ravel

–for Virginia

I.

During the quick movement, among the snowfall of plucked notes, among the brief phrases; towards the end, when the dancer had developed almost all the steps, or the flying ball gone back and forth *enough* and some one was preparing the kill; the snow-*flurry* blew in the air but the ground was unbroken white—towards the end of the quick movement of the quartet, the A-string of the viola broke, not a musical sound. At this, all in the audience started. Inserted in every program was the card,

MAURICE RAVEL, 1875-1937
Quartet in F Major

———

in memoriam

Every soul in the large audience started at the formless tone, the appropriate noise.

And during the slow movement, where there was a pause—when the bows were raised, when the snow smoothly covered the mounds; when the attention crowded into our ears to hear, but there was a pause—now the 'cello earnestly and alone spoke. In more than one, the blood rushed into tingling ears; and we, perhaps, raised a forearm, palm front, like the witnesses of mysteries in a painting.

From where I am seated in the dark auditorium, I can see above the heads of three of the quartet the lights by which they are reading!

Wonderful! there is a single footstep in the broad expanse of snow.

A flash of inward light exposes the figure of a man in a courtyard, bouncing a ball on the pavement, and catching it.

No, no, let none applaud with noisy handclaps the conclusion of the work, nor let Mrs. Nellie Tate Thomson, the stout blue-gowned patroness of the concerts, rise and take a bow.

Not to end! What a thunderbolt!

There is a momentary pause, arm half in the sleeve of the overcoat.

Again, speak again in the low note.

(The rubber ball is like a live animal, bounding away across the courts.)

Again, speak again in the low note.

You might not think it musicianly, but informal and even entirely contrary to the spirit of good quartet-writing, so to interrupt the civil conversation of the four instruments, their equal dialogue in which none speaks overmuch or too loud, to bring about a *pause,* to make the solo 'cello speak so *earnestly.* But wonderful! There is a flash of inward light—What a thunderbolt! and not to end—

Again, speak again in the low note.

2.

In June we played ball-games in honor of the composer of dance-music. The games were tennis, badminton, pelota, handball, and such other games in which on a court limited by straight lines the ball many times flies back and forth before the kill. Over all a large flat area bathed in light, these games took place, the balls flying over nets; but sometimes a wild ball bounded from court to court.

Perhaps in this composer's honor I should describe a tennis-game, game of famous elegance and coeval with the

Ravel

sarabande; and whose rhythm is One-2-3-4 Two, One-2-3-4 Two: *twang* of the racquet, silent flight of the ball, and *hop*. Meantime the players move from side to side.

But I happened to be referee of the doubles-handball game of the juniors.

The black rubber ball was like a live animal. In the hot light the boys were naked to the waist and wore silent shoes. The ball pounded the wooden wall, bounded from the cement, and was slapped by a leather glove, in the rhythm *One* and two and three, *One* and two and three: a waltz. Of these, the wood gave forth the most resounding note.

This game does not have the airy elegance of tennis because there is no silent flight of the ball, but it is more violent and precise.

Meantime the four players moved in opposite directions for the next figure. Teddy Taylor, who had just struck, fell in a step too far, but his partner black William Kelly moved across to cover his court. My lad Remo fell slowly back for the return, while his partner cast his eyes toward the uncovered court and moved across to block.

The grace of the athletes seemed even affected because—until the climax of violence—they had more energy in store than was needed for these limited movements.

Now (to my satisfaction) Remo drove a low beauty thru that left backcourt. (Loud handclaps.) The ball bounded away.

How hateful Victory is in games! puts an end to the rapid figures! What a paradox! they play to play and they play to win, but victory ends the volley.

"Good shot!" I said. "The score is now 16 playing 12."

The ball bounded from court to court.

The handclaps continued and I stopped the play. "Please omit the applause till the end," I said. "When you applaud the players now, you take them as ordinary persons—who can be praised—as if they were acting a part well. But Art is imitation not in the sense of *assuming* a disguise, but of having assumed it and unifying a new life."

The fact is that I was bitter against the intrusion of live

147

feeling, because of the thought of Maurice Ravel.

"These are no longer your friends while the game's on," I said bitterly.

"We're applauding the shot, not the player," said Meyer Leibow.

"Look at the whole at the end," I said.

"Play ball, play ball," said Teddy, who was off balance and in haste.

"The clapping is noisy and confuses the dancers."

"Play ball, play ball."

"Play," I said.

There was the thunder of the wood wall, the kiss of cement, and the leather slap. At first, as the point warms up, the stiffer movements of the players develop discrete figures, one to each triplet, but always faster, till at last there is a continuous flow of speed, violence, and precision, in great variety: the powerful soul pent in the form of the game. Now the lads have given themselves to it! a devoted offering, to the sacred dance. No *longer* our poor friends, when the game's on.

And so everywhere on the broad area, brief cries and bursts of light.

These games are in memory (I am describing them in memory) of the composer of *La Valse*, of the *Alborada del Grazioso*, of the memorial dances called *Tombeau de Couperin*.

Hateful Victory! for Remo hit a "killer," the perfect shot which strikes with a flat noise (as a string of a musical instrument might break) so low on the wall that there is no rebound. This shot was greeted with a volley of handclaps. The ball was like a lively animal: developing a bounce, it went bounding off the court, out of all restraint.

There was a pause. I tossed in a new ball.

"Play," I said.

And now could be observed something *human*, one of those mechanisms of human strategy that preserve us all from *excessive* sorrow. Teddy was off his balance; he couldn't collect himself. Remo and George, scenting the Victory, at once began to pound away at *him*; he fell to pieces and at last he missed completely. The tears flooded

148

his eyes and he felt bad, especially because he was letting his partner down. He couldn't collect himself.

"The score is 18 playing 12," I said.

"I'm losing the game," said Teddy bitterly, unable to throw himself into the swing of the game, "I oughta quit."

"No, no, play—play," I said.

"I stink," said Teddy.

But now could be observed something *human*, for black William, just in order that his partner might recover his nerve (I saw it well), *purposely* looked terrible on the next two points! the first he missed completely and the second he fell on his face. "Between the ones *I* blow an' the ones *you blow*," he said from the floor, "we're doin' good."

Here could be observed something *human*, one of those mechanisms of human strategy.

"20!" I said. "Point is game."

There was a pause.

"Listen," I whispered to my boy Remo, "don't ever put an end to this game. Even let *them* win if it's necessary."

"Play," I said.

3.

Midst of the uncircling, about to dance one round I thought—of Maurice Ravel just dead. Didn't stop, but while the phonograph played, danced the *Pavane for an Infanta Dead*, danced it while strings and woodwinds played, danced until a deathless joy possessed us both, my motion and his play.

Us fellows of the Holy Ghost the Angel cannot overcast entirely, but we live on thru each other, heart and song.

4.

Why fool ourselves? The last year before his death the composer of *Daphnis and Chloe* spent shut up in a lunatic asylum. Was not this thought a dark back drop for the games? The last year before his death the composer of

Daphnis and Chloe spent shut up in a lunatic asylum. It is hard, hard to surrender the soul to these formal dances, to these formal dances without a pause. The last year before his death the composer of *Daphnis and Chloe* spent shut up in a lunatic asylum. What a sentence to write about a musician! If there's no harmony in harmony, *where* is it to be found? Why fool ourselves? The last year before his death the composer of *Daphnis and Chloe* spent shut up in a lunatic asylum.

The works of the last years of this composer were very simple. How simple! to repeat with the *minutest* variations one figure again and again. Not to end! But why fool ourselves? The last year before his death the composer of *Daphnis and Chloe* spent shut up in a lunatic asylum. Not to end! it was necessary not to lapse into the maddening applause, but to persist, shut up, in a form one was at least sure of. This one figure, evolved by what a thunderbolt of creative effort, sure of, he repeated, with the *minutest* variation; afraid to deviate from this sure figure—lest suddenly it vanish, because a tune's forgotten instantly at the least distraction. Why fool ourselves? The last years before his death the composer of *Daphnis and Chloe* spent shut up in a lunatic asylum. What a sentence to write about a musician!

Paralyzed by a thunderbolt, of the creative spirit, amid the ordinary life: there was a pause (arm half in the sleeve of his overcoat). Shine on! speak again in the low note! How to persist in this storm-moment? and not to end or lapse into the amusing distractions (of conversations of people in the lobby); *it was necessary most of all to make the formal figure self contained*, very complete, with no clue leading outside itself. Then what a paradox, for if complete it must *end*. The years before his death, the composer of *Daphnis and Chloe* spent shut up in an asylum. I should never say it about him if he weren't a musician.

The works of this composer were very simple—to repeat with the minutest variation the formal figure, not to deviate too far from this sure thing, a tune's forgotten instantly at the least distraction. Yet not to end! What a paradox! There was a pause. No, no, please let there be no

Ravel

loud handclapping now when the composer is so ill at ease; let not the wicked patroness of the concert rise in her blue dress to take a bow. But speak again in the low note.

"Creator Spirit, come!" so have many composers said. (It is a hymn in all the hymnals.) What a thunderbolt! There was a pause—I had my arm half in my sleeve. No, no! But how am I to persist in this storm-moment and never lapse into the amusing distractions of the conversations in the lobby? Not to end! The years the composers have spent shut up in an asylum! Why fool myself? The years the composers have spent shut up in a lunatic asylum!

God forbid! Let me speak no harm of the Creator Spirit—but may He come.

Now can be observed something *human,* one of those mechanisms of human strategy that preserve us all from *excessive* sorrow. For here was the desperate poet frightened of the terrible pause; and there (as he suddenly saw in a dream) was Ravel on a sultry day during the last year before his death: he was in a broad square court of the asylum, alone; and he was playing a solitary ball-game, without outcries, bouncing a rubber ball on the ground and catching it. It was the composer of the *Sonatine.* So my eyes flooded with tears of memory and I could not put on my coat. But the thought came to me (thanks be to God, not without tears also of release)—the thought to think of my poor brother Maurice Ravel now—if indeed I must exist yet awhile in this way—and make a small trophy, as you see. Not in his honor—no no!—but mainly for my own sake. —A description of a game.

It was the composer of the *Sonatine!* I think we can, with our thoughts on that *dead* man, come to the last word. *He* won't write any new works now; we know *his* style. How sharply, among the brief outcries, broke the string! There was a pause.

[*Chicago*]
[*February 1938*]

151

The Continuum of the Libido

Well established, as they say, with a dear wife and two children—(I am thinking perhaps of Virginia and of my own home)—nevertheless, therefore, he began to feel an uneasiness in his love and in his dreams. And since he was, by the habit of good success, used to have no nonsense about such simple matters, but to adjust each thing in turn, he now began to take the greatest care, as he walked about the neighborhood, particularly from 10 to 11 PM, to find out whom it was he really desired. Looking into faces, or at the swing of a person's gait, obeying desire, he was drawn to disreputable streets.

He took photographs of the hundred visions that so vaguely drew his concupiscent attention; these he printed and compared, to find just what it was that at the present time he ardently desired. Oh, what a precious album of pictures for any one to possess! the selection of the privately concupiscible, so much more accurately pornographic than the wares of the French peddlers. Thumbing thru such a book, one is overwhelmed by a flood of ardor.

He found that he was in love with the thievish boys who live on 63rd Street. This was his present uneasiness. And as their ideal features became more precise by superposition, ancient memories of longing and envy rose into his mind's eye, to confirm and explain the conclusion. Dating these carefully, he found in his past life at least five years, from the age of 15 to 20, blank of gratification, blank of perfect gratification, and therefore forgotten. Rediscovered now. But alas! one could know *a priori* that it would be hard to get

153

close to these thievish lads and have their love—even harder now than then (or so it seemed).

For if they had not, in the first place in those times, been unattainable, they would neveʳ have become the objects of such especial longing—for we burn for what is unattainable. (It is also true that we come to burn for what we closely possess, as I have written elsewhere.) But by a beautiful causality, they were unattainable at that time just because the disposition of his character made him excel in a different sphere, different games, from theirs. Thus, he came to burn for them just because he too strongly desired something different from them. But in a deeper sense, it was just because he excelled in something different that, to preserve the infinite balance possible to a man, he burned for them. (For we tend to what we love, but perhaps we even more deeply long for what we tend from.)

But these same dispositions to excel soon developed into settled habits of excellence, and now they made a broad gulf between their existence and his. For what he had to win favor with were precisely those talents—of equity and knowledge, let us say—which could not win favor where he most desired it. That is, he shone only among people like himself; and he burned only for the others: so his early propensity was the cause of his desire and now made a fatal gulf. (So it seemed, but of course the contrary proved to be the case.)

I am assuming for these explanations the principle of the Continuum of the Libido, whereby all are enabled to love, and therefore agreeably deal with, every kind of object conceivable (thanks be to God); where love forms us to adaptability and universal success, and success assures us love, to the end of the perfect education of natural man. (It was in terms of this principle, indeed, that he so methodically proceeded to fill out all the blanks.) But now he, just by *too great* love and success in one direction at that time, had gone a fatal step too far. Then, recovering, he burned for the young thieves on 63rd Street, but he did not have the relevant success to win them. (You see, I love this causal relation between just a man's strength and his failure; I cannot often enough write down such an example of equity

154

and science, but my mind dwells on it. This shows that I am he.)

"Money answers all things." With this *universal* medium of success, he soon won the success, both the admiration and the love, desired. And further, against his expectations, once he had established the least communication on 63rd Street, money itself was no longer needed; for obviously his talents were just the ones to win him favor, since everybody honors knowledge, which is universal strength, freedom, and pleasure—and especially sexual knowledge. By sexual knowledge, and freedom, he had enormous prowess, so that—as he might indeed have known *a priori*—the very lack which had compromised him and cut him off by a fatal gulf, nevertheless and *therefore* laid a bridge across, for his excessive desire was the occasion of his developing great skill. So that once the initial advance was made by means of Money, universal medium (for which thanks be to God), he suddenly appeared in all his power to the folks on 63rd Street, like an enormous army, ultra-mechanized, unthinkable to resist, and winning immediate allegiance.

Then, well established in this easy success, sharing the reckless games and the careless language, speedily fulfilling the desires of five years, in a sketchy way to be sure—(I am thinking perhaps of Ben and Milky, and my own May afternoons)—he again began to feel uneasy in his love and dreams. Extreme longing so soon adjusted to a beautiful habit—suddenly he came to look critically and piteously at the poor lads: how unfree they were! there was not one of them who was animal-like, thoughtless and daring, as it had seemed, but each one was afraid of his father. He loved and pitied these boys because they were so respectful and well-behaved.

Scene

He was spending the afternoon with 3 lads, of 17, 16, and 15. Cristy, the eldest, had quit school for good; Henny and Milky for a day's vacation. They left the rowboat on the bank and lay on some grass along the sidewalk, and took off their jackets. Hank, he saw, was the most desirable of the 3 boys: for in every selection of a few objects of love, there is always one that attracts the most attention of desire (except in those perfectly blessed occasions of multitudinous accord). But in another selection, any of these thievish lads would be desirable, first Milky, then Cristy. He sat down so as to touch Henny with his knee. Cristy was jealous and started playing with fire to break up the arrangement: he built a tiny log-cabin of twigs and straw, and set it afire, burning Henny's leg.

"You prick with ears!" cried Hank, leaping away. "Why don't you cut it out and leave him alone?" said the older man; "if you want to touch him do it and stop fooling around." Cristy said to Hank: "Shut your drippin' hole," and he wrestled with him until he began to hurt him. "Let him alone, go fight Milky," said the older man, who desired (for Hank at least) nothing but calm and lustful suggestion. The two turned on Milky who had refused to steal some socks for them from the Five and Ten Cent Store. "I gypped these suspenders, why should I gyp for youse," said Milky; "Cristy got us into Dutch last week," he explained to the older man; and they told how last Wednesday Cristy called for them in his father's car, except that it was a stolen car, drove them around, and then abandoned the car on the Speedway.

Then they did acrobatics, not skilfully or with easy grace, but with the utmost courage, falling heavily on their heads and shoulders, with a wonderful cub grace—while he watched entranced, his longing for the one 16-year-old quite forgotten, while he sat entranced, just as if this animal-like tumbling were a portentous sign. By ducking slyly out of the way or not raising their hands to support the hurtling figure, the boys betrayed each other into heavy falls: but these tricks led to nothing but cuffs and cries of "O you shit" or "O you fuckin' bastard." But the older man was amazed—at this glory—on the May day; his heart began to pound and his vision to cloud over.

But before leaping into a double-flip, Hank crossed himself: and broke the spell.

156

The Continuum of the Libido

Some girl friends passed on the walk, pushing a perambulator, and at once the movement jarred: the thievish lads became self-conscious and were again humanity.

At last he succeeded in pulling Henny down and getting both arms around his hard body in his woolly sweater. Cristy and Milky were playing the game of Rock, and Cristy, who was much the bigger and stronger, again and again broke Milky's rock, so he rode on Milky and dug his spurs in him unmercifully. Henny refused to lie flat (anyway, people could see from the sidewalk, so it was no use); he was angry with Cris for hurting him; and opportunely, he found that Milky had unluckily left his fountain-pen and wrist-watch in his jacket-pocket. He tried to open the watch with the pen-point; the point broke; and with a triumphant smile Hank ignited the hard rubber pen and watched it vanish in malodorous smoke.—

"Why is the child so eager to castrate himself?" thought the older man. "You see, the watch is easy to open," he said to Hank, opening it with his fingernail.

A series of quarrels broke out, about the pen, about making Milky retrieve a ball, about burning a hole in Milky's jacket; but climaxed, as if tapping at last the *fons et origo* of all dissension, in a curious discussion of the girls who were loitering not far off. This discussion, more than anything else, brought the elder man to a pause and tears of pity came into his eyes, for so many well-behaved lads. Cristy had said that Hank had "got his humps off Ellen" in the boathouse. "Ooh, I'll smash you," said Hank, and he began to sob, "just like a smashed her for tellin'." "But *why? why?*" the older man persisted in asking, "she seems a real nice girl to have made." But it was just this *why,* of his fear and shame, that poor Henny wouldn't open his mouth about for all the world. There was an instant's pause of silence. "Supposin' her big brother heard about it—" then said Milky, to whom all terror took the one form of bullying and fagging.

"Every one of these lads—not one who is not—" he cried inwardly, "is terrified of his father or of his elder brother. They desire to cut off their desire, so they are caught in hesitations, rites, and perplexities; but the *real* perplexities—" so he ingenuously put it, "they never get to.

157

The poor lads thieve and break the laws, not like us others with ease and joy because *we* are on God's side—but with guilty eagerness, as a last revolt, before they succumb also to this communal authority. What a pity to see muscular lads so without the habit of success, so well-behaved and respectful, but of course this is just the penalty of that excellence. But I confess that I did not expect to see this young Irish ruffian cross himself."

By further observation and analysis, of what, for instance, led him to pay certain visits, he found that he was in love with his mother-in-law's collie-dog Tippy, and indeed with all of a class of large woolly female beasts, such as sheep and the she-bears in the zoo. He stopped short: how long ago it was he had first broken the great Continuum! But this love wouldn't be difficult, he thought cheerfully. He went to the kennels and got himself a beautiful and desirable mongrel bitch, which he cajoled and used.

And how was he to place himself on a level, and on a basis of mutual desire, with the poor dumb frightened animal, lost as to the meaning of the pain imposed on her? by what new authority? for what cause? (I am thinking of the pitiful account by Franz Kafka of the perplexed dog, wondering whence comes the food.) His eyes filled with tears as he petted the frightened bitch. Tears also for himself as he contemplated the gulf, yawning for so long a time, between himself and this desire. For he had, just by freedom and science, fatally embarrassed his perfection. But the body is a universal medium of communication.

It was necessary to crowd his attention into the olfactory sense: to sniff and smell—for the first time, as is the case with so many city-dwellers (or so he thought). But indeed, as he did so, a new world unfolded within him, of obscure reminiscences soon becoming sharply precise, tho not to be readily expressed in our visual language, and of organic longing. And his mouth at the same time began to water, and licking and sniffing became one longing. "This is of course mere infantilism," he thought, from so far off! but he clung to the beast, being thereby almost free and perfect in desire.

158

The Continuum of the Libido

His thought was so far, far off. "Eia!" he thought with joy, "I could never thus apparently quit human reason, law, and freedom—for men are only free in the intelligible world—in order to be almost free and perfect in desire with this beast in a world of bodily odors, if I were not in this also submissive to my absolute Creator. I should not dare to lie with a dog; but I, like few, am on His side! I have set *my* father so high in heaven that here I have every license and no fear. (What a stratagem!) Yet I am compelled too: for I *must* not fear or dare to deny myself in any way. Thus, for God's sake I am idolatrous; He is so great I dare not be fastidious of idols: what difference does it make? And for His sake I waste my strength in love."

[*Chicago*]
March-April 1938

Honey-Moon and Archaic Longings

I.

During the summer months, I planned to compose Olympian marriage-festivities, in honor of the new events, this peaceful countryside retreat and this, as it were, honeymoon of love. Therein would have joined all good demons in a formal design, and Aphrodite queen of love be wed to the laborious artisan (what a boastful poet!) My intention was to have the Vowels reclining on a rock afford musical accompaniment. And there would be an autobiographical debate, between Hymen and lawless Eros: ending in a solemn peace dictated by Pallas Athene. And not least: in one episode the usual Muses were to welcome among themselves, to share privacies of form and subject-matter, a new sister, for I intended also to devote the summer to paintings, along with my bride (including studies of each other).

> —Not without a dream, to compose
> Olympian marriages in rime and prose!

Uncanny depression weighed on me worse every day. (Except that I remembered the past, I might almost have blamed the change on sexual excess!) I became heartsick every morning of the week; and the country air drugged me with strange sleep and dreams, from which I awoke with ancient longings. I became heartsick every day of the week. Uncanny depression weighed on me. No art; the course of every painting I began was as follows: up to a certain point I worked carefully and with conventional talent, then vio-

161

lently I rebelled toward form and sublimity and ruined everything with a few bad strokes.

(I thought we had dictated favorable terms of peace to the wild love.)

—I came to see (so I imagined) that far from writing prose of new joy, I'd write nothing at all this summer.

Except that I see that I am writing the same unquiet strain as of old! (These new events have not proved fatal after all!) Same strain of joy, it is *my* strain. (What a boastful poet!) Everything may seem to change, except that I see that I am writing the same unquiet strain as of old. Perhaps in August, if not just now, I'll dare to describe the marriage on Olympus, but with parenthetic remarks.

—Not without a dream I'll compose
Olympian marriages in rime and prose!

Virginia, dear hope and memory
of joy, what I desire most and have,
my friend and bride, I dedicate to thee
these feasts of the fair and the brave.

When the uncanny sorrow touches me
from the heart sorely rising—
spontaneously tears flow down my face:
which moment is the end result
of the long process of Time.

2.

With a lack of foresight he began to kill the flies in the kitchen. They were sailing thru the air as if masters of the situation in every position of space, zooming past one's ear in an insulting manner. The long-handled swatter came round, and the winged corpse fell to the floor. Another fly poised his last moment on the wood window-sash and was then crushed, stuck to the wood by his blood and pulp, a wing askew.

So he proceeded, striking here and there; and the live and

162

busy zooming before long, before long was lulled. Breathing a little hard, the man dropped into his chair, leaned his head against the cushion, and closed his eyes.

The resonant music of a fly, higher in pitch as it drew near, and then deepening and fading away, resounded in the silence.

"There is a fly in the room," he said, opening his eyes.

"Oh bother it," she said, not without an edge of irritation, because he had been moving so heavily about. She was busy at the other end of the kitchen, with the last pans; and they rang against each other.

"There is nevertheless a fly in the room," he said, settling back, but with one eye open.

The insolent insect brought him to his feet, for there it was lit on the very handle of the fly-swatter. It flew aloft with a contemptuous zoom. But he followed hard with his extraordinary eyesight (that still was no foresight): the beast alighted on the fruit in the bowl. Round came the whispering wire and the fly died.

Zooooom! again. But it was the last survivor. "Ah! ah!" cried the man with joy, for he knew that it was the last survivor. The woman put by the last of the pans and turned around.

Heavily he followed the hunt (for every man must seem heavy in pursuit of a winged fly)—from wall to wall, swinging and slapping; and at last the insect in despair settled itself on the screen-door itself, trying to escape; and *Swat!* it was dead.

And now, as the true silence spread everywhere, and quick as light, into the utmost corners of the ceiling, he realized that they two were alone in the kitchen; there was no longer another soul.—

. . . "Come to bed," he said, after a moment; for it was better to be completely together than as they were.

3.

I have been sitting here in the corner of the country kitchen, hands folded on the table and my head sunk between my shoulders, whistling, trying to recall, hear again, the slow songs of Beethoven's last quartets, the deathless Cavatina, the largo in the Lydian mode. Those strains used to possess my soul, when I played the records every day at home, my old *original* home, in New York City. Now the tears flow down my face, almost "I know not what they mean"—but I know well what they mean! Every day a theme of the deathless Cavatina recurs to me, when I'm walking along the wagon-road, or weeding in the field. But no matter how hard I try, I can't remember the first part, or the modulation in F#: what is the meaning of it? Even if I were still in Chicago, even in Chicago, I could hear *some* music; there would be a radio—and who knows, by chance one turns the dial and is suddenly struck to the heart as some distant viola enters the room sounding a phrase of the Cavatina—the present falls away, Chicago is no more. At home we had not only the records, but the scores; and friends who performed the works for us on Sunday mornings.

Virginia is busy in the other room. Her footsteps and a peculiar ring of glass keep reaching me. What is she about? how to interpret it? Why should she take three steps, then pause, then suddenly two more, and rapidly return, etc.? No doubt it is routine domestic business, yet how baffling it seems in this other room! This must be a special day, when everything seems so mysterious.

No no, she ought not to leave me alone here so long; she knows my mood; and here am I sitting crooning in the last corner of the kitchen and the tears are flowing down my face. (This is bad for our relationship.)

—Here am I drifted to this back region unelectrified—I see it is by inevitable stages! I can trace the steps that brought me here one by one. How I came to leave New York because of X and Y, and because I was afraid of the police! And perhaps I left Chicago too just on account of Z! Yet what am I about? it has brought me to this lost corner, so far! so far from that neighborhood where the faces approaching on St. Nicholas Avenue struck one to the heart. I am amazed, I am amazed at the wilfulness, the determination, with which I have steered myself to this desert! (No

164

doubt here I shall be able to resist temptations of every kind.) And where next, of places void of love and music, am I going to take myself?

And here is Virginia, asking me to walk outside with her and look at the morning plants. It is my darling love; she has bent down to kiss me from above, and her arms are folded round me. She is my hope; and what I desire and also have; and my dear memory of joy. We step outside and oh, the morning heat has everywhere strewn the clouds of meadowflowers,

> —the white-eyelashed daisies and gold buttercups
> and devil's-paintbrushes in fire dipt.

Oh,

> —the morning is so bright
> the primroses look white.

4.

In the most placid June weather, in the trough of pleasure that follows on gratification, we came to a rural home to spend a summer that was, yes, as if a honey-moon. The pale sky contained a curl of mist. (Fear no tempest, reader; but if anything, expect more and more sunshine thru and thru.) The country odor cast a heavy spell, which we breathed deeply; but on the day we arrived, we did not think of the effect on our sleep of the various narcotic airs. Recently, in Chicago, I was a light sleeper, accustomed to wake easily, to find Virginia at my right side, the morning in the window. I was astonished at myself, for I never woke remembering a dream—like the man in the legend who didn't cast a shadow. (From time to time I woke from a nightmare with a cry.) Waking in the morning early, I'd half turn to kiss sleeping Virginia in the ear or throat; but I'd refrain and often try to sleep again.

—In this most conscious state of joy, in the trough of pleasure, we arrived.

But when, in the early morning, I awoke, deafened by

bird-calls, overcome by the turpentine odors of the grove, it was from an unusual, and deeper level of sleep. I thought (at least this was one incident of it) I was with Haskell at Tenafly, that time I wrote the song,

Ash-tree, O youngest tree—

if indeed that was what the dream was. But in a thick crowd (and so, more every morning, under the influence of the narcotic airs), a hundred archaic longings, surging into memory, confused me and stupefied me. And I suddenly awoke in the dead of night, with a scene of infantile lust aflame about me; and yet it was no nightmare. Perversions and thoughts of a dozen other faces set themselves up against me, where I had expected to live in perfect gratification for weeks and weeks.

How out-of-place that program seemed now! For an instant, looking askance at Virginia in the gray dawn, I imagined that the summer was spoilt.

But I became a more expert lover, polymorphously perverse. For each dreamy memory stimulated a new technique of love for our honey-moon. And I soon enough came to see all the expressions passing over her face (many of which expressions belong to the acts of love themselves)—she reviving them all, that I thought lost forever. Obviously, for it was my dear 'Ginny! And a hundred presences of her loves as well as mine were on the porch where we slept in the trees (for the beautiful weather continued, tho it became more blue and breezy). The usual acts of love, and certain dreamy desires, and perversions even tho not gratifeasible for physical reasons, all united in a tempest of pleasure, no simple satisfaction, but enormously important and ambiguous.

I came to see that the placid atmosphere, even in the moments of deadest June, was a raging equilibrium. Among the leaves there was a continuous movement; the upper airs were speeding to fill the vacuums below. In some places vapor was visibly steaming upward, everywhere invisibly. Erratic clouds of midges were signs and causes of vortices in

166

Honey-Moon and Archaic Longings

the air. There were clouds in the sky. And above the hundred flowers played the oily aromatic atoms.

[*Chesterton, Indiana*]
May-July 1938

Prose Composition:
The Minutes Are Flying
By Like a Snowstorm

From the time I first got my old car, my sky-blue car, not a week passed without repairs. I drove her from the agency, and she had a flat tire. The next morning another tire was flat, so we called her "Flat foot Floojie," after the famous song. Laboriously, under a noonday sun, and when I was not well, I changed the wheel and became ill. I got better.

Next week the horn ceased to function. Putting over to the roadside, I adjusted it, as I thought. But a moment later, when it was necessary to signal the unwary pedestrian, again the voice failed. "Hey," I cried out, my voice swallowed in the rush of air.

Next week it was the glowing headlights. Eclipsed on the highroad, with a smell of burning, they left me in the moonlit countryside.

Before long, before very long, I understood what was to be my way of life with this sky-colored automobile: that every week I could expect to repair something. To repair something, just to keep going. But once I came to admit this, what relief! to take this *property* of my car for granted, just as if forced to admit that the car had 6 cylinders.

"If you realize the car is likely to break down," said my brother, "why don't you give it one thorough overhauling?" "No," I cried apprehensively, "it's an old car and there's no way of telling—"

I began to hope to discover something broken, in order to feel secure for a few days, for a few days at least. "If only I can see something to fix before I even start out!" Thus, not without a certain joy, like a man satisfied in doing his duty,

169

I sewed up the roof before I started, or tightened the bolts where the radiator was leaking, before ever I started.

I was going on a long trip, of more than a week, to my native city. Industriously, to set my mind at ease, I busied myself with every kind of repair before starting. I fancied that the clutch was loose, the brakes were tight; I installed new wiring. But this artificial activity, of prevention, served of course only to heighten anxiety.

Once on my way, the sky-blue car began to tremble. At first this general tremor was barely perceptible, and by increasing the speed, by increasing the speed, I could deceive myself, deceive myself that it was nothing but the agitation of going faster and faster. We went faster and faster. Then, however, the noise within the car became thunderous and terrifying. Persons along the route turned in wonder, so that, as happens often, social opinion made me look to my own salvation. My hands were a gray blur on the steering-wheel of the shuddering car. I slowed down.

I drove into a garage, where the mechanic perceived that it was an old car, not easy to fix; one was just as likely to break something else as find the trouble. "There's nothing particularly wrong," said he, when I had described the terrifying symptoms—"just general looseness."

"General looseness!" I cried in anger. "That's easy for *you* to say, but *I* have to ride in it!"

I drove off, amid loud sounds, the earliest terror. "Nothing particularly wrong—" I said to myself—"at least, nothing I can remedy."

I drove into a garage filled with new and shiny cars. The mechanic of these fat, greasy cars looked at mine and burst out laughing. "What you ought to do with *that!*" he cried, "is throw it on the junk-heap!"

"No no no," I cried, about to burst into tears, "this car of mine must take me home to New York City."

I burst into tears, to the wonderment of that sleek mechanic, and I climbed into my car and drove it off.

"Ah! Ah!" I felt in mounting joy, as I stepped on the accelerator, faster and faster—"at any moment we must soon be given unto Death."

170

The Minutes Are Flying By

Having fallen into a habit of pleasure, habit of rage, I no longer knew what I was about, where I was, or who; having settled into the Indiana countryside, as does the flood, whence after bloom the flowers of the May.

Yet it was necessary for a person like me to know surely; but submerged in this torrent of ease and rage, couldn't stand to look. There was no time for any interpretation. "By death alone, I will be brought to a pause," I thought.

Therefore I laid the elaborate plans to wreck my car and slay myself at the end of summer. How unfortunate to hasten thus to self-given death, for it is famous that we contaminate the death with our own rage, so that many die yet hardly come to a pause. Yet it is not so easy, without trying and elaborate plans, to come upon the lucky chance of death; especially in a habit of easy pleasure. Here all things conspire to prevent this serious occurrence; the visits of our friends, the public health, and all fuses, brakes, and safety-valves. Here all things conspire to prevent the occurrence of any serious thing. Yet was I confident that in the jaws of death, I'd be brought to a pause.

Having sunk into a habit of joy. Having settled into the Indiana countryside, whence after bloom the flowers of the May. Into the habit of rage, into the torrent of happiness, whence after bloom the flowers of the May. Borne on the yeasty waves of the rage of aggression against my dear soul, to death, into the jaws of death, to death to death the jaws of death. Whence after bloom the flowers of the May. Here all things conspire to prevent the occurrence of any serious thing: reflex aversions, the habits of order, the public health, the habits of order, the visits of our friends. Yet come, sweet Death.

Come, sweet sweet death! I thought, for I was confident in the arrest of death. It was a commonplace of even my experience to see animals and men brought to a pause by this silent stroke, having so seen my aunt Adele and Professor Lease and George Gershwin. Even tho I had sunk into a rage of aggression against my dear self, would not I, by this arrest, by this touch at my sleeve, pause, like K. in the novel

171

who was also laid under arrest on his 30th birthday? This release of dear joy; for what am I doing here? and what am I doing *here?* Nevertheless, I cannot restrain the tears of mourning when I think of the incidents that used to be. No no! what am I doing *here?* at 1:14 AM in this dark room beside the lovely lake, etc., the page also wet with tears when I think—Nevertheless come nevertheless come, come sweet death, arrest me now. Come serious angel. Come friendly death, I thought, and touch my lonely sleeve. Nevertheless! Nevertheless! come tired death.

Therefore, with mounting joy, returning to my native city, I stepped on the accelerator, to go faster and faster, with mounting rage, to wreck my sky-blue car; and cried, "Come freedom death! serious angel."

For an instant, a present briefer than it takes to think any thought, the gleaming black messenger rode beside me, the gleaming black messenger with the limestone wings and in his hand a silent stroke, rode beside me; then was eclipsed.

"I think you know well enough where you are—" he said.

"That present was briefer than it takes for me to think a thought."

"—or you would not say, 'What am I doing *here?*' "

"Do you imagine I *precisely* know?" I said, "for there's nothing wrong with Indiana in itself or with a summertime marriage."

"With the rage of aggression—with the last pang of love—"

"Evidently I don't mean merely this present instant of 3:44 PM—"

"But the last instant of the long process of time," said the Angel, and thereat was eclipsed.

Because I was sad, he touched my lonely sleeve. "Why do you lie to *me?*" he said, "for I am too great to be contained in your lie."

"Friendly death," I said, "I am tired, and can no longer make things perfect even in energetic contemplation, certainly not in fact. I won't lie to you, because you are too great to be contained in my lie. But *shprafora besti tonieli id'iriens, ne?*"

He laughed appreciatively. And we danced the dance of the Silent Stroke.

The Minutes Are Flying By

"Try this," he said: "regularly compose your autobiography according to various formulae. For instance: leaving New York City, you brought yourself to a pause."

"But I was no better off in the new place," I objected.

"Then you left Chicago, brought again to a pause."

"At least the change of place had failed."

"Sinking into the Indiana countryside: brought to a perfect pause."

"No no, not at all!" I began to object, but he said:

"And now especially, in these moments in-between, on the highroad, look how all things have come to a deathly pause!"

"What *I* meant by death—" I cried bitterly, "was the biological destruction of this organism; *analogies* I can give you a dime a dozen. I see that all things conspire to prevent the occurrence of any serious thing."

"On the contrary," he said sternly, "you will find that all things conspire precisely to prevent the *non*-occurrence of any serious thing."

By this time I was truly terrified by the imminence of disaster and the frightful imagination of the wreck; so I drew my car to the side of the road and came to a pause. The motor throbbed slowly; I was breathing hard.

"Serious angel," I said, "you do not fool."

Now not a day passes but I am ailing; not ill—hardly ill—but with some temporary failing of perfection of my bodily machine, must be attended to, calls attention to itself; breaks in on the attending soul, a bad nail one day, a little earache the next; or perhaps one ache lingers over until the next somewhat has defined itself, with its *claim* to attention, as melodies successively *claim* attention in the flow of music. So that it's impossible just to live on a day without this slight distraction and the need, so to speak, of patching the foundation. But I used to hope for just one day without physical annoyance, and who knows? if one, many more. But now I am *glad* when I recognize what is wrong with my body today; at least it is only this; at least it is at least this!

"If I'm ill every morning for a hundred years, I will live to be an old man."

A CEREMONIAL

I used to have the curious desire to "live on" just a few days without attending to my vulnerable body. But thank God it peremptorily *claims* attention to itself, and lends beauty and interest thereby to the empty enterprises in which I engage; lends feeling and intimacy; it is meaningful to be so arrested just when I have spoken eloquently or have taken my hat and am about to leave.

I used to repress from my attention throb and pang; but now I wonder how extreme they might become, before fainting; how far can I neglect these little imperfections? how far can they take me?

I have a head-cold. First I lost the sense of taste and the sense of smell—unable to taste food or kisses, or smell hallways and houses, the strong odors of my sickly excretions, or the frosty countryside. Yet with the loss of these senses, I did not yet seem shut off from the environing world, for we seem almost to taste and smell ourselves and not objective things. But next, for 3 days I have been unable to hear: lost to the loud gongs and horns of the boulevard (so that a person like me ought not to walk outside, for fear of being hit); and in these last hours, cut off from the little noises, cracks, rattles, and hisses of my own house, so that I am indeed confined to one room. For now I have been persuaded to remain in, and indeed the grippe makes me too weak to move about. In bed, with no thought of moving toward my boy Remo, or of dancing with Carolina at the Athens Cafe, I have indeed begun to lose touch with our dear world.

Yet now my felt body is expanding to a heavy world, not well defined.

Thru all persists the desire of pleasure and the habit of aggression. In the huge and intimate sensations of our most familiar least known world, struck with this enormous and close beauty, why should we open our heavy eyes?

Here is the *desired* wreckage
the suicidal spirit
must haunt till the First of May.

The Minutes Are Flying By

I came upon this notice on a tree on a lonely road in Ohio. With a feeling of revulsion and even contempt I said to the Angel: "How despicable! You are exacting your revenge!"

"I? When you know the facts you will judge as we do."

"What facts?"

"This fellow counted One-Two-Three and plunged himself to death. In short, by a mechanical device!"

"What!" I cried incredulously, "do you judge so circumstantially, without examining the provocation or the incentive?"

"There you have it: they complain that all things prevent the occurrence of any serious thing, and then count One-Two-Three."

In the beginning, in general in my native city, the confidence I lived by would persist for a year, for six months at a stretch—until some humiliation or sudden peril disclosed the yawning error: and then the next day I was following a new safe path. But now, instant by instant, it seems, instant by instant. A conviction comes to me suddenly, and I might do anything. There is no time for interpretation. But I see that these instants are slipping away.

They are slipping away. While I have been making such elaborate plans—with what suicidal end, you know—and lying ill, lying still, concentrating on the desires nearest to nothing and planning still more closely to concentrate—suddenly this terrifying feeling has possessed me: slipping away, it is slipping away. What an incongruous reflection to occur to me at this instant—yet my heart is trembling with terror. Here am I stranded in this destructive rage, and the time is slipping away. It is slipping away. Yet only this instant—already the instant before—already the instant before that—I was planning to wreck my sky-blue car; but the minutes are flying by like a snowstorm. You might perhaps imagine that in the blessed realm of formless desire, where are no passing odors, nor audible clock-ticks, nor even the succession of the light and dusk, that there would persist a certain timeless ease. No no! I must rally my senses; it will soon be too late; it will soon be too late in any case.

Having sunk into the Indiana countryside, I must rally my prospects. It will soon be too late in any case. Now is the time, I fear, for that famous lucky chance!

Instant by instant, trembling heart trembling heart. I see 'that at first there was sent an invisible faith into my heart for six months, for three months, for a week and a half, whereby in crimes and acts of love I persisted and even thought I knew what I was about, until the yawning error—But now there is no time for any interpretation. I must do it quick if I am going to do it at all; it is already too late in any case. Do not imagine, friends, if sometimes I seem to be paralyzed (and then you ask me, "When? when?"), that I am always to blame; only this instant it was too late in any case. And what a cruel question, to ask: "When, when, trembling heart?" Do not, friends; *I* can ask that question more closely than any one, because has not suddenly a terrifying feeling, etc.? Having sunk into the Indiana countryside, I must rally my prospects. It will soon be too late. It will soon be too late in any case. Now is just the time, I'm sure, for that famous lucky chance!

Whence after bloom the flowers of the May. The minutes fly by like a snowstorm. Whence after bloom the flowers. See, here is the desired wreckage, trembling heart, trembling heart. Whence after bloom the flowers of the May.

When, when, trembling heart? I seem to myself as tho I might do anything. Instant by instant! having sunk into the Indiana countryside. A quick blow, a happy phrase, a false step, not necessarily an evil gesture. You might imagine, it is even a commonplace, that there is many an act that cannot be acted instant by instant; these demand consideration, research, organization, execution. No no! a quick blow, a happy phrase—is not this instant the end result of the *long* process of time? determines the past, determines the time that is slipping away; when an invisible confidence comes to me suddenly—but there is no time for any interpretation.

See, it is an image of Ludwig Beethoven, inventing the end of Opus 135, I mean the last part of his last work: you know he quarreled with his tailor and told him, "It must be!"—and do you think that the next instant he did not

The Minutes Are Flying By

thereby determine the quarrel and the quartet and the Archduke and all the life slipped away, crying: It must be! It must be! Instant by instant, trembling heart trembling heart—

The quick blow, the happy phrase, the false step, the gesture not necessarily fatal. The false step, the recognition of necessity, the yawning error. The quick blow, the happy phrase. When when, trembling heart? Instant by instant is invented even the quartet in F Major. Now is just the time, I'm sure, for that famous lucky chance.

Whence after bloom the flowers of the May. Now now is just the time, I'm sure, for that famous lucky chance. Whence after bloom the flowers. See, here is the desired wreckage, trembling heart trembling heart. Whence after bloom the flowers. The minutes are flying by like a snowstorm. Whence after bloom the flowers of the May. Having sunk into the Indiana countryside—whence after bloom the flowers of the May.

[Chesterton–New York City]
1938-1940

Saul

What giant? Saul. We are trembling with pleasure, to describe a beloved larger than human. From his shoulders upward he stood higher than the soldiers. He spoke like a prophet, having wisdom as well as strength.

The white-haired Samuel, near his own death, poured oil on the boy's head and kissed him; and said that at Bethel would come down a band of angels with musical instruments: "and thou shalt prophesy with them," said the prophet, "and be another man." And "let it be when these signs are come unto thee *that thou do as thy hand shall find*, for God is with thee."

To do as the hand shall find!

To be another man!

When Samuel was able to say these words, he trembled with pleasure, as we writing them tremble with pleasure, desirous of describing a beloved larger than human.

"The spirit of the Lord came mightily on him." He did what came to his hand.

Then consider such a giant, whose lot was not to fail, but to do as his hand should find. The people said to Samuel: "Make thou us a King"—asking for a man of habitual success, not an inspired agent as occasion arose (for there are many inspired agents as occasion arises). But on Saul the spirit came *mightily*. Samuel said to the people: "See, there is none like him."

179

None like him, none like him, who had (so to speak) a convertible use of the auxiliary verbs will, can, ought, do, have, and be; so that in a given case, he will do it, he can do it, he ought to do it, he does do it.

He is another man. What giant? It is Saul. All the people shout: "Long live King Saul!" trembling with pleasure in the face of their beloved larger than human.

In anger he scattered Nahash the Ammonite so that no two men were standing together. He took the kingdom over Israel; he fought against Moab, against Edom, against the kings of Zobah, and the Philistines. "Wheresoever he turned himself, he put them to the worse." In anger he scattered Nahash the Ammonite. He smote Amalek. He put to the worse the Kings of Zobah. In anger he scattered Nahash the Ammonite so that no two men were standing together.

O our exemplar of the possibility of success, do thou, do thou as thy hand shall find, for God is with thee. What a hope for all, not to fail! but to be another man, in wisdom as well as strength. We are trembling with hope, that there may come down a choir of angels, and we prophesy among them if the spirit come in might. Amen.

In anger he scattered Nahash the Ammonite, and he smote Amalek.

To what a height of grandeur! to what a height of grandeur is our beloved now raised, who even at first was head and shoulders above the people.

He took Agag, king of the Amalekites, of whom Samuel had said in God's voice: "Slay him." Then Agag was brought before King Saul in chains, and said: "Surely the bitterness of death is at hand."

Saul drew up his sword and paused, and he slew him not. "For me to obey *not* the Voice is also divine," said King Saul.

(But Samuel hewed Agag in pieces before the Lord in Gilgal; and in anger he went to Ramah and never again beheld Saul.)

To what a height of grandeur! Saul, without any priest, laid hold on the burnt offering and offered it to God at Gilgal. Hereat in anger Samuel went away to Ramah-naioth and never again beheld King Saul.

Saul

"Let there be no diviners by a ghost in Israel," proclaimed the King of Israel; "is not the future whereto we turn our hand?"

And why do any longer what the hand shall find? At such a height of grandeur, where he will, can, and ought—our beloved hero gigantic!—it would be a *small* thing also to do. For "why is the King come out? to pursue a flea?" This is the height of power. (We are trembling with pleasure.) The people desired of Samuel: "Make thou us a King." Here is King Saul; you see there is none like him. He has taken the kingdom over Israel: all the people have shouted: "Long live King Saul!" He has fought against the kings of Zobah. Then why do any longer what would be a *small* thing? Our hope! to what a freedom of competency come! he has the habit of being another man. (The people are trembling with pleasure.)

At this time there was again a war with the Philistines. Again again. In anger he scattered Nahash. Again again again. At this time there was again a war with the Philistines.

"Why is the King come out? what is he pursuing, a dead dog? a flea?"

This is the tedium of starting again (the 4th and 5th time) the contest victoriously carried through: the novice opponent lays himself open by the very *same* error; but the animal spirits fail.

—"Go," Saul said to the boy, "and the Lord be with *thee*." And he put a helmet of brass on his head and clad him with a coat of mail; and David girded on a sword. And David tried to go, but he could not, for he had not tried the armor. "I cannot go with these," he said, "for I have not tried them." "And I cannot," said Saul, "because I have."

Who are these coming forth? (We are trembling with pleasure.) It is the famous choir. Nay, is not Saul also among the prophets?—In these days when Saul turned himself to prophesy, he spoke no longer in the usual words. Therefore the people began to say that Saul was insane, saying: "Saul also is among the prophets."

And here is Saul the King—from his shoulders upward greater than all the people: you see there is none like him. All have shouted. The spirit has come on him with might. He says no word. He is another man. It would be tedious to turn his hand. The fact is—it is a secret. It is King Saul; all are trembling with pleasure; you see there is none like him. He says no word; it would be tedious to turn his hand. What a hope for all! to say no word. The fact is—that the spirit has come on him with might. King Saul is standing at the open gate, with one hand on the door of the gate. (Do you know his secret?) O our exemplar of the possibility—of not turning the hand. Not to pursue a dead dog, a flea! What a hope for all! He says no word. Our beloved has come to what a freedom of inability.

Looming in the open gate, with one hand on the door of the gate: the spirit has come on him with might. The fact is—it is a secret.

The next instant, this King is without power. Everything has moved on a space.

"Dear God," prays King Saul, "let me not go mad. Which sacrifice must I bring unto the spirit, to leave me not? Nay, *let* me be mad."

The next instant, the very next, is not the slightest possibility of the smallest success of any kind whatsoever, such as to kill a flea; it is out of the question. (For to succeed, it is necessary to turn the hand to it and never pause. Otherwise the means of action: the movements of society, and movements of one's own wit, move on a way: one is out of touch. Even King Saul, who could do anything, must do this or that—) yet pause. Why do this tedious thing?

The least thing is now out of the question. (We are trembling with pleasure.) Just because he turns his hand to it, he cannot do it. He speaks in no language whatsoever, so the people say: "Saul also is among the prophets."

What least passion has overcome the King if not *envy*?! (Do you know his secret?)

Powerless and yet full of memories, remembering that once he scattered Nahash, he recognizes the spirit

182

Saul

everywhere (for there are many inspired agents as occasion arises)—so that the least exploit, that a boy might perform, becomes a great thing in his eyes. Then what least passion has come over our King in the height of his grandeur, if not envy?

While King Saul was standing in the gate, the women came up from the battle with musical instruments. They never noticed the haggard figure in the gate, but they sang loudly and shouted:

> "Saul hath slain his thousands
> and David his tens of thousands."

What looming figure, what giant, is it in the gate if not King Saul? Never noticing the haggard figure in the gate, they shouted. The King was displeased and very wroth; he said: "They have ascribed unto the boy ten thousands, and to me they have ascribed but thousands; and all he lacketh is the kingdom" O my exemplar—what a hope for all! to lose so easily this kingdom! we are trembling with pleasure—do thou, do thou, do thou, fear not, what thy hand shall find, for God is with thee not. Do thou it, it's safe!

An evil spirit came upon Saul.

Haggard, tears flowing down his cheeks on either side, and his heart pounding, he stood in the gate. "Where am I? where am I?" he asked, finding himself in this strange place. There is no longer the expert tedium for this absent King. We might have warned the careless women not to disturb the delicate balance of the spirit with even playfully brutal words.

The blinding tears streamed down his cheeks until he felt the courses of their flowing. He wept when he remembered that he smote Amalek. Everywhere he recognized the spirit, in even the exploits of boys. He wept when he remembered the songs he used to sing.

2.

When the evil spirit was upon Saul, David, who was musical, took the harp and played; so Saul found relief.

David bowed on the side and said: "May the words of my mouth and the meditations of my heart be acceptable to Thee, O Lord."

Saul was crouched in the corner fearfully, and his huge spear stood by its point in the floor.

David turned his hand to the 10 strings and was about to sing. But since Saul was lost in the ordinary world, it was necessary first to adapt the ordinary world to his insane soul, in the form of music; to make familiar the strange place; as if to renew for the madman the creation of the Six Days. Therefore (how strange!) David first formalized Chaos itself by way of a string-prelude, twangling all the chords—but this brute matter was already numbered in thirds, fourths, and fifths.

He then sang in a clear voice: "The heavens declare the glory of God and the firmament showeth His handiwork. Day unto day uttereth speech. Night unto night revealeth knowledge. (Neither is their voice heard!) In them hath he set a tent for the Sun, who is a bridegroom coming out of the chamber and is glad, like a strong man, to run the race. Nothing is hidden from this heat!"

Awakened by this much to the common universe, Saul looked with clearer eyes. Then David said earnestly in a speaking voice:

"The Law of the Lord is perfect, restoring the soul; the testimony of the Lord is sure, making us wise. The fear of the Lord is holy; it endures forever. By these is thy servant warned; in regarding them there is great reward."

"As what?" asked King Saul sharply, "I don't see any great reward."

"As follows: *who otherwise can discern errors?!* O clear thou me, Lord, from hidden faults; keep back thy servant from presumptuous sins, that they may master me not."

"This is a well-known answer. I too thought of it."

"Sing to me now about Saul," said the King; "it is not

184

enough to sing of the work of the 1st to the 6th days; because we've come a long way from that to this."

"I have not yet made a poem about the King."

"Then recite the history."

David did so, elevating the meaning of it by allegories. He told how Saul followed the asses; the strayed asses, that roamed through the hills of Ephraim and Shalishah and Shaalim to Zuph, were a man's lost thoughts that lead him on, nevertheless, to seek aid of Samuel, who here represented the Lord Himself.

"No," said Saul, "the story merely means that it is by chance that a man becomes the King."

Not so, for did Samuel choose any comer? It was when he beheld Saul, larger than human, that he said: "On *thee* is all the desire of Israel, and on *thy* father's house." The hero answered: "Am I not a Benjamite, of the smallest of the tribes of Israel? and my family the least of all the tribe of Benjamin?"—nay, but ıt was *just* here that is to be found the King; by choosing always the least of the least, you come on the one who is larger than human head and shoulders; none like him. By a divine way, through the Minimum finding the Maximum.

("There is no particular method, the boy is in error," thought Saul.)

"It is not as a man sees," cried the stricken King, "for a man looks on the outward appearance; but the Lord looks in the heart."

"Oh," said David, "so Samuel said to my father."

"When did he so?" cried Saul wildly suspicious and leaping to his feet.

David stood simply, with his arms at his side and his harp hanging from the right hand. "Here is thy boy David to do with; do not hate me."

Sensual love restored the King to his right mind.

He seized hard the dancing (though stationary) figure of the child; by so doing, knew where he was; he brought down, to kiss him, his great head and mouth on the boy's, yet did not cease to stare wildly. But David, measuring the time and allowing for the beat of heart and breathing to become formal, then artfully slipped his cool tongue between Saul's lips—which Saul tasted with surprise, as if he had forgotten to eat. And now flooded the majestic pleasure and colossal smile of the King.

He smiled and laughed.

"What did Samuel say to *you?*" asked King Saul.

"I am ashamed to tell," said David.

"Tell it!"

Jesse had made the 7 brothers pass before the prophet, but none of these fitted Samuel's preconception. "Are here all your children?" "There remains yet the youngest, and behold, he keeps the sheep."

(At this instant the resolve formed in the bottom of Saul's heart to sacrifice this lamb David.)

" 'Send for him.' But when I appeared," said David, "he was disappointed, because I was slight."

"This time the smallest from the largest tribe!" cried the King merrily.

"But he consoled himself by muttering that I had beautiful eyes!!"

Like a waterfall, Saul laughed loudly and joyously.

David cried: "Everybody knows whom Samuel is in love with: it is King Saul!"

"The little conqueror of Goliath with the big eyes!"

"I slung a stone and hit him in the head; that was his weak spot."

"No, no."

The King could not contain his joy.

He laid hands on David and sensual pleasure restored him to his right mind. His joy began to mount a climax and he made some verses:

> "Thou, child David musical,
> art my sufficient reason still:
> between successive breaths wind-music,
> between successive footsteps dancing."

"The holy spirit has come over the King," said David; "take the harp too."

Saul said:

186

Saul

"David formal David woos with strains
of music the unquiet spirit, with
his presence musical in pose refrains
my career headlong to self-given death."

"Let the King live forever!"
Saul's joy rose to such a height of grandeur that the sense of absolute ease oppressed and paralyzed him.

"David, do you imagine, does the people imagine, that this King is envious of you or any one else?"

"My lord, Samuel said: 'Do as thy hand shall find.' "

"I am not boasting like the other witless giant; but the King lives at such a height of grandeur that he has not these or any other feelings."

"We stand before you," said the flattering youth, "as before a mountain, and wonder about the region above the clouds."

"The medium of ordinary activity, I mean your social and personal world, breaks down before the plans that I and the Lord make!"

"Then the King forbears to turn his hand."

"Nor can language express it."

"He does not speak."

"The fact is—it is a secret."

So these two came to a pause.

The King fell back into his fixed habit and wild stare, looming in the darkness beside his long spear fixed by its point in the floor.

Patiently—for there was no single moment of either cure or despair—David again preluded on the strings.

"Play something from the days among the sheep, my lamb," said Saul, darkly following his own thoughts.

David preluded; and he sang:

"The Lord is my shepherd; I shall not want. He makes me to lie down in green pastures; He leads me beside the still waters. He restores my soul; He guides me in straight paths for His name's sake.

"Yea, though I walk through the valley of the shadow of death, I will fear no evil! for Thou art with me! Thy rod and Thy staff comfort me!—"

187

In the height of triumph David now said: "Thou preparest a table before me in the presence of mine enemies! Thou hast anointed my head with oil!—"

"*This ought you not have boasted!*" cried King Saul, and the spear was ready to his hand. "Lord, as my hand shall find—Thou saidest it!" And he flung it.

But David avoided it, and the hungry spear stood quivering in the wall. And David fled from the presence of Saul.

Fear not, Saul; but *do* thou as thy hand shall find, for God is with thee not.

"Let not this musician reappear," cried the King, "to distract me from this infinite confusion."

He came outside, to seize upon some beast as a sacrifice instead, but there was none formal enough, not even Jonathan.

3.

"And Samuel died; and all Israel gathered themselves together, and lamented him; and buried him in his house at Ramah."

I SAMUEL XXV, 1.

4.

Saul *chased* the young man—a human relationship grounded in the fact that bodies occupy space! (The condition for a chase is that while *A* moves from *L* to *M*, *B* moves from *M* to *N*.) He chased him into his daughter's bedroom and found in the bed—a dummy with goat's hair! Foiled again! He chased him to Naioth, but suddenly became inspired to take off his clothes and prophesy; meantime David ran off to Nob. Saul hunted him from Naioth to Nob. Then David, after some dubious dealings of his own, came to En-gedi. What a chase! Here he cut off Saul's skirt!

The condition of the Chase is that both *A* proceeds from *L* to *M* and *B* goes from *M* to *N*. When *B* has failed to leave *M*

188

on *A's* arrival, he is in general Caught. On the other hand when *A* fails to proceed to *M*, where *B* is, we say that *"A* has *Given Up* the Chase."

You would imagine that the King could easily catch a fleeing lad in his own kingdom. No no! he was far beyond the least possibility of the slightest success of any kind whatsoever. While the King of Israel was running from one town to another, David slipped off to Achish in Gath and there pretended to be mad.

"What's here!" cried Saul, rushing into Michal's bedroom, and with a ferocious oath brought round his heavy sword. *Glunk,* rang the dented sword on the wooden dummy.

Beyond the least possibility. Beyond the least possibility of the slightest success.

The whole of the King's army, under Doeg, took part in the wild pursuit, hallooing across the Holy Land. They closed in on En-gedi: here David cut off Saul's skirt when the King was asleep in the cave.

Beyond the least possibility of the slightest success of any kind whatsoever.

Standing across from King Saul, David held out the skirt on the tip of a spear. Beholding it, the soldiery burst into gales of joyous laughter. Amid the uproarious onlookers, King Saul stood across from the youth.

"What is my father pursuing?" asked David humbly, "a dead dog? a flea?"

Saul stood naked from the belly downward.

"After whom is the King of Israel come out? What is my father pursuing?"

The loud laughter penetrated to the wit of the bewildered hero.

"Is this thy voice, my son David?" he asked; and he wept boiling tears as he stood naked before the young man his son and all the people, in En-gedi.

Next, David fled into the wilds of Ziph.

The spatial condition of Coming To some one is for *A* to move to *M* where *B* is resting (and this either in friendship, to Go to Meet, or in hostility, to Attack). Coming to Meet Each Other is the condition where A moves from L to M and B moves from N to M. Being Together is, in general, for A and B both to be in M. On the contrary, to Avoid has as its conditon that A do not move to M if B is there, and vice versa. To Be Apart is for A to be in M and B not to be in M. To Miss some one is for A to proceed to M and B has left M; to Miss some one is a peculiar combination of To Chase and To Avoid. To Wait For some one is for A to remain in M on the expectation (on the hope) that B will proceed to M. To Hide From some one is for A to remain in M on the hope that B will not proceed to M.

Now it was night in the cave, and the Prince David cowered in the obscurity in the belly of the cave. Meantime outside, the round moon shed its glorious illumination among the spacious clouds and the clear stars were scattered widely through the heaven. But within, it was so totally black that the young Prince came almost to exclaim in terror; yet he did not dare to go outside into the fatal illumination where the soldiers were hallooing near and far. Here, at the height of his triumph, he invented the famous Psalm of the Cave:

> "Awake, my glory—
> I will awake the Dawn!"

While he was singing, Saul came into this cave to refresh himself, bringing with him a lantern that shed soft golden light about the cave. Lulled by the song, the King fell into a deep sleep.

The Prince appeared, with a drawn sword. With infinite care he cut away his father's skirt.

The rough soldiers burst into a thunder of laughter when they saw the King in En-gedi, naked from the belly downward. Standing across from the King, David held out the skirt on the tip of a spear, while the surprised soldiery burst forth in gales of joyous laughter. Amidst these uproarious onlookers, King Saul stood naked from the belly downward.

"After whom is the King come out?" asked David humbly; "what is my father pursuing, a dead dog? a flea?"

The storm of laughter penetrated to the understanding of the bewildered hero, and he wept boiling tears, as he saw he was beyond the possibility of the slightest success of any kind.

What a chase! (beyond the possibility of the slightest success of any kind). From Zion to Ramah-Naioth, and from there to Nob, to En-gedi, and into the wilds of Ziph— beyond the least possibility of the slightest success of any kind. You would have imagined that the King could easily catch a fleeing lad defenceless in his own kingdom— beyond the least possibility of the slightest success of any kind whatsoever.

5. The Witch of En-dor

Now Samuel was dead and all Israel had lamented him, and buried him in Ramah, his own city. And Saul had put away those that divined by a ghost, out of the land.

And the Philistines gathered themselves together and came and pitched in Shunem; and Saul gathered all Israel together, and they pitched in Gilboa. And when Saul saw the host of the Philistines, he was afraid, his heart trembled. And when he inquired of the Lord, the Lord answered him not, neither by dreams, nor by Urim, nor by prophets.

Then said Saul: "Seek me a woman that divineth by a ghost, that I may go and inquire of her." And his servants said: "Behold, there is a woman that divineth by a ghost at En-dor."

I SAMUEL XXVIII, 3-7

(En-dor. Hither comes Saul in the night, with a lamp and says:)
SAUL: Witch!
I am disguised, not like the King. In other raiment than the King, and with no crown. You would not think that this was the King of Israel. I am afraid. I have no authority at night. How bitter cold it is! My heart is pounding,

missing a beat. I ought perhaps to have eaten.

The Lord refuses to inspire me with a suicidal prophesy. Let this witch do so.

(The Woman of En-dor appears, and seeing the King she says to herself:)

WOMAN: Here he is! I see it is my beloved Saul, larger than human; but a formless ghost is larger still. (He knows this.) Wonderful! he stands head and shoulders above any of the people and he pretends to disguise himself by taking off his crown.

SAUL: Witch! *(to himself)* I am without capability of any kind. No one even comes when I call. I used to imagine that if I put myself to it, I could do anything whatsoever; but recently I have tried without success to do the very simplest things. Now at last, the fear of death takes precedence over every other preoccupation of the King. Witch!

WOMAN: Young man, why have you disquieted me at midnight?

SAUL: Mother, divine to me by a ghost, and bring me up whomsoever I shall name.

WOMAN: No no! for King Saul said: "Let there be no diviner by a ghost in Israel: is not the future where we turn our hand?"

SAUL: *(angrily)* Why do you mock me with the name of Saul? What have I to do with that King?

The Lord does not inspire *me* with any next prophecy.

WOMAN: If you would not insist only on your own death, He would inspire you. This we are not allowed to foretell to ourselves, or to consummate with our own hand.

SAUL: I used to think that if I put myself to it, I could do anything whatsoever; now I cannot even put myself to it. Not even! not even!—thus it is with respect to every act. And now I am preoccupied with nothing but my own death.

WOMAN: Whom shall I bring up to thee from Hell?

SAUL: Bring me up the prophet Samuel.

WOMAN: Traitor! thou art Saul! why dost thou deceive me by coming in these rags without a crown?

SAUL: Nay, Samuel! bring me up Samuel!

Saul

(He draws his sword.)

WOMAN: Put back your knife, which now has no desire but suicide. Do you think I did not from the beginning recognize the King, head and shoulders above the people at Mizpah? tried to disguise himself by leaving off his crown!

But beware; a formless ghost is larger still.

SAUL: Nay, nay, bring me up Samuel.

(When he asks it of her a 3rd time, she cries out:)

SAUL: What is it you see?

WOMAN: A godlike being coming out of the earth.

SAUL: In what form is he?

WOMAN: It is an old man, and he is clothed in a robe.

SAUL: *(in an ecstasy of excitement)* Is not this robe rent away? I did it with my own hands!

Thanks be to God who has taken away from me this kingdom! Samuel! Samuel! (I am going to fall upon the ground in terror of the death)—nay, but speak, and say it!

(It is the Ghost of Samuel.)

SAMUEL: Here he is! I remember it well: this was our example of the possibility of success.

WOMAN: See, the visible breath in the night air streams about the gigantic head of the King of Israel, but of the ghost not.

SAUL: Damned breath of hell, go down! Thou prophet!

WOMAN: Blessed be Thou, O Lord, who quickenest the dead. And let us say—

SAUL: And let us say, Amen.

(Now summoned, Samuel says to Saul:)

SAMUEL: Why hast thou disquieted me, to bring me up?

SAUL: Between us, Samuel! between us! which of us two has disquieted the other? I am not speaking of only the time when I was King of Israel, though from the very first you then doomed me to this moment.

Between us, Samuel! it was not I who, following my father's animals, chose a King (though I see now that I pursued them too stubbornly on that day, up to this moment at En-dor).

SAMUEL: It was the people said: "Choose us a King!" (for at last the people are responsible for everything, both good and evil). They hoped (nor did I sufficiently discourage them)—

SAUL: *(sharply)Why did you not?*

SAMUEL: I *did* demur, yet my soul was not against it—

SAUL: Ah!

SAMUEL: After all, it was the *first* time, and who was I to prejudge it on merely abstract principles?

SAUL: What did they hope?

SAMUEL: The fools! hoped that they might be the lucky ones! after all it was the *first* time!
Our hearts were set on a beloved larger than human— who would have the habit of success!
Then I chose him, on whom was all the desire of Israel, head and shoulders above the rest.

SAUL: By what right did you do it? I was pursuing my father's animals in all simplicity.

SAMUEL: Now thanks be to God for the example of failure!

SAUL: *(enraged)* Chose a Saul of dreams! you evil people! you evil prophet!
How dare you judge me by your Saul of dreams? Do you think that this sacred flesh, which is my divine portion in the creative work of the Six Days, is your *idea?*
Laugh, all you future world!—the Israelites and the prophet Samuel have set themselves up as the judges of success and failure.
If you knew where it is I set *my* success and failure, you would never call this a failure.—
Look look,
how far the conqueror of Agag has come!
Here he is!
(At these remarks Samuel smiles with great benignity.)

SAMUEL: Boy, do you need to tell *me* this? You have come so far, but I have gone also as far as Hell.
It is also true, nevertheless, that no matter what King Saul and the prophet Samuel recalled from hell may know, this may yet serve as a merely human example for future generations.

SAUL: *(laughing)* See, I now live all my life—for these few hours—in the territory of jokes: of sophistical reasoning, fanciful associations, and tell-tale slips o' the tongue.

Saul

Everybody can see the ridiculous accidents that befall the King of Israel; the soldiers cannot contain their laughter, and I too am one of the soldiers.

(whispering) They do not hear the secret conversation.

SAMUEL: *(quickly)* Hush—

(He indicates the Woman of En-dor and puts a finger on his lips.)

(She walks apart, and says:)

WOMAN: Let me never hinder
by my presence profane
a secret conversation

a secret conversation
invention of a song
let me never hinder

the acts of love
a secret conversation
invention of a song

by my presence profane
the acts of love
a secret conversation.

(Meantime, while she is saying this, King Saul and the Ghost of Samuel perform a ritual posture.)

WOMAN: They are dancing away the life of the King,
I can no longer hold my boiling tears.
This was the beloved of the people
whom God made lunatic by grandeur
—to be a famous example!

(With a cry of passion, as though his heart were burst, Saul now says, in answer to the question: "Why hast thou disquieted me?")

SAUL: Father, I am distrest; for the Philistine makes war against me and God is departed from me and answereth me no more, neither by prophecy nor in dreams. Therefore I have called upon thee, to make known unto me that which I must do.

SAMUEL: Why dost thou ask of *me*, seeing that the Lord is

departed from thee and become thine adversary? Now the Lord hath wrought for Himself; and He hath rent the kingdom out of thy hand and given it to thy neighbor, even David. Moreover, the Lord will deliver Israel also with thee into the hands of the Philistines; and tomorrow shalt thou and thy sons be with me in Hell.

(Now hearing this, Saul falls straightway his full length upon the earth; and he is sore afraid, because of the words of Samuel.)

And there was no strength in him; for he had eaten no bread all the day nor all the night. And the woman came unto Saul and saw that he was sore affrighted, and said unto him: "Behold, thy handmaid hath hearkened unto thy voice, and I have put my life in my hand, and have hearkened unto thy words which thou spokest unto me. Now therefore I pray thee, hearken thou also unto the voice of thy handmaid, and let me set a piece of bread before thee; and eat, that thou mayest have strength, when thou goest on thy way."

But he refused, and said: "I will not eat."

But his servants, together with the woman, urged him; and he hearkened unto their voice. So he arose from the earth and sat upon the bed. And the woman had a fatted calf in the house; and she made haste and killed it; and she took flour, and kneaded it and baked unleavened bread thereof; and she brought it before Saul and before his servants; and they did eat.

[Chicago]
[1938-1939]

Prose Composition:
The Sea! the Sea!

I.

"The Sea! the Sea!" cried those fugitive Greeks. "Land ho!" say the joyful sailors. Poets desire to start with an exclamation-point, like the Spaniards: "¡"

> —Oh! oh! at the beginning
> instead of at the end.

The end is the most important thing, because everything is done for this. The most important thing is the beginning, because from this everything flows. ¡Oh!

"Ah, I have found it!" cried Archimedes, with the elegant principle, running dripping thru Syracuse.

"I've lost it," said Melisande, as she dropped her husband's ring into the well.

Nothing at all. Not to begin: to bring to a *short* end; this is what we poets—rivals of the Creator of the Heavens and the Earth—desire.

In full flight: "The Sea! the Sea!" Nothing at all. A *"flight* of stairs," as we say, descending from the top of a building to the street, like swift birds, in a series of *flights.* What a long and empty street; who is there, after watching him under the corner-lamp for accurate appraisal, to pursue? It is the dead of spring.

On the First of May has come the fearful blizzard; the air is

197

thick, and the tiny flowers are gorgeously

   ridged inch-deep with pearl.

We residents of the dead of spring go "about the woodlands" taking notes. The sea is fixed in its unrest: Proteus photographed with one foot in the air. (Those in close pursuit won't fail to catch up now!)

Never fear: *in the gorgeous sunshine we poets have gotten onto the floating iceberg that has melted from the shore, and are sailing off into the golden warmth.*

Nothing at all. "I've lost it," laughed Melisande, as she threw her wedding-ring into the well. Oh, don't cry, girl; only don't cry. No, but cry, cry, if that will do you good. Tears are flowing down on both cheeks. The ice is melting underneath our feet. The black little violet has a nauseating odor, but you can hardly sense it, such a little squeak.

The whispers o' the sea: the play o' the waves: the music o' the winds: the play o' the waves

Here's an empty corridor of doors. Enter Number 4-0-7. ¡Oh oh

2.

Room 407. Haskell lives here. He lives at 470 Audubon Avenue, and at this time my boy would be about 15. Glad that I have come and already desirous, already desirous, he draws me into a large oyster-shell where we lie curled up together. Breathing in my ear like the noise in a sea-shell. Nothing of him unchanged. His skin is mother-of-pearl. Rocking from side to side in the play o' the waves. Oh oh: O's of love-pleasure.

Rocking from side to side. The noise of the heavy loads of water on the rocks: and faint and clear, and clear, tones of pipes. Confusion of the brine and sand: and faint and clear—Look, it is the Proteus himself—

Membranes of flying spray blind my eyes, until in black voids oh blinded eyes; salt-stifled; and tumbled. Perhaps 4 o' 7? what disaster is it that all are subject to in this ratio? 11! One one one: fucking in an out.

198

The Sea! the Sea!

Here on his rolling wagon, attended by the mermaidens and pipes, is the Father Ocean himself—All's lost in the blinding spray.

I have no memory of anything fresh except brine; otherwise than by a heavy wave I was never thrown down.

Here is the Father Ocean himself, on his wave-wheeled chariot with the loud horns, with the wreathed mermaidens blinded by the foam, by the slapping waves, by the whistling wind, deafened by the whistling wind.

3-parts buried in the sand and absolutely immovable; but the moving sea and sand will move it on its way, on its way.

The whispers o' the sea

A strong whistle thrills amid the rigging of the ship, in long-drawn vibrations. "Land Ho!" cry the joyful sailors.

There was a strong whistling in the room. Gleaming between the ceiling and the floor, frozen in the blinding salt and hanging from the ceiling by a piano-wire, was the joyous Father Ocean himself in his wave-wheeled chariot. Under the bed was blown a snow-dune. I was coughing.

Haskell was standing at the window, looking at the blizzard: "It is the dead of spring." The whistling wind keyed our attention high. I was continually coughing. Outside the air was thick and the thin snow drifted thru a crack.

It was photographed with a foot in the air; it was the dead of spring. There was a strong whistling in the room. Almost fresh, the keen odor of the drift keyed attention high, but you could scarcely perceive it, such a little squeak.

[Chicago]
February 1939

199

The Mean, The Maximum, and The Minimum

The maximum, the mean, and the minimum
are all good wisdom and destroy us
without sin!

P_{ay-day}, three young householders find that last month cost them only $42.50 each, for rent, food, etc., etc. We say "only" because this was an amount they were more than used to, but there is a mean in your life too.

Th˙ doorbell rings. Enter Normal and Robber and sit down without taking off their hats. Now there are five and Lew says: "Five of us could live like kings on $10 a week." Normal cries: "If I could get out of business, it would be Utopia!"—he is a little salesman in the commercial world that tends always to the great Extreme. Liv says: "We could play ball every clear day from April to October."

They are fascinated by the question of the Utopian life: to heighten by art, by juster proportions, a possible existence, an almost possible existence. What their life would be if they could pool just a few dividends!

Normal takes off his hat and opens the top button of his trousers; but Robber keeps his on because he has a date.

Liv's little brother is standing in the doorway secretly grinning.

They start with clothes: It isn't necessary to wear a tie; there are no buttons to lose on a pullover sweater; mocassins have no heels; and corduroy pants last forever. Robber looks distastefully at Liv's filthy yellow corduroy pants, gaping at the fly and ripped symmetrically at the knees. Liv wears these for a certain purpose and to be amusing.

"It might be better to live in sunny Italy," says Henry Faust. "No, there's no big-league ball." "Cincinnati's warm, but the Reds stink on ice."

201

"It's practical!" Normal insists passionately; "you don't take it seriously, but I take it seriously. Where there are so many billions of dollars in Chicago, couldn't we come into $10 a week? But when you try to *earn* it, you soon have to try to make $18 or you're out. And where do you stop? Where do you stop? Once I thought if I had $10 a week, I'd be independent; I wouldn't know what to spend it on. But by the time I was making $18 a week I was thinking in terms of $35."

"Where do you stop?"

"The only thing is to go back to what you wanted when you were little."

"Ha!" thinks Liv's little brother in the doorway grinning, "that's what *he* thinks!"

"—a little regular income; the main thing is to be regular, so you know where you stand. I'd be satisfied with $8."

"If there was ten of us, we could live on $5."

"Where do you stop? Where do you stop?"

Liv has planned out the daily routine: "Our daily routine could be as follows: in the morning a game of ball. I could be captain of one team and Norm of the other. After lunch some reading. . . ."

He slips into the routine of a boys' camp he went to, and these are his juster proportions. (It was there he wore the yellow pants.)

" . . . In the afternoon a little scrub-ball until the big game about four. At night you sit around and talk just like we're doing now. Every Sunday we go to see the Cubs or White Sox, whichever is at home." "I think we ought to do a little socially useful work just to make you feel right," says Normal; "two nights a week I'm willing to canvass for Labor's Non-Partisan League." "How many young men in 1937, dissatisfied with their jobs, are thinking of a life of the Golden Mean!"

Robber gets to his feet. "What about women?" says he.

"I knew you'd start that!" Normal cries. There follow the many dirty jokes. Anyway some women have sense and might even become Utopians. "Oh oh, trouble."

"Generally speaking," says Liv, "to be honest with ourselves, we go with girls just for screwing and not for companionship or talking, and they can't play ball."

"Well Abyssinia," says Robber, "I have a date."

"Oh wait awhile," says Loose, "and I'll drive you."

Now Robber and the nameless little brother are standing in the doorway. In this pause—

In this pause, the formalities of baseball suddenly strike with force: "When the outfielders swing to the right, when the left-hander comes to bat—" "Nobody looks so good as a self-possessed catcher who holds the runners close." "What about the centerfielder starts at the crack o' the bat and takes the ball moving without a hurry—I'm thinking of Tris Speaker, the Gray Eagle o' the Indians."

"Last week he fell off his house drunk and broke his head," says Liv's little brother.

"Oh, if you're talking about individuals, what about the Babe striking out?" "Herb Pennock, the Silver Fox of Kennett Square, stalling for the rain."

"The hit and run."

"The double-steal."

"The home-run that breaks up the ball game."

You see how the variety of both extremes is held within the rules.

"But the trouble with *our* game," says Norm and the tears start into his eyes, "is that nobody can play it; nobody but us five can get off from work; no matter how hard you try you can't escape it."

"Maybe we could organize them as Utopians. We could have a number of separate units."

"No no no. You can't find more than half a dozen who are willing to be reasonable. I see it in business every day."

"To you," says Robber, "it's reasonable; to me it stinks. I don't want to miss a thing."

"When they begin to talk baseball," thinks Lew, "I get so bored stiff."

THE GOLDEN MEAN

The Golden Mean is to have just so much interest as a person is adequate to and turn to it his full attention; this isn't much, and demands rule and repetition.

How the Mean Serves God

To know where one is, proportioning the self and the objects of desire, is prayer. Measure is the same as saying Grace.

How the Mean Is Both the Maximum and the Minimum

Thru the Mean we avoid the importunities of desire, which denial would make rage only the more, exposing us to impulses and accidents. Thus it is thru the Mean that we attain the Minimum. But the Mean reconciles warring opposites and avoids waste. Thus it is thru the Mean that we attain the Maximum.

Loose and Robber take their leave. "Lew, take me along!" screams Liv's little brother, vanishing downstairs after them. "Hey, where the hell do you think you're going?" cries Liv.

Norm says, "Robber's against Utopia."

"Yes, and he'll soon talk Lew out of it; that leaves only three."

"I didn't think your little brother was very much impressed either," says Henry Faust, "if you noticed him standing there laughing in his sleeve."

2.

Liv's little brother makes them let him off in the Loop. They can't understand what the 12-year-old boy can be after there, so late at night. But he goes straight to the great Department Store.

Here he knows the Night-Watchman, and for the price of some trivial intimacies is free to play thruout the great store. Besides, the watchman has a 14-year-old daughter whom the boy ardently loves.

Everything is in the great Department Store! to be got by the infinite power of money, which is exchangeable for all things and alone proportioned to the infinite appetite. The Department of Canned Fruits! the Department of Polymorphous Love! Little brother puts on a pair of roller-skates, to move more swiftly from pleasure to pleasure.

(It is Charlie Chaplin who, in *Modern Times,* invented the idea of a Department Store as earthly paradise; in *Modern Times* he skates about the store like a graceful comic angel; in one scene he balances blindfold on the edge of an abyss, a comic angel. It is of course comic to have everything pell-mell, like Adam in the garden: for instance, an elephant with a writhing proboscis.)

Like a giant little Roy sits with legs outstretched—the wheels still spinning on his feet, not unlike the fluttering ankle-wings of Hermes—on the floor among the toys in the Toy Department. Here's a toy farm, a house, a barn, orchard-trees, and animals. Put the man and his wife together in bed, take the cow from the field and put her in the barn; and dim the light: it is Night. Here is an illuminated electric-locomotive clattering on the rails. Here is a little War.

Huge Roy plays with our machines, with a derrick, an alcohol steam-engine. Here's a whole town; pell-mell he scatters the collection of so many houses, motorcars, and men and women about him on the floor. And here is a War, with tiny cannon that actually fire thru the empty store a loud report.

Here are the undistributed letters of a game of anagrams (the players of which do not realize how much they betray themselves in the words they create).

—Sailing on one foot with the other comically lifted behind, soaring with wide-stretched arms and baggy sleeves, speeding from pleasure to pleasure, comes our Charlie Chaplin, and when he does so, no one can refrain from tears.—

On the fourth floor is the Furniture Department. In a silk-furnished ebony Empire bed in the form of a Sphinx, is sleeping the Night-Watchman's daughter. Roy kicks off his wheeled shoes. He loosens his belt and his trousers fall to the floor. Already his little penis is erect, like an inquisitive little animal.

Each of the polymorphous acts of love strives to the maximum; if a boy is well-educated by early corruption, they do not give way to each other. Each kind of pleasure, struggling to be more and more, passes finally into uncontrollable excess. The little body is afire, and now is the time for flaming thoughts. To play with the toys until an orgasm of uncontrollable excess. And to arrange the words to a moment of maximum pleasure.

THE MAXIMUM

To *have* each thing, to *turn* the attention to each thing, into each thing—is the Maximum. It is always in excess, for there is no room in the soul for a comparative measure.

Excess is the only prayer, because this is the thing that is given to us and not made by us; as it is said, "The earth is the *Lord's* and the fulness thereof."

Thus, it is thru the Maximum that we escape our too dear selves and so enjoy the Minimum.

The little boy is asleep, has escaped from the powerful desires of his dear body and soul. (Do not think that he is now without a strong and sweet sensation.) But it was necessary to undergo many arduous joys of the intelligence and lust to come at last to this home most have lost, on the very edge of death.

Six o'clock in the morning! With a loud clangor of the burglar-alarm the Watchman wakes the two children. Everywhere in the store is the daylight. And already—how soon!—as he takes the iron wheels from his shoes, the boy is laughing in his sleeve all day.

206

The Mean, The Maximum

3.

Desiring to do without—perhaps as a method of punishment, and disgusted and weary with the continual consumption of goods in which he and every one else were consuming their lives, and not without a little envy of the rich, and also because he thought it was right to add this particular force to the general social conflict—Henry founded the National Industrial Boycott, an organization to destroy the bourgeois structure of society. The plan (a classical one, dating at least as far back as the *Fable of the Bees*) was simply to buy and consume as little as possible, the Minimum, and to spread this resolve as widely as possible. Then, since the productive system was geared not to necessities but to widely advertised superfluities, it would soon crack wide open.

To hear it *crack!* Henry confessed to himself that he had a lust for this particular sound.

A critical friend said: "Even granting, what is absurd, that you could get a following with this scheme of yours, can't you see that it's not capital that will be hurt first, but labor? You might as well recommend a war."

"Yes, a war of attrition, minus the violence (which always flies to the Maximum)."

"You mean: all the poor people are to starve by principle as well as necessity."

Not answering, Henry cried: "All the same! If we don't all learn how much they have bullied us into needing, we'll still have subways even in the Socialist republic."

He took to wearing one suit and to living on the diet figured out by the experts of the Relief agencies.

He was a 1940 urban Thoreau, but omitted the idea of individual independence which to the transcendentalists had seemed the highest good, but to Henry pure egotism. "I wonder what deep desire to see their fellow-citizens doing without inspired *them*?" he asked himself; and with nervous joy read Hawthorne's biting observations on Brook Farm; "yet Hawthorne was the first nihilist of them all, too Calvinist to approve even of privation!"

207

Doing Without

All the same! N. I. B. gained a little headway and they began to *nibble*, as they boasted, at the economy. Several thousand bourgeois Americans, who were sympathetic to any and every effort to destroy the existence for which all had the deepest unconscious disgust, decided to keep their 1939-model automobiles for another season! These cars, built to last one year and be traded in, soon broke down; whereupon the manufacturers, by way of counter-propaganda, instructed their mechanics to be insulting to all who drove in for repairs, and even to be "out of stock" on those old parts, and they waged a safety-campaign in the state legislatures. There was a certain amount of chaos: fly-by-night mechanics set up shop; some drivers, having used the omnibus once or twice, neglected their cars altogether.

Likewise, among these same people, there spread a movement to read the books on their book-shelves instead of buying new fiction. All were amazed to discover the pages of Anthony Trollope, etc., completely unopened; and soon there was much lay literary criticism, contrasting in "meatiness" the 19th-century masters and the 20th, represented by Margaret Ayer Barnes. Clifton Fadiman loyally championed the moderns, but soon lost his job anyway, since the publishing business was so leaky that it couldn't survive even this tempest.

But there were a few poor people who for a time were freed by the suggestion not to want certain things obviously desirable. They experienced an enormous relief of competitive tension—a relief almost like that of evangelism. (And perhaps in the long run this experience will still bear some influence.) But these people were not large consumers in any case; nor could they transmit their free feeling to their children, but rather an even stronger lust which comes of being deprived of what one sees all about.

In the end all lapsed from N. I. B., perhaps even into excesses that they had never before practised. (Perhaps also this was the measure of success desired by Henry.)

He complained bitterly: "Once they have experienced a sensation, all—all except myself—find it impossible not to have at least this satisfaction as well as all the rest. How can you hope for political reform with such people?"

His friend said: "On the contrary, yours is the self-defeating plan. Why do you want to overturn the state? Because the people have too little; and to accomplish this you teach them to want even less. On the contrary the great hope for change is just to demand *more;* this is what the profit system can't survive."

Henry said: "Do you think that the way to the Maximum of pleasure is not always thru the Minimum? Let me tell you a parable.—

"There was a Zwinglian minister during the Reformation who decided to dismantle his church. (Indeed he determined to tear down the building.) And first he dismissed the choir and took off his vestments, and stripped the altar, and took down the paintings, and burned the illuminated manuscripts. With a sinking heart, he thought of dispensing with the organ; he recoiled from it, but since the Holy Ghost had once put the idea in his head, he had them take out the organ also. In anguish he shattered the pictorial windows with stones; at first he said he would replace them with plain glass, but now that there were not even windows, it was impossible to go back. Instead, he secretly decided to push down the walls! He was afraid to announce this to the grumbling congregation. He waited until a Sunday, when all were within the church and could not see what was taking place outside; and he ascended the pulpit to preach. Then his workmen, not profaning the day with this destructive work—for the *Lord* said, Make No Graven Image—proceeded, amid loud noises, to tear down the edifice. Bricks and plaster fell on the worshipers. The walls fell outward; the frame rent and collapsed amid the shrieks of all; there was a loud *Crack!* And there, roundabout, were the broad fields and the orchard trees, the village, the clouds, and the sun. . . ."

"Very pretty," said Henry's friend. "You remind me of a celebrated argument of the philosopher MacTaggart on survival after death. The fact that all experience is sensory and that the sense-organs decay, says he, is no proof that there could not be experience after death; for this is like saying that we cannot see without windows just because a person inside a house cannot see except thru windows. Rather, MacTaggart asks, who knows what our experience will be like when once we have got rid of these sense-organs!"

"Do you think that is such a stupid argument?" said Henry, laughing up his sleeve.

Chicago
[February] 1939

Prose Composition:
Waiting and Endless Pleasure

Waiting is in general the act of A at P in so far as his desire or fear is to come to P, but is not at P. (Or will come at a time T, but it is not yet T.) Here is the attentiveness of directed desire, the frustration of impossible attainment, and a determinate conclusion. Thus, if the desire is strong, if the waiting is strong, there is a painful distraction from what is present, yet we cannot sufficiently concentrate on what is not present—for if a mere imagination satisfies the desire, then this object is present and there is not waiting; but if more than a *mere* imagination, then we have nothing on which to center the attention. This is impatience. The next phase is boredom, *ennui:* as the many present objects, toward which the desire is not directed (the passing moments in which desire cannot rest), become monotonous, large without interest. There is also possibly anxiety, the fear of disappointment. But very often the pleasure-loving soul will not fail to make use of these pangs of annoyance or anguish to dissipate the energy of desire itself; in this case the expected arrival is greeted finally with a "cool reception."

The brothers in charge of the parking-lot down at Johnson's beach, waiting for the job to be over, for everybody to *be* there, so they could go inside and dance. *I* was not impatient since, with my well known affection for farm-boys, it was their company I desired, or at least that was sufficient to contain me in peace. (Unless perhaps my

211

vivid awareness of their impatience was my suppressed impatience.) Welldon, the younger one, wanted more cars to come: if they had to wait around, they might as well be busy. I pointed out judiciously that there were many items of interest all about: a painter, for instance, would be interested in the colors of the lake; it would interest almost anybody to study the dents in the fenders of the automobiles; and I could wish, I thought, that they were as interested in me as I was in them. But they wished it would rain, tho the sky was clear, so that *no* more cars would come. Thus in waiting, we depend on some one else's act, for instance the North Wind's; therefore we naturally imagine impossible wishes and fears. "What difference does it make," I asked Dick, "whether you sit here or somewhere else?" "I want to go inside and learn to dance." "Who's teaching you, just all the girls?" "No, Elenor Johnson." Out of good nature, and as a classic amatory device (especially where a kind of friendliness is all that is aimed at), I circled the conversation around Elenor's graces: she wasn't stuck up altho her father owned the whole beach. There were repeated lulls. "It won't rain," said Welldon again, and there was the repetition of half a dozen other such isolated remarks—for of course this was the main talk, the conversation of intellect elsewhere, the dialogue of distraction, which unlike my contemporaries, I do not present in full (since first our master Lardner made it clear!) "Say, you must think I'm a girl!" was one of these quodlibets of Dick, as I caressed him offhandedly and he failed to dislike it.

The fiery tedium of waiting for M. was a kind of pleasure to set the teeth on edge. And soon, in our relationship, was conditioned by a passionate anxiety of disappointment. Secondary passion of waiting for the clock to go round to the hour at which I would "give up waiting"; that is, waiting for my own limit of impatience: we set this limit on the clock and objectify the waiting, as if we were waiting for 4:30 PM, but when it is reached, we extend the limit (and soon the whole afternoon is waited away). This very bitter *after*-waiting, waiting for a person who is already late (sometimes he is "already late" even *before* he is late!), waiting for our own decision, when just what is material for

212

Waiting and Endless Pleasure

a decision, namely some other desire, doesn't exist. And Anxiety, which is the momentary overflow of that enormous interior sea of anxiety, the desire dammed up by our first loss; so that this momentary anxiety tastes of more than a thousand loves and losses, and is more powerful than sexual intercourse with M., who need therefore now never come! or would be greeted, coming, by a "cool reception"! A French humanist, Saint Simon or La Rochefoucault, in the intervals of cooling his heels at court, used to jot down his observations and reflections; to dissipate the tedium of waiting by an independent activity (sprung from himself): this shows of how little importance he regarded that court. But now, waiting for M., jot down what thoughts? What! to interrupt the teeth-chilling thrill of this anxious tedium with the wan pleasure of literary composition! as well advise me to read the Bible! for if I could read and write, I should not now be waiting for M. (But let me not belittle the excitement of literary composition, whereby often it is an annoying interruption when the doorbell finally rings. And then, what pent-up rudeness of the host!)

In general, we "blunt the edge" of waiting, as they say, by finding something present to attend to. In the extreme case, where we are occupied in every present moment, absorbed or carried away

now, now, now,

we are never waiting. And conversely, let us once divert our attention to any future moment or absent place, and we are at once *waiting*. Thus it is dangerous to buy tickets for a concert next week, the more so the better the music will be; it is bad to have a dinner-engagement; to make a rendezvous is fatal to the day before: to spend the time wishing away the time; being bored in pleasant company because of the *imagination* of being elsewhere. And likewise, to shorten the interval to what I most dread and hate (and this makes me wonder whether the fears and pangs of my pleasure-loving soul are not the more delicious longings suppressed, so that if only I could attain what I *least* want—) What then, instead of waiting? to attend to the

213

well-known world roundabout? God forbid! this would be an intolerable distraction; strong waiting at least saves us from this. By strong waiting crowned with disappointment, how many things I have escaped—where now I see my friends entrapped (where now I see myself excluded), who did not wait or were not disappointed. If only I may wait out my last disappointments before the pleasure-loving heart is corroded with despair, I'll be safe (tho I see clearly that these two events come at the same time and are the same).

We "lie in wait" when our friend is coming to P, but he does not expect to meet *us* there. We "sit cooling our heels" when the object of desire is in no hurry to arrive: (then is the time to jot down little observations in a note-book). We besiege, we obsess, when our friend is unwilling to come, or come out, but we know he must. "Haunting" is the obsession by spiritual beings, such as the Furies, who first lie in wait, then haunt. To "lure" or, sexually, to "camp" is a kind of *hunting by waiting,* in which we expose ourselves or some other promised joy as bait. We "stall" when we prolong our waiting by indulgence in the monotonous present, in the hope of a more favorable outcome, sometimes not clearly envisaged. The opposite of all these is to "go out to meet" or even to "pursue." To "stalk," to "beat the bush." We go out to meet our friend when he is at Q and we proceed from P to Q knowing that he is there. We pursue when, while we are proceeding from P to Q, he moves on from Q to R.

2.

We, as the merry-go-round goes round, have the growing pleasure of pleasure renewed in a variety that makes no difference; that is various enough to be starting over, so we may have the same pleasure over and over. There is no threat of an end. For such pleasure, the elementary movement itself must be exhilarating and pleasurable, such as this bounding up and down on jolly horses; and there must be no threat of an end, so we may allow ourselves without fear to be carried into this present movement. They say that

Waiting and Endless Pleasure

we are thus carried away into the most ancient smile-producing and sleep-inducing lusts of infancy. The famous jingly and piping sounds are unlike music in that they do not set up the internal probability of a beginning, a middle, and an end; but when the nickel ride is elapsed, just break off. This is intolerable, and there is every temptation to stay aboard and ride out another nickel, in the double rhythm of bounding up and down on a jolly horse in the circle.

In this class of pleasure is the endlessness of ballroom dancing; of roller-skating in a rink (wheels on wheels) where the couples go round with a fixed look, the young man on the inside to take the sharper turns; of bed-time stories. Of Skater's-waltzes; Schubert marches; and such overtures as the one conceived by Frank Sullivan for *Der erste Glopper vom Vicksburg*, where calm gives way to storm, and storm to calm, calm to storm, and storm to calm—till the last late-comer is seated and the curtain rises. . . .

Specifying further: there are two opposite kinds of endless pleasure: that in which you are borne steadily along past the varying scenery, and that in which you stay still and the variety passes by. While the noise of wheels or of a motor serves as an assurance of continuous motion—it must not alter nor attract attention to itself (itself composed of monotonous variations), the flickering scenery meanwhile attracts attention to itself, yet must not attract too much attention. There must be no famous ruin or scenic beauty to make you put your head out the window and look back. There must, further, be no threat of an end, as when the commuter knows that after the Bay come the Salt Meadows and soon New York City: such a ride is nothing but *waiting*,

immer
noch von Erwartung zerstreut—

always distracted by waiting. But we must conceive a new longing at each moment, somewhat looking back as on we speed; yet not be let down at the next, lest a pang of longing form in the heart. Such a ride, such an endless ride, along the rocks along the Lake in the summer afternoon, where the bathers form an endless frieze; the effect of the frieze to make scenery of these naked figures; if only there is not one to remind me *too* vividly of V. or M. or heavenly Ganymede.

The other kind includes: to lie watching the waves and the flames; to stand on a bridge and watch the cars stream under; excavations; night-noises. We do not move nor think about ourselves; the hot firelight and the noisy waves distract us enough for the transition from now to now so we do not turn suddenly upon ourselves. Yet unless we are drawing mainly on ourselves, we might become too attentive: the dark car passing will precise itself into a problem. There must be no threat of an end. To sit all night in the restaurant and watch the changing clientele; those who come in for late confidential dinners; the theatre-goers who come for talkative suppers after the three hours silence; those who come after midnight dances; those who return for a drink after the acts of love. The one with no place else to go—with whom we soon set up a kind of understanding, he in his corner and I in mine. But if you gaze too attentively, you give offense; some one objects to being stared at and there is a brawl.

At every moment we may beguile waiting with endless pleasure because the monotonous world is present. It is present

now   now   and now

and there is no threat of an end. It seems that there is no threat of an end in the endless changes because each one turns out in the end to become something else, as you see. But the fact is that we *both* beguile waiting with endless pleasure and are waiting.

This endless pleasure is not the determinate pleasure of Art, because there is no internal probability of a beginning, middle, and end; and yet it is necessary for the effect of Art to keep the reader in this endless pleasure *also*, to

keep the reader in so sweet a place.

Waiting and Endless Pleasure

But I see that in *my* Art (for the most part) I fail to lull even the agile reader; but he follows me in *anxiety*, then not at all. It is necessary to provide *both* endless pleasure and the threat of an end: the *second* may take the form of anxiety, as if a poem were a firecracker, but why should the reader drive himself when there is not also some animal pleasure to be got? The endless pleasure is given by actions and speeches in character, when the character is known and not always being revealed; by adventures without catastrophic reversals; by grammatical diction and meter. By enumerations, provided that each new member does not involve a change in point of view and a new common genus. The desire to please, on the poet's part, is the source of your endless pleasure; but the desire to create something involves the threat of an end, and the poet's pleasure is your anxiety.

At every moment I beguile my waiting with endless pleasure because the monotonous world is present still. With the repetitive pleasure of essays of art—but there is something dangerous here to my continued ease because every poem is harder to begin. With the continual pursuit of pleasurable boys and girls. With the acts of love. With theatres and games. But there is something dangerous here to my continued ease in the examples of failure, loss, and oblivion; except that in every case, by the grace of the Creator Spirit, there turns out to become something else, and I am given another respite, as you see.

3. *Firecrackers*

With the deepest fascination and fear, my little friend Ira Deott, who is eight and at the beginning of the age whose sentiments I understand, like my own which have not changed—lit a firecracker. He darts back, holding his fingers in his ears. There's a pause; now he's afraid it *won't* go off, or be a mere sizzler. Squinting, steals a glance over his shoulder. It goes off with a bang! What a *different* moment! ecstasy of a *real* change (not a sizzler!). To what? The tiny smoke has blown away. Ira is now even *more*

217

frightened, but he can't resist—resist preparing another explosion, celebrating the Declaration of Independence.

Others keep preparing a sudden stroke of good luck, to come with a Bang! bang! to change that way of life we've become expert enough in to capitalize on misfortune, for a glorious novelty probably fatal. Everybody knows who these are.

Others long for a good disaster: we express this persistent longing by cries of joy when we read of the floods in the Ohio valley, by a sportsman's interest in the Central European wars. By driving thru traffic-signals, and by drowning. You would imagine that we all believed in the life to come.

But I, these summer days at the Dunes beach, look only to avoid the accident. Not that I falsely estimate the value of this happiness, which is what it is; let it persist and persist, even so. And let us say, Hallowed be the *Ordainer* of the world: thru Whom may I avoid the undertow and other error, no tree fall on us, and my wife bear with ease our child long awaited.

Chesterton
June-July 1939

218

A Statue of Nestor

–for Susan

Of all who sailed to Troy, only one has lived to die in a bed. It is Nestor; and now he is about to die, at home in Pylos with no untoward circumstance.

This quiet sentence makes itself known like a thunder-bolt, in the little world ringed by the horizon. This heavy sentence of death is heard by his friends with a somber, fierce joy, for we (we all are his friends) have been waiting out our generation to hear it. Shall we not send a commission to witness Nestor's death and certify that there is no untoward circumstance? Then he shall have been the proof of our hope, that it is possible to live in grandeur and die in peace; for he at least committed it.

As Orpheus invented harmony and Theseus established the political laws, Nestor will be the norm of our generations; but they were heroes and Nestor is every way a man. Therefore the unobtrusive fact, that he is about to die, etc., breaks on all the circumscribed world like the rumbling of thunder.

King Agamemnon came home to what he had hidden behind the palace front.

Queen Helen came home to the pool in Sparta and looked in it, and she was the witch Phorkyas.

The character of Achilles was not to commit himself, yet in the end he perished in the shrieking butchery like Priam.

The giant Ajax went mad. And forever and ever Ulysses twisted his mind and, as poets have said, he cannot now remain but must drown in a twisting wave.

Nevertheless! *all* of these violent causes do exist in the

219

world together and are, in so far, at peace. Yet this vortex of violence has engulphed every soul that crossed to Troy. Only Nestor knows the right raft!

Perhaps the *fierce* joy of the friends of Nestor (all of us are his friends!) is that that living reproach to us all will no longer *be* there. When he dies we say *Oof!* This is the kind of thunderclap that clears the atmosphere.

There are persons in agony, driven by their fates and furies, who cannot afford the luxury of cheap resentments and have come humbly and hungrily to Pylos to hear a useful word.

In the anteroom there is such a rout that you would think it was the gluttonous suitors. The representatives of the cities are continually arriving, under strict commission to observe whether there is not an untoward circumstance that can be taken as even a symbolic or oracular violence. (I myself am one of these representatives.) Some are gathered in a knot about the physician, Machaon. Others are eating. Everywhere are hushed conversations, but a large crowd makes a buzz.

This crowd of the friends of Nestor wishes that Nestor would die *soon*, the better to avert any untoward circumstance.

Almost *we* are the untoward circumstance, by whom Nestor cannot die at his own time in peace.

"In the end he will *fail* to die and be rapt away like Oedipus."

"We'll all be back next year."

"What role did he play at Troy? He was a kind of adviser."

"Yes, by that time he was already old. The time he fought was during the preceding generation, shoulder to shoulder with Pirithoüs."

"Nobody took his advice."

"He foresaw this. He gave the advice in order that they should rush to their doom with their eyes open and not be foolish as well as demented."

The rout is not disrespectful, but just as at a funeral a large crowd makes a buzz.

220

A Statue of Nestor

In this home there are four generations of Nestorides.

The son Antilochus (some say there is no such person, for he died at Troy—this I must check), even in the time of Troy the son of Nestor was called "a second Nestor," when he won the chariot race.

But the grandson Neleus is a man in his early thirties like myself, and I think that I know what he is thinking, standing alone against a wall:

"Either these persons are fools, taken in by a public reputation; or, what is more likely, this is a public demonstration for a public reputation, and my home has become a place of fraud and shame."

In thirty years the grandson of this famous wisdom has heard him say mostly commonplace things, sometimes grudgingly and hesitantly, sometimes in garrulous profusion. More rarely the old man made a violent paradox, as though he were trying to be witty. Once or twice he said something that seemed to be the motto and oriflamme of a new age; then Neleus recognized with a thrill of pride the blow of the decayed power. But he cannot see (as I find it hard to see) that all these sayings might be equally true together.

He sees that his own father absolutely abdicated and ceased to be, as if swallowed up by the old serpent. (It is said that Antilochus died at Troy shielding the old man with his body.) The grandson lived as a child in a family whose hieratic forms he did not comprehend. (I, who had no father, find this hard but not a subject of resentment.)

Meantime there is a fourth generation, another Nestor, growing up and crowding him from below. And still the ancient serpent is not dead! Do we not have the right to resent at least this, that we are so soon being crowded out of life?

He wants to shout out, attracting all ears in the sudden silence, *"There are furies also in this house!"* He begins to say in a high and strange voice, "You say that there is nothing untoward—"

(Would this have been an untoward incident? No, not if this is the case in every house.)

But standing across in the doorway is Orestes, the son of

Clytemnestra, a young man like ourselves. With Nestoride discretion, we do not compare our situation with his, our potential furies with his actual furies. Is it living in the house of Nestor that makes just this difference? Abashed, we stifle the outcry and bow to grandfather's guest friend.

Now a quick silence falls, as when the light breeze suddenly departs and leaves the water glassy smooth. On the arm of the physician of Troy appears the old man Nestor. Let us see: no posture in the doorway, no anxious glance around. Good. But what! does he not even seem to shrug his shoulders at the peculiar scene? Is his gesture the commonplace, or the violent paradox, or the motto of the new age?

From time to time, as I observe here, there is a blank moment.

Raising the cup of wine, he says in a clear tired voice the following prayer:

"To the Creator:

"And to Mother Earth and the Sky, not ringed by the horizon, but they are the horizon:

"And to my great-great-grandparents Time and Flow, the Serpent swallowing his tail, and the Swallowing by the serpent of his tail. All men are free in the age of gold, and there is no threat of a change. He has a scythe to sever that unendurable duration. His children are being savagely devoured one by one:

"And to Compensation and the Bones and the Blood and Holiness and Heat and Nourishment and Vision:

"And to the Gods, who have authority in art and nature:

"And to the Giants in the earth and in the soul:

"And to the Heroes—(I myself was a comrade shoulder to shoulder with Theseus who slew the mixed man in the south; for by the courage of Pasiphaë and the art of Dedalus, the giant in the soul was lured forth into a vulnerable body):

"And to the Tragic Men, those who sailed with King Agamemnon and those who did not sail and also those who dwelt in Troy, for rage made no distinction of them all who acted in their own persons what they did not know they knew:

222

A Statue of Nestor

"And to their Furious Sons:

"—To them all I give thanks that I am what I am."

He poured the drink and without another word or sign (there is here a blank in my perception)—he was moving on the lawn toward the sea, waiting always for Ulysses to come.

An excited buzz rises among the glossarists:

"By Time and Flow I take it he means Saturn and Rhea; but what are the Bones, the Blood, etc.?"

"Iapetus and the original Ocean in our bodies, whereby we first jumped out on the land like frogs. By Compensation he means Themis. These are all the Titans."

"Easy for *him* to know where he is at!" cries one fellow in a loud and bitter voice. "In these few generations he can count back to his great-grandfather the Time. But what about us who have lost the count, and all we know is that there was miscegenation on miscegenation?"

"Is the confusion theirs, my boy, or yours?"

In blank horror the young man Neleus has been staring at the ancient serpent looming before him, involving us all in his coils and placidly chewing his own tail in his egotistical mouth. Could hear nothing further than the threat: "The Serpent swallowing his tail, and the Swallowing by the serpent of his tail." Or if he hears anything, it is the promise that a blow of the knife will free mankind—before he stifles—

(Would this be an untoward circumstance? No, for a man is not responsible to the third and fourth generation.)

I fell to the ground, gasping "Air! air!"

They hasten to loosen his clothing.

—When we are lulled into awaking out of sleep (for there is a more regular rhythm than these nightmares), it is to look up, lying head in her lap, into a wondrous timeless face, time-ravaged, such a face as could be maiden, mother, queen,

Maiden Mother Queen
Goddess.

223

Ulysses

Now the python Nestor slowly unwinding his haggard coils is sliding down to the sea. Shining, more brilliant than fire, each scale wide as a mirror framed in gilt and verdigris, in which a man might see himself if he would shield away the light.

The voice of the man Ulysses is gasping and wailing, "Poseidon! *Ai!* Poseidon—Poseidon—" The dragging weight of the water is falling back to the deep, but his claws are clutched in the weeds of the rocks.

He can no longer see the world as it appears, except a shiny world a man's length away, for the salt tears or the salt sweat blinds him thus much; or the brine of the exterior sea is dashed in his face as he wipes it; and a fourth kind of salty blindness is blood in the eyes. The shiny wall by day is streaked with rainbows, but by night it is a gulph of woe.

The music of the sea (for music is measured noise) does not have the harmony of the tetrachord of Orpheus; nor would you distinguish out of it the pitch, the timbre, and the volume, for all of these are the forms of the booming and hissing notes; but the beat is distinct.

This is the Dialogue of Ulysses and Nestor:

"Which gave the wiser advice at Troy?"

—Among the Greeks at Troy it was thought that Nestor had a golden, honeyed tongue. All the while he was giving a dry recital of the facts of the case in the fewest possible words. For how can the nature of the case fail to charm: it has such order and plausibility; it is almost persuasive; it is so unburdened by the tiresome details of the expedient that it seems to fly; yet it has the curious, pleasant complexity of the irrelevant. Sometimes when Nestor spoke they broke into a thunderclap of laughter, the laughter not of ridicule but of delight.

—Captain Ulysses knew them one and all, and in a few blunt words beside the point he advised them according to what they did not as yet know they wanted. He called this his collection of rainbow tales. Nevertheless, in the deathly comedy of the war, his advice was often good enough, because the adversaries shared with each other the same impassioned world.

Ai! Ai! Poseidon—Poseidon—Wherever is a crevice the salt sea is flooding in. The ripples in their thousands are passing like a great thought over a great face.

This is more of the dialogue of Ulysses and Nestor:

"Which is the more violent man?"

—I violent? gulps the baleful Python. How can it be? I hold the opinion that "everything is what it is and not another thing." Therefore I address myself to each thing in itself . . . in turn . . . or even several at a time. How could I violate anything? (On this principle he has swallowed whole three generations of mortal men.)

—I do not even address myself to things, insinuates the Old Man of the Sea. I politely pass in between them, wherever is a crevice. I do not make a gory mess.

—Neither do I make a gory mess.

—Neither of us makes a gory mess.

Aiaiaiaiaiai.

The ripples are arrested, in a black frown. On the streaming swell (the waters are flowing in sheets down the mountainous body of the water), the man is eased, is loosed from his despairing clutch of the weeds.

"*Nestor! Father Nestor!* help me. . . . *Ai* Poseidon—Poseidon—"

So far as I am concerned, that frightening old man himself could again uncoil his folds and continue on his way and slide into the boiling foam. But what did I expect? that it would *not* be monstrous to have descended into Hell with Theseus, and held the hand of raving Ajax, and to be a father to Orestes—and still live on?

The Theory of Non-Commitment

The dilemma of non-commitment is well known: that not to commit oneself to doing or not doing a thing is the same as committing oneself to not doing it, for it is not done. Either one commits himself to do the thing (and in fact does do it), or he has committed himself to its not being done, even though he has not committed himself to not do it.

Therefore the man who would make a non-commitment must do so positively. He must not merely refrain, but must invent new circumstances in the issue, a sharper form of the issue, so that even after he has not committed himself either to do or not do, and so faces the consequences of not doing, nevertheless the consequent issue is not settled after all, but *it* must still face the issue of whether or not he will commit himself. Thus if, as is often the case, a man is non-committal because he does not want the issue to be settled at this time or in this form, he does not retreat from it or merely look on, but advances to a quite different position from which, when all seems to be over and done, he is still forcing the issue more essentially than ever, and is non-committal. Certainly it requires a man of resources to invent the "new circumstances"; but it is just such a man who is dissatisfied in the first place with the issue as ordinarily presented. If he brings into the open the grounds of his dissatisfaction, he soon finds in them "new circumstances" and the principle of a new non-committal position. This, then, is the *aggressive non-commitment*, which proceeds from an apparent commitment not to do, yet *still* remains non-committally alive.

Now, contrary to this is the method which proceeds from an apparent commitment to do (or to not do), yet still is non-committal: this is the *limited commitment.* It is used by the non-committal man dissatisfied with the issue in the following cases: when it seems that nature or history cannot present the issue except in these unpromising alternatives (to me this seems unlikely); or when it is likely that the issue will clarify itself but he is not master enough of the situation to force it to do so by an aggressive non-commitment; or best, when he judges that the true issue is actually involved in the presented issue as in a matrix. Then, as the issue clarifies, he can still become non-committal. But the danger is that, though he commits himself with a limitation, the force of his commitment (to do or to not do) is positive and definitive, he becomes too involved, etc. No; for the person of resources can occupy such a position by his limited commitment that unless the issue clarifies itself to his satisfaction the issue proves (by his doing) not to be committed after all.

If he has no resources, and can neither invent new circumstances nor occupy a potentially inhibiting position—how does such a person claim to be a non-committal man, and dare not to commit himself to issues that have more reason in them than he has?

Thus, alternately, aggressively non-committing himself and committing himself with an inhibiting limitation, the non-committal man undergoes a life-gradual growth to his absolute commitment.

Helen

Lulled forth from slumber by rhythm, as if there were a better quiet than those nightmares, the young man falls awake. He opens wide his eyes to look into the face of Queen Helen.

His head is between her knees and she is stroking his forehead.

Now they are conversing in whispers. Now she is crooning "Lullee lullay," and her voice comes from that deep place where the nerves are knotted that, when you hear it, the apparent world is ringed in gold and the five senses are standing equally at their distances, in the air, at attention.

The persons in the room he sees, upward from below, large and clear as if they were at no distance at all; and he hears their conversation close to his ear.

But what are *they* whispering, the two? But mostly she is singing that new aubade: *Lullee–*

> Lullee thou tiny little child,
> awake! lullee lullay,

as if indeed there were a better quiet, etc. And she says:
"Is it not unwise for Grandfather to piece out our world so, into those Titans and Gods, and Giants and Heroes, and

227

yes, the Tragic Men and their Furious Sons; and not say further that these are all the creatures of superabounding love that burns and revives the grass?

"The easy flooding of longing that needs no urging, it is itself the urging—little child, it has the forms of resentment, jealousy, murderous wrath; disgust, guilt, suspiciousness, self-castigation, anxiety; inability, overestimation, cruelty, disregard, scrupulousness, inconsequence, emptiness: all of these (I read them off at random in my heart) are the forms of superabounding love. No matter where you longingly look about—turning to each thing after it has struck—you see the causes of your dismay.

"But if you shut your eyelids—lullee—and turn your eyes backward in their axes, then you will see all these things coming friendly toward you like the countryside whose trees are visibly sprouting flowers, and the reappearance of the grass.

"Oh, but don't cry, little child, don't cry, and I shall tell you what I have seen: I have seen Tantalus eating grapes, and the daughters of Danaus easily bringing the water!

"Do you think that it is a hard thing to stretch out a hand? See, stretch out to me your hand. So. And cannot great King Tantalus stretch out his hand and eat?

"I have seen a lover wish her beloved well and speak to him kindly and with regard for him, and without thinking of his death, and take delight in their pleasures together without fear and be confident of herself, and easy at heart, and full of thoughts, and congratulating herself on her good fortune, and judging rightly—all these are the forms of superabounding love. Do you think it is hard for a lover to wish well to a beloved?

"In a blinking of the eye! all of the lusts of the age of thirty are the forms of superabounding love," whispers Queen Helen, stroking his forehead. His head between her knees, stroking his forehead, and lulling him forth from slumber by rhythm, as if there were a better quiet, etc.—he falls awake.

But it is the witch Phorkyas, the time-ravaged lust, of whom once they cried out in despair: "Let her go! let her go!"

228

A Statue of Nestor

And she is wailing: "Nestor! Father Nestor! help. These little pleasures are these miseries. Do you have a better secret?"

Orestes

"You do not see them, but I see them."
It is the saying of Orestes when his furies stir and wake. We are stupefied to see him move. I do not think it is by any arrogance that he distinguishes himself from us. But at the risk of saying what is peculiar—and even sharp—he is making an effort, he making an effort to speak according to common notions. The next moment he cannot make this effort and he sadly calls out, not in English.

As when a demented man, who sees every person as a hound-dog, comes to the physician and tries to explain to him his hallucination, but the physician is sitting in front of him a hound-dog: next moment he cannot help but call out.

I do not think it is by any arrogance that he distinguishes himself from us. We in turn, stupefied to see how he moves, do not compare to it our life-gradual growth into absolute fury. We also falter back a step. —"Perhaps I ought to try to convince him that nothing is there," says the very person at whom Orestes is looking with peculiar horror. Next moment he calls out and we falter back a step, as if he were calling out the figures in a dance.

"*I* see them," says the old man Nestor (it seems to me that there is arrogance in his voice), "for there are Furies also in my house.

"*Good* dogs—*down,* lady! down, miss! *down,* now. There's good dogs."

With a wink he says, out of the corner of his mouth, "I'm a good caller. Sometimes I dance along with 'em.—" He falters back a step. *Aiiii!*

"*Down,* miss; DOWN!—

"Why not? Everything—" he is wailing and gasping—"is what it is"—in a voice of anguish—"and not another thing."

229

These wails and gasps he is now accompanying by a regular beat of his right foot on the fourth count: 1 2 3 4. (But when he comes to dance himself, it will be in the self-contained abandon of choriambs.)

The figure he is calling is the Gracious Host Speeding His Guests (as if we were taking our departure and not he):

"Again soon! friends! let us see you,
calm in our house the furies around you,
make one of our days happy with you
again and soon!—"

"There's good dogs. There, there—lullee. Orestes?"
"Sir?"

"Our prowling silent furies play
with your ferocious dogs away.
Shall we renew the holiday
again and soon?"

"Yes, sir."

"We'll teach by practices of order
these dogs to dance outside the border,
we'll speak of peace instead of murder
again and soon."

'Aì Λίνε, σῖτο Λίνε: "Woe to Linus! Death to Linus!"
What sudden lament is it that makes an old man of Nestor before our eyes and his wrinkles deepen to the skull? The tears are flowing from his eyes onto his knees. It is the outcry for Linus dead and for my own lost youth, and he says:

"He died for *me*, to be an early-dead forever, lest every lovely boy degenerate into a change. Now is it the dead of spring and the violets arrested.

"Look! there in the grass is the numerable body deflowered by their jaws. Let's stand and look our fill, lewd eyes, and cry *Woe Linus!*

230

A Statue of Nestor

"Linus! by your contrast I habituated am, long since too heavy for canonic grace."

'Οῖτο Αἶνε.

"Come, yelpers, come now. What! 's there not flesh enough to make one bite? So long as still I'm unoffending? Then I'll dance with ye. Why not? Everything is what it is."

(No no! it seems to me that he is proving that something at least is not what it is.)

He calls savagely:

> "We'll fiercely dance the dance together
> of the men and dogs in gather
> that formerly fled one another!"

And now Nestor dances with the dogs. He is dancing the Dance of the Hounds and the Man. This sight most of us cannot bear to see, and we turn our eyes to the wall. Some of us hide our faces in our cloaks. But one or two of us are looking humbly and hungrily on.

These yelps, these snarls and grunts, these commitments—are not English. What does it mean?

It means that the past with its curse is still blessed.

Therefore I cling like death to what I might forget.

It has brought me at last to not less than I am.

If I'd lie like the dog with my nose on the ground, *then* I think the tiredness'd slip from my shoulders.

It means that the past with its curse is still blessed (when I lie like the dog with my nose on the ground); it has brought me at last to not less than I am (when the tiredness slips from my shoulders like thunder).

"What! why am I calling the figures if there are so few willing to join in our general dance? If you will not come dance socially with my furies, why have you come from so far to the deathbed of old Nestor?" This quiet sentence—is pounding in every heart like the rumble of thunder.

(Is this an untoward incident?)

"To the Creator and his absolute commitment: and to my Fury-Dogs: and to Courage."

When I consider how two or three times already I have, with my strongest will and my best ingenuity, maneuvered

231

myself into the very same impasse, then I say, "I know this place; why do I not consider it beforehand and cure the error that will bring me here again and again until it is too late?" But this correction, to be sure, is just what I cannot bring myself to.

But no; if *once*, with manly courage and clear principle, I should face my fear through and act my role out, if not with faith at least with art! then perhaps I could be done with the repetition. For I cannot propose to myself some other way than the same temptation day by day unvarying that is all my resources. The way is the difficult ease.

Logia of Nestor

"He wishes to speak to his family." The physician lays a finger across our lips, for there is little breath left in Nestor.

Nestor says to them, "Goodbye to you, little Likely. Let's play the game of statues."

The small child does not make a sound when he sits back motionless, and we also do not.

Nestor said: "In my household, if for a day I was perfectly good and easy, then insensibly but swiftly this goodness turned into a stone statue."

He said: "To a young man, to be true to himself is the way of difficult ease; afterward it is easy but it is not the way."

The Master said: "During the first generation I committed myself, during the second I was non-committal, during the third I made limited commitments."

Coming to Achilles' tent he found him seated on a stone staring out to sea, and he said: "If you are waiting for remorse or any other feeling to stir in somebody else's heart, you must choose a comfortable seat; remember, he is occupied, you are not; your long time is not the same as his long time."

Of Ulysses Nestor said: "He is reasonable in everything but desire; he is quick at attaining everything but his ends; he is resigned to everything but living on a little."

During the butchery after the fall of the city, Nestor said: "This is what no one wills and all desire."

He used to say: "To have the useful is good, to have the needful is best."

Said: "The word that heals as it violates."

The Master was an observer of natural things and noticing the parallax of moving things he remarked: "The nearground backward flies, but the background onward, unless farther back you take a grander background to refer to. To see all move look at the sky."—This is why, pretending to be garrulous, he used to mention Theseus and Pirithoüs.

2.

The Master said "Clear to loneliness on his hilltop ringed by the hills shines the way of difficult ease! Among the people he does not forget it, but his divided heart is darkly boiling: Therefore he cannot take the wandering step ordained with the beginning of the world, nor stretch the hand whereby the heavy things fall of their own weight, nor speak the word that heals as it violates."

He asked: "To use the power by which each thing is what it is, stored there from the beginning of the world, is this the way?"

"What is the way?" said the Master. "During the first generation I learned to be true to myself; during the second generation I achieved immortality; during the third generation I came to be at peace—*still* I have not found the way." Asked concerning immortality, the Master replied: "It is to draw on the I-creating energy." Asked concerning peace, he replied: "It is the art of dancing with one's furies."

It is said that when he exclaimed, *"Still* I have not found the way!" he became invisible in the room; and at this moment he was riding the whirlwind. Most often he was inconspicuous where he sat, and silent and apparently swift as the wind when he moved, for his behavior was without indecisive gestures and divided intentions.

3.

It is said that the Master assumed many forms. In the form of a python he ringed the horizon with his tail in his mouth.

The Master said: "What is the use of dancing? I should have lived when several suns sailed through heaven, before he swallowed them down; then there was light enough in the world and it was possible to judge by shadows. When the mountains had not settled it was possible by art to bring a heavy body down. When the Gorgons were wailing, there was a use in honeyed speech. What is the use of balance when all is flattened out? What is the use of dancing?"

He used to say: "Each moment is the end result."

At Troy when the Ethiop Memnon pressed him close and Antilochus shielded him with his body, it is said that Nestor revived him from the dead lest there be an imperfection in his own household.

The Master said: "What is the use of dancing? It is no longer the way."

It is said that he could make the branches bloom visibly before one's eyes.

He used to say: "The word that heals as it violates."

Finished at Quaker Hill
1939-1944

A Goat for Azazel

1. *The Sitting Together of the Brothers*

When Jimmy first lived in our neighborhood, he was always the center of happy gatherings, of parties that collected without premeditation and the orgies of malicious wit that heartened us against poverty and saved us from envying success. His house was the place of midnight coffee detracting from the next day's work. It was the place even of pandering to careless love. To disburden ourselves of resentful feelings—and who among our energetic but socially alienated friends was without resentment and strong aggressiveness?—we all of us came to happy Jimmy's home; and here the evil could explode in laughter, there was plenty of alcohol, and more truth than appeared in the bourgeois press. There were dreamlike conditions that easily released the energies of our intelligent selves.

Here we felt violently at ease, more so surely than we would have wished. When we left we were ashamed, though usually nothing particular had occurred to which to attach the scandal. But it was in the atmosphere; it was in *leaving* the atmosphere, for no one felt ashamed when staying in that heartening atmosphere. But the hour was so late that one could resent at least the ruin of the next morning. This did not prevent anyone from returning in a week, and each one was sure to meet his friends.

Then what was at Jimmy's? It was not beauty or wealth or

wisdom that made him our darling; for I think that we were then too proud—whatever has occurred since—to be clients, disciples, or lovers of a beauty (which he was not). And if it had been any of those, all would have been bitter rivals; but this was not the case, for all were friendly together; because Jimmy gave what nobody would even ask.

It was his daring!

How could this be? It is daring that stirs precisely resentment in those who don't dare.

But Jimmy dared and did those things that we did not even know we desired.

In this way we all were always learning something, disconcertingly about ourselves. But since it was about ourselves, in the end we were as if never at all subjected to learning anything. This was "freedom" and "being violently at ease."

I am referring only to daring deeds of ordinary life. Daring to be in earnest with regard to the level of entertainment, so that it was not really necessary to have an opinion on the ten great works that appear in America year by year. To indulge the sexual promptings of charity or fancy, as to gratify the coach-dog when the owners of the street bitches drove him off. And so forth, no great matters.

When we did not even know we desired the pleasures of bestiality or pederasty, what an effortless self-discovery it was for each one to see these taken for granted by our dear friend Jimmy! Who doesn't like to be constantly finding out—especially when there are no immediate consequences?—to be touching on archaic desires, just as everyone likes to talk about his childhood?

Just because the satisfactions he seemed to enjoy were far from our daily needs—but they were always *less* far, and this was where Jimmy and all of us were heading for a fall—none was envious of Jimmy or self-conscious of his own impotence. It was in only a confused and hardly embarrassing way that every one of us was enjoying Jimmy's life by proxy; and it was hardly by proxy, because in the dim regions of *these* desires of pleasure and purity there was not so great a gulf between one ego and another. So long as we remained at this distance and at this nearness!—

236

A Goat for Azazel

So long as we remained at this distance, "far from our daily needs"; I mean to say that such behavior was so far from the ordinary perspective in which the acts themselves were suspect, that it was innocent, playful, and even obvious.

When the boy Warren was urged to woo the Widow, it was that such a relation was obviously called for "in principle," so long as everybody, including the boy and the woman, continued to regard it in this perspective; and anyway the matter had already been decided beforehand under the influence of alcohol—therefore *in vino veritas;* and why should they not have a week of good pleasure instead of remorse? because Jimmy's genius lay just in making a blessing out of a *fait accompli.* . . .

So long as we remained at this *nearness,* lest, the enchantment withdrawn, our universal resentment solidify into a blow of hate.

We were strangely at ease when we dared by proxy to judge according to our best thoughts. I am referring to nothing more esoteric than bearing in mind some of the distinctions of the classical philosophers. Perhaps this social ease came from the fact that among those true ideas and those simple lusts there is no use in setting up one ego against another.

Sharply Jimmy turned on himself and asked by what right he was so easy-going when all of us were so miserable. (For the *fact* was that, like others who sometimes touch on simple ideas and primitive desires, our Jimmy was wracked with anxiety and guilt concerning his daily behavior. This was where he was heading for a fall, for it is impossible to keep it up.)

Then he often used to say conveniently: "It's not *I;* after all, it has nothing to do with *me!*" But this was the case! and the most beautiful thing—the reason why I love him still when the others have turned against him—was that *at that time,* though since he has become proud and fanatical, he was able to say without boasting that it was not he.

"It has nothing to do with me"—because he persuaded himself that he was subject to the small child in him still, and this happy child happened to have clear eyes as well as wide eyes. What was there to boast of in that?

Today he is always angry; he is protecting his integrity and lives by points of honor. But at that time we saw him angry only once, and then suddenly. It was when L. like a fool, said, "I'm impatient with these people who refuse to grow up!"

He was referring to us all, and from that moment we ceased to be his friends.

But Jimmy—God defend and prosper him at last!—cried out: "What *you* mean by growing up is agreeing to moderate the illusory ideals of adolescence to the hard conditions of the environment. Then you achieve—if you do!—those very adolescent ideals, which nobody really wants, in a realistically flat form, and most often at a time when nothing makes much difference any more. But what I mean by refusing to grow up, is to *go back*, consciously and trying to avoid the risks of regression and fixation, to our early years of childhood, so that we at least know what it is that we really want and can challenge the world—whose conditions are now seen to be not so hard but very wonderful—with our whole desires. These satisfactions are rapturous and are not too rare. And if we are liable to regress in any case," said Jimmy with a little smile, "is it not less generally dangerous to meet the social demands with the impractical hopes of a little boy than with the almost possible wishes of the age of fifteen, which are nothing but the existent repressions glorified by acceptance? The first is the case of the gentle people who live in secondary elaborations. The second is the resentful, ambitious, and compromising herd—no offense meant—who almost remember what they imagine they want."

"No offense meant," said Jimmy, describing a general condition, which therefore could not possibly apply to any living personality, especially when he was sitting in the room talking to you; but another person sometimes finds it hard to feel that what is said of all the members of his class is not also said of him.

"No offense meant," thought Jimmy, as he wrote the epigram that caused us all our woe:

When the energies in love I now exhaust

238

and so am known as kindly for the most,
are for the pleasures of aggression freed
when I am middle-aged—then take heed,
you liar L. and D. you thing of dirt
who injure us today and go unhurt.

"Very nice!" said L., "but why, pray, are the conditions hard for the likes of me, but not so hard for *you*, so that you have satisfactions that are rapturous and not too rare?"

"Did I say that?" asked Jimmy, whose resentment, muse of unflattering comparisons, had vanished. "I must have meant that it is because what the childish people really want is ease, affection, lust, and such things; and therefore to them all the great world of arts and sciences and social institutions, with the rewards of progress, created objects, or positions, are merely so many supervenient graces; but *therefore* they are free to all and can be chosen as objects of concern, to be consolation for the unavoidable despair. But if a person should think that *these* are what he really wants—they are really nothing but surrogates—then he approaches them in the wrong relation of conqueror, and there's no peace in them."

2. *Doubts*

The next moment the atmosphere of faith (which makes possible all things) was dissipated, when Jimmy went away to work in the Arsenal at Springfield. The events that now occurred fill me with shame; but it is only because I know that *I* had no share in these scandals that I now dare to report them. To report them with hate—for I report them in order that, if all the others are at fault, I also shall be. (It seems to be impossible, when all the others are destroying themselves, not to do likewise; and this goes back to the original agreement by which I associated myself with these people.)

As soon as he had gone away, the others (not I!) turned on my darling Jimmy with ferocity. (He was now *my* darling in exclusion of the others; and this I desired from the very beginning.)

But in order to *innocently* share the evil, I turned not against him but against our relations with him. And I saw that the little desires of which he had so pleasantly reminded us—like the jewels of the *Phaedo* which we encounter by surprise as if they bore no relation to the ordinary rocks and dirt, but they are a nagging reminder of the materials of the courts of Jove—these little desires were suddenly the enormous passions which each one would never admit to himself, but projected his disgust for them, and his unsatisfaction of them, on far-off Jimmy. I am speaking always only of such passions as to review my daily life fundamentally or to cohabit with beasts.

The fact was that we had come to *rely* on our pleasant evenings at Jimmy's, as an addict does on his specific drug. If we perhaps thought that it was alcohol that had the power to release the soul, we now found that there was no satisfaction in these mixed drinks. I therefore asked: Did our friend have the *right* to deprive us of himself if once he had become so necessary to us? What was to become of the energy of craving that used to be so pleasantly consumed on week ends? But it was this very energy that the others were turning against our host—how could it be otherwise?

Perhaps it was not a great amount of energy, but not much is required to blacken character and lay burdens on a scapegoat. But the full satisfaction of unsatisfied desire, I think, still came to each one privately in self-disgust; and it is this energy that I am exhausting in memorial writing.—

I thought: (1) in the end it was Jimmy who was at fault. For like an immature person he had behaved vis-à-vis his friends with no regard for what was possible for *them*. In this he undertook a *presumptuous responsibility*. What an enormous responsibility it was to unsettle my resignation in my boring daily work by seriously advancing an occasional counsel of perfection! More deeply: it was even *criminal* to touch, almost to tamper with, the sexual ideas that we others had luckily quite forgotten—forgotten except in outbursts of inexplicable irritability, moods of distraction and masochistic mistakes in making a living.

A Goat for Azazel

It is because I allowed myself to indulge in such cowardly reasoning—namely: that Jimmy should have tempered the wind to the shorn lambs!—that I am torturing myself with this memorial writing.

(2) But was it not *most* likely that Jimmy's behavior vis-à-vis his friends was rather the result of thoughtlessness, which amounted in the circumstances to callousness? He behaved as he wished and said even what he meant just as if he had never made an agreement to associate with these people. From my own experience I knew that this was most likely the true explanation, for it has several times occurred to me that someone confronts me with a face and voice contorted by hurt pride and rage, although—that is because—I hadn't been thinking of *him* at all.

(3) No, no! the most charitable and obvious explanation, and the one with which I finally satisfied myself, was that Jimmy was always *taking for granted* that we saw everything in the same light he did. This was not presumption, nor even callousness, but simply inexperience. He took it for granted, when we asked about the movie, that we meant: "is it of the order of Racine?" He took it for granted that the feeling of Warren for Mrs. K. was only fatal desire, and that it was at least desire.

So! I concluded, my friends are perfectly in their rights to be impatient, and my dear Jimmy is also blameless.

By such reflections I expressed by own resentment against Jimmy.

But the others were more direct.

Pasty-face D. and the fine gentleman L. wrote letters to Jimmy in which they urged him to pursue his course and corrupt also the children of Springfield, Massachusetts. In the words of Agrippina, they said in substance:

Poursuis, Néron . . .
par des faits glorieux tu te vas signaler.

"Keep it up, Nero, and you'll distinguish yourself."

I think that there were two letters. Yet there might have been ten. There were twelve of us; but Warren and I did not send these letters. What my way of resentment was we have seen.—

At the end of the summer, before returning to school, the boy Warren tried to kill himself by taking an overdose of sleeping tablets and slashing his wrists.

The reverberations of this drama were enormous. It was at most conceded that Jimmy was not immediately responsible for the razor. They observed a propriety in the fact that it was just the youngest who had succumbed; and they suffered remorse for not having protected the adolescence of each one. And at last I was privileged to hear in somebody else's mouth my own reflections about "presumptuous responsibility" and even "tempering the wind to the shorn lamb."

(4) But the *fact* was that out of charity Jimmy had given me the benefit of the doubt; he had offered not to take as fatal my agreement to associate with these people. He took it for granted that I still hoped, as indeed I did! to be one day perfectly happy, and not that I was resignedly content with substitutes for gratifications of tertiary elaborations.

If he was callous, it was to the importance of the accidents crippling me.

And if he was presumptuous, it was that he presumed that I was his living friend, which was indeed the case. Was this inexperience?

While he was living in our neighborhood, our instincts of ease proved to be more persuasive than our worst ideas.

The fault in my relations with Jimmy was that I judged in a limited way what he was up to; and also what I was up to. But it would have been better to have put more trust in the feelings we had experienced in company. In any case, these feelings survived; they were the materials and memories for new revaluations; so that I could *still* "make up my mind" again and again. It was not too late to become the dear friend of Jimmy.

I thought: "Perhaps we have our dear friend Jimmy to thank that this was an attempted suicide and not a suicide. Attempted suicide and suicide are not even of the same kind of symptoms (though deceptive accidents may occur in either case). Often what they call the exciting cause of attempted death is nothing but the saving ray of hope."

A Goat for Azazel

3. *A Solitary Deed*

When he came back, Jimmy was tired to the death.

For three years he had worked in the accursed Arsenal, during which time he had ceased to have the energy to exteriorize new thoughts in conversation but learned to answer merely "Yes" and "No"; lost also, therefore, his little smile of novelty of conversation. Yet it had been necessary for him to remain there, where he was destroying himself rapidly, because everyone had to take some part in the war—just as now he was taking another part in the seemingly endless war.

Being almost in solitude there, as it seems, he was able to question himself closely on the problem of why it was that he was so easy-going when all the rest were so miserable. And he now thought that it was long back that he had agreed to take a fatal loss, or at least knew that he was taking a fatal loss; therefore, it seemed, he could be careless about the later things. That is, he could exploit them of their full resources of peace—which is given when you don't seek it. (Meantime he was involved, less and less innocently, in the seemingly endless world-wide war.)

His heart was so strongly weary as to sap the freshest joys to its own pause—

> as Moscow vast laid waste
> exuberant Napoleon.

But as for me, I was now willing, when I met my friend again, to sympathize without evaluation with *any* behavior of my friend. His action whatsoever would question me and not I it, as if to say, "Will you again make the mistake of deciding what we are up to?" And I was not deceived by the patience, *with no false move*, of my poor tired friend; but now for the first time I came to admire him—except that I was on edge.

When he saw how this was, Jimmy said to me: "Harry, I'll tell you what I'm up to, in order that you shouldn't expect

243

anything else of me just now." His voice was very tired. "I remember that I used to do what I wished and even to say the things I really meant. But these days I'm willing to limit my actions to the circumstances *set by these people.* This is how it is. *Except that in these circumstances,"* said Jimmy proudly, "I decline to do anything improper according to my best instincts! I will not speak the truth; I will not tell a lie. On such a negative principle, I won't go far, I think. For the most part, I won't commit myself; where inaction is a commitment, I'll act as I must. In the end I might go even to the limit of what good motives can do among evil alternatives! Perhaps you don't realize that this is an exquisite way of self-torture. It is a matter"—he said in a low voice—"of integrity."

He said: "I've found a way honorably to express my resentment against my positive faith."

He began to tremble, and he said: "You see, Harry, my ancient resolve used constantly to suggest new positive little triumphs to me; you remember, they were not much. But now, since I know myself better, I have only the ideal of a negative check, like the conscience of Socrates."

The fact was that he did not trust me or my intentions. This meant, from his point of view, that he would not intervene in them. Thus, he declined to commit himself on the war policy—though surely, one way or another, he must have committed himself—because he would not in the *least* influence my behavior. About the revolution he would no longer talk at all.

But I saw—I hope without envy!—that it was otherwise with young Raymond! (for *he* had committed "attempted suicide," it seemed). Once I interrupted these two in conversation. Jimmy's face, though attenuated, was alive, and he was saying: "No, no! if you can't rule out this suspicion, follow it! do it!"

So far as *I* was concerned—let me repeat this—his attitude was *heroic* in my eyes. But—what next? how much longer could he remain in this *nice* situation without attenuating into nothing at all?

All at once I remembered that once before in my life I had been forced onto this edge of anxiety, anxiety of a spectator who obscurely knows that his own hope is at stake. It was when I was the accompanist of our friend Schneider the violinist, at the time when, as he thought, his talent was gone forever. Then, at his birthday concert, happening on one note truly bowed, he played this note seventeen times; the string broke; and he fell in a faint.—

The next moment Jimmy's reserve degenerated into mere violence.

Something astounding! for us who had never seen him in anger, but always smiling, even recently when he was tired.

(At the same time, was he not the author of that epigram:

> When the energies in love I now exhaust

etc.?)

This L. mentioned in the epigram, a smaller man than himself, he beat unmercifully and in public, unprovoked, and quite beyond the expectation of his character. There was no doubt something thrilling in this. It seemed that this was the pleasure of aggression he had promised himself when he should have decided that he was "middle-aged."

"I call this my Honor!" he said roughly to me. "Have you any objections?"

I threw wide my hands.

"Since I'm tired of diffidence, dismay, disgust, despair— I'll openly display my public blazon. You haven't seen this before?

"Perhaps I'll operate honorably among these persons by annihilating my enemies among them! I am reminded of the Suicide of the Egomaniac—"

"What was that like?"

"The Egomaniac wanted to leave this world. But how could he turn on himself? Therefore he systematically set about destroying all the rest in order to be at last alone!"

"This was a long method."

"Yes, yes!" cried Jimmy in self-satisfaction. "I like this idea of Honor because it is endless; it is perfectly indefinite and you may carry it as far as you want or have the power; it won't let you down. It used to mean simply that one had the right and duty to defend the name and perquisites of one's status; but now since that order of statuses is outmoded and only the Honor remains, I can invoke it in *any* situation. There's no such thing, and it's always at stake in the changed world that no longer recognizes any of the old perquisites. Who can disapprove of what I do if I see that my Honor is involved in it? This is terribly convenient."

So far as *I* was concerned, it was somewhat thrilling, momentarily thrilling, just to see the inwardly accumulating energy strike out once before suffocating.

"Harry," said Jimmy slyly, "let me tell you a secret. Do you know why previously I could not do the least thing, and now I can with *ease*? It's because I used to be paralyzed by guilt at the very moment of stretching out my hand! And now for a year I have made *no false move*! My conscience is clear for the first time since I was two years old! It takes twelve months to clear the conscience. Then, now I'll act right out."

"Do you call it action to knock a little fellow down at a bar?"

Jimmy smiled the live and easy smile that I hadn't seen since long ago.

4. *The Scapegoat*

For three nights running he dreamed that he was the Scapegoat in the Atonement ritual of Leviticus xvi.

At 5 AM he called me by telephone to tell me about it.

"I don't mean that I dreamed in general about being this goat—by the way it's only the *kid* of a goat—" he said, "but I dreamed it as it's described there, correct in the main details: the High Priest in a white robe enters the sanctum just once in a year; there are two kids, one for Jehovah and one for Azazel—whoever he may be; the Priest kills the first kid and then—Let me read you the passage. Hello?"

"Yes," I said, hoping I would not have to answer anything further at 5 AM, rudely awakened.

He read: "*21. And Aaron shall lay both his hands upon the head of the live goat*—that's the kid for Azazel; hello?"

"Yes."

"—*and confess over him all the iniquities of the children*

246

A Goat for Azazel

of Israel, and all their transgressions in all their sins, putting them upon the head of the goat—hello?"

"Yes."

"—and shall send him away by the hand of a fit man into the wilderness."

"What do you mean by a fit man?"

"Listen. 22: And the Goat shall bear upon him all their iniquities into a land not inhabited: and he shall let go the goat in the wilderness."

"Let him go?" I said in amazement. "Then what do you do?"

"What do you mean, then what do I do?"

"I mean in the dream—after he lets you go, then what do you do? Hello?"

"Yes, I'm just trying to remember. Then I don't do anything. No—there I am with a little beard and twinkling hooves, and then I wake up."

"Well?"

"Who or what is Azazel?"

"Azazel is a local devil," I said positively.

"Is that what it means to go free—to be left to this devil?"

"I suppose," I hazarded in the manner of 5 AM, "that it means that the goat reverts to wildness, with his long beard and his twinkling hooves."

"Oh."

"So? . . . Hello!"

"I was wondering what the dream means."

"I'll analyze it for you later."

"No no!" said Jimmy. "I understand where this comes from perfectly. What I want is to *live out* this suggestion. For a change!"

"I beg your pardon?"

"The thing to do," he said firmly, "is to look up the glosses. Then I'll know the possible meanings. I'll tell you what I find. . . . Hello? Harry?

"Harry, this is Jimmy. As I was saying, I'm not satisfied with the other role I made up for myself."

"You ought to have a cup of coffee," I said.

In the mail he sent me half a dozen glosses; but what

247

conclusion he himself arrived at it was impossible to tell by such a method of communication. The fact is that after this letter, the matter was never again referred to; it withdrew into the same secrecy—not quite the same secrecy—from which it had emerged. He wrote:

"These two goats were Nadab and Abihu, the sons of Aaron, who had just been consumed by the Lord's fire because of an error in the service. (Chapter xvi begins: *And the Lord spake unto Moses after the death of the two sons of Aaron, when they offered before the Lord and died.*) But such a judgment was intolerable; therefore, as always, the ritual was composed as a compromise interpretation of the event, a kind of bargain; only one of the kids was slain (was the Lord's), the other got away. Of course it was admitted that *he* was terribly guilty; in fact they were both guilty. But one was lucky!

"More generally, then: these goats were types of the long line of pairs of brothers in Genesis, Cain and Abel, Ishmael and Isaac, Esau and Jacob (Barabbas and Jesus), of whom one either was killed or inherited, while the other became a wanderer in the wilds. But the ritual is a shrewd commentary on the history, for we see that there is nothing to choose between the goats; they are assigned by lot. What is really given here is not an original crime, but a reciprocal relation between bearing the sins and being excluded: the stranger is the guilty one. The other one, meantime, is good and dead.

"The goat for Azazel is the wild strain in each one's blood; it reverts to its wildness—led there by a 'fit man.' This wilderness is called Azazel and is peopled by wild strains. But what does the 'fit man' see and do there, when he is bringing the wild goat to be let loose? His adventures would make a remarkable romance. But in any case (v. 26), before he returns to the camp he must wash his clothes and bathe his flesh in water. . . . At least there *is* still a wilderness in which the wild

248

strain may live; but later, in Jerusalem—for the urban society is more exacting—the goat is traditionally taken to a cliff top and dashed to his death on the rocks. Thus they're both dead.

"If Azazel is the *name* of the scapegoat (as the A.V. seems to think), then the other goat, 'for Jehovah,' *is* Jehovah. Jehovah they slay in his house while the desires of all the people are let free outside! What a day of triumph! It's no wonder that this is the Day of Atonement, for the affliction of the soul. A day of rejoicing! (Is it so easy to dispose of the creation of the Heavens and the Earth?)"

"No!" wrote James in the margin. "In that direction I've gone far enough! Try the other way." And he continued:

"When they have at last got rid of this wild and guilty goat, the people feel that they are purged and free. And this is the condition for their *beginning over,* as they must, for it is the season of the New Year, the Day of Atonement being the climax of the celebration of the New Year, season of sounding the horn. To begin over in freedom, it is necessary to agree to take a loss, lest the new life be corrupted by the old. In order to look out again, for a moment, as if at the fresh creation of the Six Days. It's therefore an occasion for breathing freely when they can bid good-by to the desires that interpose between them and the created heavens and earth. These desires are all the past, and they commit it to Hell, for Hell is nothing but the past; Azazel is the prince of Hell. But on the part of that Scapegoat: is it not generous of him to keep away and not trouble the camp further? The people are no doubt cruel to enjoy their purity and disburdening at the expense of the other one in Hell.

"But there is a remarkable commentary of Rabbi Moses Maimonides. He says: the Lord allows the goat to escape to Azazel because He Himself is *generous;*

249

since He has His share, He does not begrudge to give something also to the Devil! What can be the meaning of this odd opinion? (Not without reason the Jews say of Rabbi Moses that 'the Rambam has strong shoulders!' if he can carry even an opinion like this.) It means that there is room also, place also, for all the iniquities and transgressions of the people; these are allowed to exist and move in their own way—though of course in due separation and distinction, for everything is what it is. If they are banished to the past, as they must be if we are to start a New Year, at least they are not hounded there, but are *let go;* this generosity allows us to forget them, not merely to repress them. In this way we can begin over, without dragging past time ever lengthening, yet without disowning past time like shallow persons. For we say: There is a superabundance! one part is committed to Azazel and there is *still* more! . . . Such an opinion rightly belongs to the Philosopher of Creation, as we must call Rabbi Moses: he who insists *both* on the unlimitation of God and also on the 'Work of the Beginning' and 'Work of the Chariot' or Cosmic Universe. The goat for Jehovah is slain, because what use has the secret Lord for a goat? but the goat for Azazel lives on just because it is a usual thing in the wilderness of the ordered world.

"Both of these goats, separately and together, signify our Savior. Guiltlessly slain as the one, he can therefore atone for our sins, as is well known. In the beginning they are not *his* sins—he is really no way involved. But now when they become his, he can go free in the forest; this forest is the Hell to which he descended, and the Heaven where he is sitting at the right hand of his father. There, it seems, our sins are transfigured; our Savior in Heaven is no longer without our sins, even no longer without our guilt? though these desires exist now in the angelic way? No, no! his *innocence* is to be *incarnate,* within the human precincts, and to die. His heavenly freedom is his guilt. What a sharp contrast with the secret God, whose incarnation is an abominable idolatry, so that the Creation itself is *almost* to be considered as His *fall!* But our Savior's incarnation is his justification, whereas his resurrection and freedom are merely the assumption of the ideal of our desires (realized at last! this is why he says that God has forsaken him). He is not blameless where there is no law, in the wildwood, but just where there is a law, within the precincts. It seems that he is the only one who is perfectly incarnate! all the rest of us suffer from spiritual delusions and are day by day undoing the work of the Creation. (This brings the matter of these goats home too close to us.) What a hope for all!"

He wrote finally,

"This New Year's, of which the Day of Atonement was the ending, did not fall in the beginning of the year, but in the Seventh month, half way through the year, when there was already something for reconsideration, as if the latter half of the year were a time for *second* doing or even systematic *un*doing. In the ancient calendar, the first month was the beginning of the Spring; that could not be the spiritual New Year. But on the first day of the seventh month—calling to order—they used to sound the horn.

"Jacobus."

5. *The Goatherd*

By means of glosses, he seems to have satisfied himself vis-à-vis the Goat, for when next he dreamed, it was about the Fit Man appointed. He dreamed that if he had paid close enough attention he would not have lost the love of his friends. But his companion reassures him: *"One cannot notice everything—"*

A CEREMONIAL

(Scene: Azazel)

CHORUS: One cannot notice everything,
the resentful blow unlooked-for falls.
JAMES *(wandering):* I do not know the way, I do not go the
way:
therefore love and longing are lapsing from my heart.
CHORUS: Has not the same wild chase of what fled you
again into the same impasse betrayed you?
why are you mourning for the lapse of longing?
JAMES: Where, unattracted, shall I take a step?
if I do not go at all, I shall not go the way.
CHORUS: Perhaps you might awhile, like many another,
be less near in your ardor to the goal,
your ardor always to the single goal.
The means of life
are also part of the time of life.
JAMES *(choking):* Aa—how the nausea
of the divagations of these persons from their hearts
is rising in me—
like a drowning flood. *(He vomits.)*
CHORUS: So. Like the rest of the experts in avoidance, this
fellow has persuaded himself that the original elements
of the world are clean and clear and very simple—great
barber-surgeons with Occam's razor, but no physicians.
And now their stomachs cannot bear the valves, the
vulvas, and the blood-greasy sockets of even the first
mechanical analysis. And what if they should come to
lay hold of the absolute violence of a reality. Uh—*(He
chokes.)* This fellow will never ride the whirlwind; nor
will I.
JAMES: I am much refreshed. What's the matter with you?
(Sniffing.)
Blood! That's what it is! I am not squeamish.
And? and? *(Sniffing.)*
Goats! goats! but such a noisome litter
of the gaseous Chimaera herself—
    (He sees the GOATHERD.)
Fo! what is this unwashed heap of rags
exhaling. I'm sick again. So fascinated

252

by disgust that I am feasting on the spot.

CHORUS: Your heart no longer runs along the way,
maybe your flesh will creep along the way.
This is a way to advance on the way.

JAMES: Creator Spirit! look how the vermin
are spontaneously crawling into life
out of this monstrous vitality.

CHORUS *(sharply):* Nothing from nothing comes.
Be thankful also for the things o' the Fourth Day.
(James vomits a second time.)

GOATHERD *(recreating the scene):*
Victory bleating and with twinkling feet
he danced his way into the wildwood
hung with strong grapes. The rotten apples
were sweetly expiring on the ground
while I was blowing loudly on the horn.

CHORUS *(for* GOATHERD*)*: Tekyoh! Tekyoh!

GOATHERD:—My curly horn I blow.
Rotting fruit is not so fair
but the liquor in it is afire

And into flame the clusters
of the rotting grapes have burst.

Tekyoh!

JAMES *(alert):* Ah, do you think if I pledge you in a glass of
this fire I'll go the wandering way of the beginning of the
world?

CHORUS: Perhaps—in your case. But I hesitate to advise it.

JAMES: Backwards! Extraordinary. The causes are leaping
backwards after the effects. First I was sick at the
stomach, and now I'm drunk as the Master. Will I come
to be thankful in the end for the things of the beginning?

GOATHERD: And when we came into the wildwood heart
then free—unto Azazel—I let go
that wild and dancing kid.

JAMES: Eia! Eia! *(He dances a step.)*

CHORUS *(prostrate):* Blessed art Thou, O Lord, who hast
commanded us to let the scapegoat free.

JAMES: Will I not come in the end to sit again in the trusting
company of my witty brothers?

CHORUS: How goodly and how pleasant is the sitting of the
brothers together.
GOATHERD *(voice of anguish):*
But because we have sinned we are exiled from
our native land and simple heart;

and ease and joy and brotherly trust to us appear
as disgust, dismay, and despair.

We who in an instant might stretch our hands and
touch the creator work of the Six Days

lose heart in the struggle with the hobgoblins of these
people and their things that do not exist.

I was a fit man and appointed to let the
wild kid free—

(James vomits a third time and is purged.)

JAMES: Foul goatherd! why did you not cleanse yourself of
my sins? Is it not written that you must wash your body
and clothes in water, and *afterwards* you may return into
the camp?
CHORUS *(sharply):* Hush! Do you expect him to shock you
according to your taste? This would be precisely *not* to
shock you.
GOATHERD:
In the worldless in-between
the camp and the wildwood
maybe this carelessness
is ceremonious.

PART 2

*(The stage darkens and glows with almost natural light.
The horns are calling Tekyoh, Teruah.)*

254

A Goat for Azazel

CHORUS *(for the High Priest):* In the Seventh Month at the
New Moon there shall be to you a blowing of horns. It is a
new beginning. *(The* GOATHERD *is transfigured and is the
Fit Man appointed.)*
DANCER: Half of my year is rolled away.
Let me live out the fall
in unravelling the summer.

(Somewhere my child-heart—)
The kid is trembling
in the grip of the Priest,

he smells his brother's blood
his beard is quivering
and he is bleating high-E.

You would think that this frightened animal
was a little old-man child.

Don't fear, little old-man child,
for I shall set you free.
(A Catechism of the Ritual.)
DANCER *(for the High Priest): What is our guilty ease?*
JAMES *(as if suggested to):* We take pleasure by proxy in the
guiltless freedom of our darling.
DANCER: *Who is the Scapegoat?*
JAMES: *He* is our darling, now the object of all disgust and
dismay.
DANCER: *Why is such a one let free?*
JAMES: Because otherwise the people would wither away
and die.
DANCER: *Who is the Fit Man appointed to lead him into the
wildwood to Azazel?*
JAMES: A man who because of his wisdom has a dispassion-
ate heart may therefore interpret to the people what he
has seen in the wildwood to their advantage. He is not
squeamish.
DANCER: *Who is Azazel?*
JAMES *(indirectly):* Only our savior is perfectly incarnate.

DANCER *(insistently): What does the Fit Man do afterwards?*

JAMES *(excitedly and unsuggestible):* As I already *told* you! he must *wash* his body and clothes in *water,* and *then* he may return into the camp.

CHORUS *(describing the scene):* Oy
The High Priest has now brought forth the great sack into which are to be loaded the sins of the people. It is bound on the shoulders of the kid: surely the burden will be too heavy for him, and the people wail.
Oy
Oy.
And first the sack is charged with our guilt. With distrust.

JAMES: Ai.

CHORUS: And dismay.

JAMES: Ai.

CHORUS: And disgust.

JAMES: Ai Ai.

CHORUS: And despair.

DANCER *(loudly):* But *these–*

CHORUS *(suggested, in a loud and thrilling voice):* But these are nothing but the forms of superabounding love, the same as is the tonic of the flowers! and why should not the goat *therefore* twinkle his feet?

DANCER *(laughing):* Ha! and afterwards they pile in the enormous burden of the things that do not exist!

CHORUS *(laughing):* These do not weigh much!

DANCER: One's shoulders need not drag!

CHORUS: Is this the whole of it—of that gruesome repository?

JAMES *(breathing fiercely):* Yes! yes!

CHORUS *(for the* DANCER): As forth he boldly dances
led by my silken cord,
the parti-colored streamers
ravel our favorite.
His eyes benignly peering
shed radiance around
and his horns lie on his shoulders
as he lifts his triumphant nostrils.
(Tekyoh. Teruah. Shevurim.)

256

A Goat for Azazel

(There is a pause.)

DANCER *(gravely, simply, in walking motion, and speaking for himself):*
Now have we come into the natural world
where there are no things that do not exist
and, not by a miracle, the tree and beast
draw from the measureless creation their
strength and beauty. And because they do not think
that the impossible is possible
men do not find (with fright) how all their possible
has suddenly become impossible;
but glorious wit and serviceable power
spring not by chance but from what a man is.

And here I see—how goodly and how gracious!—
the unsuspecting brothers sit together
(is this impossible?); exert each man
without remorse his strength (is this so hard?)
in the collaboration afire.

If then some brother, moved by his best love,
gives aid and judges by the facts of life;
and another notices the time is flying by
and keeps in mind the instant death, and serves
—what amazes you? is this so difficult?—
they are not made the scapegoats of the tribe.

So. Into this natural wildwood heart
I led the happy kid and let him free.

(Let the light flicker briefly, into daylight—as the one ripple moves across the endless calm sea.)

DANCER *(in awe):* Azazel . . .
my ears and eyes are useless to me
my touch is suffering the illusion of the
    moving pin points.

CHORUS *(for the dancer):* Not too rare for sense,
but like a heart-easing blow.
I desire what is possible
why am I paralyzed?

257

My desire is actual
and *then* I stretch my hand.
I think I am clenching my fists
but I am grinding my teeth.
My thoughts are only facts
why do they seem future? future?
CHORUS *(for himself):* I am only a man, therefore too much
   a spirit disembodied.
I cannot see what is,
my thoughts do not exist.

Even a commonplace desire
is too angelic—damned,
as when the Morning Star
flickered in the sky.
DANCER: Our savior is flesh.
CHORUS: He is not a champion against the Creator of the
   heavens and the earth.
DANCER: He moves mountains.
JAMES: Alas, I have made works of art.
CHORUS: (Even so! do not say a word against the creator
   spirit.)
DANCER: If I could be attentive, love would not cease to
   flow.
CHORUS: It cannot be helped.
DANCER: Shall I *therefore* return to our camp and wash
   myself? *(Exit.)*
JAMES *(with momentary conviction, a sentence of
   W. C. Williams):*
   "The ideal is a lie and in the end it will kill you."
   (Then, on soberer consideration.)
And the real is true and will kill you in the end.
This is because in the end is the end.

Into statues of art I have frozen on the way,
when you get what you want you freeze on the way
: this is the way we advance on the way.

Committing oneself (to a limited extent)
to an obvious folly, just to live on

258

A Goat for Azazel

: this is the hope in there's life there's hope
: this is the hope that will kill in the end
: this is the art that has frozen into glory.
—But what is the way? where is the way?

for "never to die" is no longer the way
and "courage! courage!" is no longer the way,
"happy if I suggest it to myself"

this is no longer the way.
I do not know the way, I do not go the way,
therefore love and longing are lapsing from my heart.

Surely the ending of music is stillness
and the ending of orgasms is still sleep
(though no desirer has such a thought)

: if I pledge you in a glass of fire
and lose, who have and therefore can, myself,
shall then I walk with wandering step

the way of the beginning of the world?
Of fools and drunkards God takes care
: take care of me, my watchful Lord.

6. The Boy Framed in the Doorway

To my delight—I was the only one who could see any significance in it—Jimmy now took to wearing a red goatee beard and looked, especially when he put on a pair of spectacles, like James Joyce the poet or Trotsky the inventor of insurrection.

He took the initiative and buried the hatchet; buried it, that is, in the ground, not in somebody's head. (It is remarkable how a lucky pun has almost driven from common usage the old meaning of the courteous Indians.) This was easy to do—I mean to bury the hatchet in the ground—because Jimmy's spell of violence had put him in the wrong, and among peaceful folk two wrongs make a right.

So several years had passed and all our peaceful acquaintances were once more *friends.* –

We gave a *surprise* party for Jimmy on his thirty-fifth birthday.

He came into the darkened house, and suddenly was blinded by all the lights switched on and deafened by all the phonographs and pianos sounding at once. We sprang from behind chairs and shouted "Happy *birthday!*" and this was a complete surprise, because he had not been thinking of the fact that it was his thirty-fifth birthday, so that he momentarily faltered.

He momentarily faltered with the shock of the heart that we aggressive persons inflict on our dearest friends with cruel surprise parties.

He joyously blew out the candles with a circular puff, leaving the thirty-sixth in the middle to burn a little longer, while he cut the cake. (It was in such athletic *cortesia* as blowing out the candles with one puff or tipping his hat on a bicycle or halving an apple neatly with his fingers that our Jimmy excelled.) It was a white-haired cake, of coconut shred in marshmallow icing, but the center was golden and made from the oranges of the Hesperides.

Among the gifts piled on a table were a beaver motorcycle seat, a silk hat, and for a joke a huge black-horn spectacles frame such as Ed Wynn the comedian used to wear. A score of Händel's *Partita in E-Minor* autographed by R. Schneider; a worst seller (that I shall not name).

The liquor flowed so fast that almost immediately we were phoning out after some more.

Meantime everybody began to dance; and in this circling company, in the golden alcoholic haze, in this circling company, in this circling company, at last the multitudinous relations among so many persons—there were twelve couples—I mean the relations that keep their terms apart even more strongly than they unite them, these relations began to be dissolved in the haze; to be unwound, in the circling company, in the uncircling company.

It could be shown how the several thousands of complicating relations were unwound, sometimes one by one, but even six, ten, seventeen at a time.

A Goat for Azazel

A more violent and intoxicating chaos yet was produced when we began to play two phonographs at the same time, one revolving out Oscar Hammerstein's *The Last Time I Saw Paris* and one pounding out *The Mahogany Hall Stomp.* In the end it was only Dick and Diana—who used, under that same name, to tour the vaudeville circuit in "ballroom with lifts"—who could successfully thread this compound rhythm, stepping independently, but coming together on the double bar-lines.

Somehow—"I know not how" as the poet says—I was able to see from the perspective of near-the-floor that all the feet were twinkling on the white floor.

When Jimmy put on the huge horn frames, he was a *strange* goat, for his beard was red whereas the eye-circles were black.

Among the gifts on the table was one which I had begged for the occasion from Arthur Eliphaz, who had bought it from his unwilling father for sixty dollars. It was the Wallet of St. Francis with its contents! a broken crucifix, a boy's top and tangling cord, a tape-measure, and a copy of the *Song of Songs.* This wallet was made of kidskin and could also be used (as I intend to show elsewhere) as a large tobacco pouch. But at present, who could deny that it appropriately belonged to Jimmy? and it is on this principle that we apportion sentimental property among our friends.

Amid wisecracks, Jimmy was now explaining to a group in the corner that when he said "You Liar L." and "D. you thing of dirt," it was merely for purposes of alliteration that he had chosen these initials, L. for "Liar" and D. for "Dirt."

Among the gifts that were stored up for Jimmy in the cellar—

The liquor was running low; where ever was the boy with the new supply?

The last 2368 relations among the dancers unwound all at once when they began to reel; as a watch spring does when you release the sprocket. There is a little zzz.

If this narrative is beginning to run down along here, it's because it's hard to know what to say when there is so much agreement.

Zzzz.

261

I mean to say, the mechanism of animosity by which all little by little could gratify themselves is released. Zzz!

Suddenly Jimmy *agrees* to regard himself as the scapegoat. Zz.

All had sat down now, and they were slowly chattering in different groups. Jimmy was explaining something to Raymond and Esther, but he broke off to call to me: "Harry?" he called slowly.

I waved across to them.

He said: "No. Har-ry?"

Finally I carried my glass over. *They* were drinking some mixture of gin or so (there is nothing to do but mix it), but *I* was drinking, as always, Wayne County Applejack.

"It's Harry," he said. "Look, Har-ry. You—have to hear, what I—have to say. Because after all you—and I—" This was all accompanied by gestures. "Look, *you*—said you knew, where *I*—was in the wrong."

"*I* said it? Oh no!"

"Yes."

"Raym here—I was telling Raym and Es where I was in the wrong. But you—have to hear too. Because you had a *theory*! I know. Yes. A theory!

"Where was I?" he asked, perplexed.

"You were going to say where you were in the wrong because I had a theory," I said with lively interest.

"Don't talk so *fast*," said Jimmy. He appealed to the others, "Thinks he's smart because he can talk so fast. Ha.

"*I* have a theory too!" he cried. "Raym—I'm telling this to only you; *he* mustn't listen. Because his theory's wrong, but my theory's everlastingly right! Yes. That's my theory."

"What's your theory?" I said.

"What you listening for?" he cried indignantly. "Raym—I'm telling this to only you and Es. Everlastingly *right*!"

"I'm not listening," I assured him.

"Theory is:" and he spoke in a loud voice, so that even some of the others stopped talking, "Got to keep it up! Shouldn't go away! Shouldn't let 'em down! Mustn't get tired! once you start—that's the theory."

A Goat for Azazel

"Everlastingly right!" said Raymond enthusiastically, who had committed attempted-suicide when he thought that he had been let down.

z.

Like Nancy and Sluggo in the cartoon, we saw a Thrilling Chase: On the floor out of the kitchen slowly crept a mouse slowly pursued by a listless cat who was in turn being followed by a tired dog.

The doorbell rang. The party sprang alive. It was the boy with the liquor. The party sprang alive. "Happy *birthday!*" we all shouted. We greeted him with tin horns. (The mouse, by the way, scuttled safe into a hole.)

Zzz.

Jimmy opened the door to the boy.

His drunkenness slipped from him so suddenly that I could almost see it standing there independently.

(I alone was near by.)

It was a boy of eleven framed in the doorway in the foreground of the umber night. On his left arm was resting a magnum bottle; at his right foot lay a basket. He had a wise little participatory smile curving from the lower left to the upper right, and on the thumb of his free hand was a small bloody bandage. He had a shining sweater, and his trousers were worn-blue.

But what about this charming sight was so remarkable that my friend should say, "So!"

It was this: that while the boy stood there with his weight on his right leg, Jimmy looked at him and thought: "I see from behind *his* eyes that now *I*'m the celebrant in the house to whom I'm making the delivery. So! *I*'m the man with the black motorcycle who early in the morning, when we're on our way to school, lets me climb behind on the sheepskin seat and hold on tight to the tobacco-smelling leather jacket, while he whirls me half a mile. *I*'m the one in my top hat, for whom we'll interrupt the ball game to let me pass, on my way to church to attend the baptism."

7. *Jimmy's Surprise-Party*

The conspirators laid their plans well for Jimmy's surprise party. They occupied the subtlest places of ambush, beneath the bed and in the closet where the liquor was kept, behind the softest chair and behind the case of books. One crouched outside the window on the fire escape to the avenue. Close to hand, lurking in the dark, they had the switches of the full electric daylight.

Most often, because of the inconveniences, a man is not surprised in his own home; they lead him on a pretext to the home of a friend. But these terrorists understood that it is only in his own home that a man is intimately surprised. In a strange house, if there is an unexpected appearance and a deafening shout, there is always the ambiguity that these might be the custom; they are unexpected to him but not unexpected in the nature of the case. And one has not there laid himself open, giving way to fatigue, to expect only the expected, as a man does when he turns his own latchkey into his own foyer, thinking either "Now I'm back to this" or "Home at last." In a strange house, in the dead of night, the cracking of the woodwork is absorbed into one's defenses-in-depth; but at home it may penetrate to the pang of terror of the third year, of the zero hour.

They had copied his key and sneaked in beforehand, while their agent kept him away until the hour. They knew his ways.—

It was Jimmy's happy birthday!

A man touched by Luck is sacred. One may not approach him except sacrally and bringing gifts. (Afterwards one must wash.) The contagion of his luck is dangerous and vitalizing.

It was on this day of the revolving year that he had first had the luck to fall heir to the heavens and the earth and to draw on their power conserved from the beginning of time, of which that moment also was the end result. Surprise! surprise! to inherit so young the force of life, whose first characteristic is that it is inherited.

Therefore carefully, in panoply, with expectant weapons

264

and breathing aggression, the conspirators were ready for their host the child of Luck, pledged to support each other lest strokes of luck destroy them one by one.

But when happy Jimmy came to the door and turned the key, he was deep in thought, thinking, "It is my birthday and no doubt they have prepared a surprise party for me. My old friends will have been thinking of the day for me, hoping that I have not been thinking of it myself. But now half of my life is unrolled away, and I am long well into my middle age, defined as the time when we get what we carelessly longed for in our youth. I know what that's worth and indeed I watch with horror, but powerless, each satisfaction come into being one by one; therefore I cannot think that my birthday ought to be celebrated with a party. Nevertheless!—"

Thus he expected to be surprised with a party, this was his fatal mistake. For when a rational man is simply surprised, *un*expectedly surprised, then his immediate reaction, at the very instant of shock, is to hunt for a cause, and in this salutary effort he keeps the courage from draining from his heart entirely. But if already beforehand he has made this effort of reason and become habituated to it, and *nevertheless* he is surprised—for it is a surprise!—then he has no more defenses. (We saw it well how those who step by step forebode the outbreak of the war, had no more courage and were overwhelmed when the war broke out.)

—"Surprise! surprise!"

When the child of Luck came into his home, the full electric daylight blazed in his startled eyes.

Out of the closet of liquor leaped a person crying, "happy birthday to you!" The books, the wisdom of the western world, fell from the shelves. And his dear bed of lust and sleep finally rose to confront him.

A grin cut off the escape to the avenue.

They also had secret weapons: The beloved of his careless youth, who had been best forgotten. And his only enemy smiling advancing with outstretched hand.

"Happy birthday to you! happy birthday to you! happy birthday, *dear* Jimmy—"

And when he was overwhelmed and there was no more courage in his heart, they came around him crowding with their gifts.

Chesterton–New York–Norwood
1939-1944

Textual Note

Goodman published four collections of stories during his lifetime, *The Facts of Life, The Break-Up of Our Camp, Our Visit to Niagara,* and *Adam and His Works.* The last was a collected edition and included most of the stories in the other three as well as a few "new" ones. Many other stories appeared only in magazines, and still others were never published at all. When he reprinted a story in a collection, he usually revised it, often extensively. Others were tailored to the needs of novels in which they were to be inserted.

In preparing this complete edition of all of Goodman's stories and sketches, I have returned to the earliest printed versions for my texts. Much of Goodman's revising was done twenty, even thirty years after first writing, and his style had changed enough to put his revisions at odds with his original conceptions. The general effect was to make all the stories, early and late, share a diction and syntax that is mere patina, spread thin over the variety of literary voices and manners he explored during a long career. His last and fullest revisions—for the majority of stories in *Adam and His Works*—were undertaken years after he had stopped writing fiction altogether, and after his style had undergone a journalistic refurbishing for his mass audience as a social critic.

I think that in every case his original stories are better than these later revisions. Moreover, since this is to be the definitive edition of his short fiction, there is good reason to represent his career as accurately as possible in its range and

267

its development. The revised versions mask and blur the relevant distinctions. And in any case they are already widely available in *Adam and His Works*, whereas the original texts are scattered among dozens of ephemeral magazines, and in books published in tiny editions, long out of print. Moreover, it would make little sense to print side by side stories written in the same year, one as it first appeared, the other as it was altered after decades had elapsed. Many of Goodman's stories did not find their way into any collection, and so were never revised. The four-volume edition, of which this is volume two, includes twenty previously uncollected stories, nineteen never before published, and two dozen others that have appeared only in the special issue of *New Letters* magazine I edited in 1976. The establishment of an historical canon for all of these will make it possible to study the unfolding of Goodman's career by bringing together works that although written in the same period, repeating the same motifs, and even referring to one another, have never been available within the covers of a single volume.

(In the case of *The Break-Up of Our Camp*, I have used the text of the first publication of the entire work, rather than of the individual stories, to preserve its overall unity. In order to sustain similar values in *Johnson*, I have accepted the manuscript version as my basic text. Only two of the *Johnson* stories were published at the time of composition, and while retaining the substantive changes—not many—of those, I have emended the spelling and punctuation of the published versions to conform to the manuscripts. Still another chapter, "Martin, or the Work of Art," was published many years later, greatly altered, and since the original manuscript no longer exists, it has been treated here as an appendix.)

One further principle of selection needs to be mentioned. As the title of this collection suggests, it includes a number of works that are not strictly speaking stories, though they are not quite essays either but something in-between. A comparison of "The Father of the Psychoanalytic Movement" and "Golden Age" (see the edition of Goodman's psychological essays, *Nature Heals*, Free Life Editions,

Textual Note

1977), will illustrate the shading of one genre into the other, and my cut-off point: the former I include here among his fictions, but not the latter. On a slightly different basis I have excluded "The Diggers in 1984," a political tract disguised as fiction; Goodman himself so regarded it, and did not include it in *Adam and His Works*. I have also excluded separately published chapters of novels unless there is good evidence that they were originally intended as stories. Thus there is nothing here from *Parents' Day*, although some of it was first published in a magazine, as if a story; contrariwise, "Eagle's Bridge" and "The Continuum of the Libido" are included because they were conceived as separate works. The two adventures of St. Wayward and the Laughing Laddy, from the abortive fifth volume of *The Empire City*, represent still another category, works that were intended as parts of a novel but became short stories instead—as indicated by Goodman's including one of them in *Adam*. And of course I have included his two novels-in-stories, *Johnson* and *The Break-Up of Our Camp*.

Of the unpublished stories I have printed all that cannot be classed as unfinished or juvenilia. This is a matter of judgment. My own conviction is that Goodman's maturity came at a normal age for writers of fiction, about his twenty-fifth year. Anything written after *The Break-Up of Our Camp*, his first major novel, I have regarded as mature work even if Goodman never published it; stories written before 1936 have been considered on their merits. A few pieces published in high school and college periodicals have been omitted, but otherwise I have included everything of his apprenticeship that saw print, as well as several that he tried to publish, unsuccessfully. The manuscripts for a couple of dozen others, chiefly exercises of his undergraduate days, survive among his papers.

In editing this large body of work, I have tried to preserve Goodman's original intentions so far as they could be determined. Publishers took various liberties with his texts, and where I am sure Goodman preferred some other reading, I have adopted it. Thus I have restored "obscenities" censored by cautious editors, and have rescued the ending of "A Prayer for Dew" from the hell-box where its first

269

printers dumped it when it would not fit the page.

Goodman's spelling and punctuation were somewhat idiosyncratic, especially during the first two decades of his career. Some publishers made his prose conform to their own style-books, others did not. I have not attempted to sort out his usage from theirs, for there is nothing to go by, case by case; he usually discarded his manuscripts as soon as a work had appeared in print. In most of the early stories "though" is written "tho," "through" is "thru," etc., according to Goodman's habit. Exceptions probably represent editorial changes, to which he may or may not have agreed. Punctuation is even more difficult to deal with, for his own practice was sometimes inconsistent and careless, sometimes purposeful if eccentric. I have regularized a few recurrent patterns according to the modern usage that he himself sometimes followed, changing the old-fashioned "such-and-such,—" and "so-and-so;—" to "such-and-such—" or "so-and-so—" and sometimes "so-and-so;" depending on the sense. And I have made the use of quotation marks consistent, dispensing with them entirely for passages already marked as quotation by indenting. I have printed such indented passages in the roman font, even though Goodman often set them off by italics. (In making such emendations I have been instructed by particular instances of regularization in *Adam and His Works.)* Aside from these, and the correction of obvious typographical errors, the texts are as they first appeared.

Goodman ordinarily entered the place and date of compositon at the end of each story. I have included these whenever I could find them appended to any version of the text, and I have supplied them in brackets for those stories that must be dated by extrinsic means.

The following is the publishing history of the stories included in this volume; reprints in magazines or anthologies are not listed unless of special interest. I wish to thank those publishers below who have given their permission, or otherwise facilitated the publication of stories which first appeared under their imprint. Admirers of Goodman's work should be grateful to David Ray, editor of *New Letters,* for first making so many of the unpublished

Textual Note

stories available. I also want to thank my co-literary executors Sally Goodman, George Dennison, and Jason Epstein for their help, my three generations of proof-readers, Holly, Christopher, and Mary Stoehr, Ruth Perry, Maurice and Charlotte Sagoff, Black Sparrow's Seamus Cooney, and my friend John Dings.

Collections

The Facts of Life (New York: Vanguard, 1945).
The Break-Up of Our Camp and Other Stories (Norfolk, Conn.: New Directions, 1949).
Our Visit to Niagara (New York: Horizon, 1960).
Adam and His Works (New York: Vintage, 1968).
The Writings of Paul Goodman, ed. Taylor Stoehr, *New Letters,* XLII (Winter-Spring 1976).

Publishing History

"A Cross-Country Runner at Sixty-Five" (1936), *New Directions in Prose and Poetry 5* (ed. James Laughlin, Norfolk, Conn.: New Directions, 1940); *Facts of Life*, 1945; *Adam*, 1968.

"Remo" (1936), *Christopher Street*, I (July 1976).

"Peter" (1936), unpublished.

"Night" (1936), *New Letters*, 1976.

"Prose Composition (sustained—rapid—jokes—slow—forthright—and disturbed)" (1936), unpublished.

"The Birthday Concert" (1936), *Break-Up of Our Camp*, 1949; *Adam*, 1968.

"Tiberius" (1936), *New Directions in Prose and Poetry 7* (ed. James Laughlin, Norfolk, Conn.: New Directions, 1942).

"A Prayer" (1936), unpublished.

"Frances" (1936), *Kenyon Review*, III (Autumn 1941); *Facts of Life*, 1945.

"Vic McMahon" (1937), *Break-Up of Our Camp*, 1949; *Adam*, 1968.

"A Ceremonial" (1937), *New Directions in Prose and Poetry 5* (ed. James Laughlin, Norfolk, Conn.: New Directions, 1940); *Facts of Life*, 1945; *Adam*, 1968.

"Orpheus in the Underworld" (1937), *Facts of Life*, 1945.

"2 Pastoral Movements" (1937), unpublished.

"Prose Composition: Virginia" (1937), unpublished.

"Ravel" (1937), *New Directions in Prose and Poetry 6* (ed. James Laughlin, Norfolk, Conn.: New Directions, 1941).

"The Continuum of the Libido" (1938), unpublished.

"Honey-Moon and Archaic Longings" (1938), unpublished.

"Prose Composition: The Minutes Are Flying By Like a Snowstorm" (1938-1940), *New Letters*, 1976.

"Saul" (1938-1939), *New Directions in Prose and Poetry 8* (ed. James Laughlin, Norfolk, Conn.: New Directions, 1944).

"Prose Composition: The Sea! the Sea!" (1939), *New Letters*, 1976.

"The Mean, the Maximum, and the Minimum" (1939), *Partisan Review*, VII (September-October 1940); *Break-Up of Our Camp*, 1949; *Adam*, 1968.

"Prose Composition: Waiting and Endless Pleasure" (1939), *New Letters*, 1976.

"A Statue of Nestor" (1939-1944), *Facts of Life*, 1945; *Adam*, 1968.

"A Goat for Azazel" (1939-1944), *Facts of Life*, 1945.

Printed August 1978 in Santa Barbara & Ann Arbor for
the Black Sparrow Press by Mackintosh and Young &
Edwards Brothers Inc. Design by Barbara Martin.
This edition is published in paper wrappers; there
are 750 hardcover trade copies; & 200 special copies
have been handbound in boards by Earle Gray.

Paul Goodman (1911-1972) the well-known social critic (*Growing Up Absurd, Compulsory Mis-education, People or Personnel, The New Reformation,* and many other books) had several careers before his fame in the Sixties. He was trained as a philosopher at the University of Chicago, taught literature in various colleges, became an expert on community planning with his architect brother Percival Goodman, taught ninth-graders in a progressive school, founded with Fritz Perls the Gestalt Therapy Institute and practiced psychotherapy, married and raised three children—all while living on an average income about that of a Southern sharecropper (when he started doing therapy in the early Fifties, his income jumped to $2,000 for the first time in his life). But these were really just his sidelines, and the reason that he lived in voluntary poverty rather than following one of the more lucrative callings open to him was that he regarded his work as a creative artist as his true vocation. Among his thirty-odd books his novels, plays, short stories, and poems would fill a shelf by themselves. His masterpiece is *The Empire City,* a comic epic written in the tradition and with the zest of *Don Quixote.* His *Collected Poems* contain, among hundreds of fine poems, the extraordinary sequence he wrote in mourning for his son Mathew, *North Percy,* probably the most moving elegy in American letters. Even though they never made much stir during his lifetime, Goodman knew the worth of these works, and yet he himself spoke of his short stories as his personal favorites. He gave one of his volumes of stories to a friend in the mid-Sixties, and wrote in it that it was his best book. When asked why he preferred it, he said, "That's the book I think is lovely—*Our Visit to Niagara*—I just like it, everything in it. That last story—'The Galley to Mytilene'—it's enchanting, I love to read it."

The present four-volume edition of *The Collected Stories and Sketches* includes all of Goodman's previously collected stories, plus dozens that have never appeared in book form, and twenty new pieces, written during every stage of his literary career and published here for the first time.

5.00